The Bondage Club

By

Alexandrea Weis

This is a work of fiction. Names, characters, places, and incidents are products of the author's imagination or are used fictitiously and are not to be construed as real. Any resemblance to actual events, locations, organizations, or persons, living or dead, is entirely coincidental.

Copyright © Alexandrea Weis 2014
First Edition Alexandrea Weis July 29, 2014

Licensing Notes

All rights reserved. No part of this book may be used or reproduced in any manner whatsoever without written permission, except in the case of brief quotations embodied in articles and reviews.

Book Cover: Bookfabulous Designs
Editor: Maxine Bringenberg

Chapter 1

The glare of the overhead lights only amplified the hangover plaguing the lean man in the fitted black suit as he strolled down the aisle of the Los Angeles Convention Center. Keeping his head down, his bloodshot green eyes stayed focused on his black leather loafers in hopes of easing his queasiness. As his long legs kicked out, he noted how the black carpet beneath him was already worn and dusty, despite it only being the second day of the convention. To the side, various booths and tables set up by book retailers, authors, publishers, distributers, and other ancillary services catering to the book industry were packed together, vying for attention at the annual Book Expo. The din of a thousand voices filled the convention center despite the early morning hour, making the attractive businessman feel as if he were already running behind before his long day of meetings, marketing pitches, and backroom deals had even begun.

Ahead, he sighted a dark blue banner with a sixteen-pointed gold star, designating the Donovan Books exhibit. A Greek symbol made famous by the Argead Dynasty of Alexander the Great, the company logo was designed by Jim Donovan, the founder of the publishing house. An absolute nut about the ancient conqueror, he had insisted that the star would bring success to the company he had started over forty years ago.

Beneath the banner, a gray-haired man with sharp features and an impatient frown stood checking his expensive stainless steel watch.

"You're late," he snapped.

"Back off, Chris." The green-eyed businessman pulled back the sleeve on his black suit jacket and checked his own stainless steel watch. "I'm right on time."

"What was her name, Hunter?" Chris pestered. Placing his hands behind him, he rocked back and forth on his fancy black Italian loafers.

"Who?" Hunter Donovan grinned, making his five o'clock shadow highlight the boyish dimples in his chiseled cheeks.

"The blonde I saw you doing shots with at the hotel bar last night. I figure she's the reason you look like shit this morning."

"Miranda, I think." Hunter's eyes skimmed the convention floor. "Or it could have been Melinda."

"It's a good thing you're my little brother, Hunter, and not some schmuck Dad hired to run the company, or I'd fire your ass," Chris told him, reaching inside his gray pinstripe suit jacket.

Hunter peered over at the arrogant man next to him, wondering if they were actually related or if he had been switched at birth. Despite being a few years younger than Chris Donovan, Hunter always felt the world-weary shadow in his brother's blue eyes made him seem much older than his forty-nine years.

"Yeah, well, I didn't want to run the company, remember? You talked me into it, so you could go and kiss ass with the authors," Hunter countered, running his hand through his thick mop of curly brown hair.

"And be thankful I did make you take over the company." Chris waved the cell phone in his slender hand about the convention center floor. "Otherwise you would be like all the other writers here, trying to hawk their books." Chris's eyes twinkled with disapproval. "You're a better publisher than a writer, Hunts."

"Don't call me that. I hate that name." Hunter's wide mouth turned down at the edges. "You know I never got a chance to be writer."

Chris chuckled, sounding more aggravated than amused. "You got your chance. You spent what? Three years living with that photographer, Kathleen, while Dad footed the bill, but you never finished that masterpiece you kept telling us you were writing. You have to actually finish writing a book before you can be considered an author, little brother."

Hunter glared at Chris's smug grin. "Are you finished?"

"Finished?" Chris snickered. "The point is you never finished anything, Hunter. How many sports did you go through? How many art classes, music lessons with I can't remember how many instruments? And then there were the chess lessons, and—"

"I get it, Chris," Hunter edged in. "You don't have to be a dick about it."

"Hey, I stuck with things." Chris pointed to his brother. "You didn't. That's why Dad wanted you to run Donovan Books. You had to do something with your life."

Hunter noted the way his brother nervously tugged at the sleeves of his freshly pressed designer suit. "So where is he?"

"He'll be here." Chris's condescending eyes ran up and down his brother's wrinkled suit. "Did you sleep in that thing?"

Hunter patted the front of his jacket. "Not quite. It spent the night on the chair by the bed."

"Have you ever heard of a hanger?"

"Sure have, but I never bothered to ask her if she had any." He placed his hands in the pockets of his black trousers. "I was kind of distracted at the time."

"Stop being such a smartass, and for once try and concentrate on the business. We need to impress this writer and you show up—" Chris shook his head, clenching his teeth. "This guy is already a New York Times Best Seller, and if we can sign his next book, we could cash in."

Hunter stepped closer to his brother, dropping his voice. "I don't know why I have to be here. You're the salesman, not me."

"He needs to meet the president of the publishing house. I just manage the talent."

"Manage? Is that what you call it?" Hunter snorted abruptly. "You didn't manage Monique Delome too well. You're the idiot who lost us her latest book. *A Chance With You* hit number three on the NYTB list. Do you know what that would have done for our company? Haley Books raked in millions on it. Just because she dumped your ass for that oil guy didn't mean you had to let her go as our client."

Chris's blue eyes appeared as if they were going to pop out of his head. "Don't bring her up again. I told you we needed to wash our hands of her. That last book she wrote was nothing but bondage and rough sex, and not what Dad ever intended for our company."

"Dad is seventy-one and not up on the book scene anymore. Everything has changed since *Fifty Shades of Gray*. We need to get edgier with our books."

"No, Hunter, we need to stay true to our old man's vision. Jim Donovan's ideals are our ideals."

"Chris, unless we pump out some meatier books with a lot more hard core sex in them, there won't be a Donovan Books."

"Bullshit!" Chris glanced to the booths surrounding them and lowered his voice. "There's always going to be a market for the kind of books we publish. Values haven't gone in the toilet for everyone just yet."

"Have you been watching the news lately?" Hunter hurled back.

Chris waved off his comment as a stocky man with thick-rimmed glasses approached. He wore an ill-fitting blue suit, brown shoes, and a blue woolen cap. Hunter thought he looked as out of place as a donkey at The Preakness.

"Here he is," Chris whispered to him. "He's from Charleston, so emphasize our interest in Southern fiction."

Hunter scowled. "We don't have an interest in Southern fiction."

Chris plastered a fake smile on his face. "We do now."

Hunter waited as the man waddled up to them and shook hands. Unimpressed with his woefully weak handshake, Hunter instantly tuned out anything the Tennessee Williams wannabe had to say.

Why are all these aspiring Southern writers short, dumpy, and donning berets?

Hunter stood impatiently to the side as Chris put on his best salesman persona.

"You will be very happy with Donovan Books, Mr. Mallory," Chris began. "We're progressive and hooked into both chain and local bookstores across the country. Our list of book reviewers includes some of the top names from the *New York Times, Chicago Tribune, Los Angeles Times,* in addition to *USA Today*. And I can assure you as your manager that we will get you spots on all the primetime news networks, as well as the morning shows. At Donovan Books, we look at all our authors as family, and want you to stay with us for many years to come."

The drab little man feigned an indulgent smile on his pasty white face. "Well, I am in the market for a new publisher that can get me into higher-end bookstores," he replied in a nasally voice, making Hunter wonder if he had sinus problems or was actually trying to sound like an intellectual. "My books are better suited to upper-class readers; the kind who want to pursue philosophical discussion about relevant social issues."

Hunter suppressed a hankering to laugh. "All that is fine on paper, Mr. Mallory, but can you pursue that philosophical discussion on your pages with a smattering of sex? We need sex to move the book."

Chris shot him a dirty look. "We are avid proponents of important books that push the edge of modern-day thinking is what my brother meant to say."

Mr. Mallory turned his Coke-bottle covered brown eyes to Hunter. "Yeah, it's got a lot of sex in it. I'm not an idiot, Mr. Donovan. Sex sells and I have bills to pay, you know?"

Hunter smirked at his brother. "In that case, we'd love to publish your manuscript, Mr. Mallory. If we can work out a deal, I can guarantee you a two-year contract for print and e-book release, with another two-year option to follow if the sales are good. We would own character rights if you were to write any sequels, world wild distribution, and will pay for all the PR, pre-release copies to reviewers, and set you up at the Book Expo next year for a signing."

"That all sounds fine, but you haven't read my manuscript, Mr. Donovan. So how do you know you will like it?" the confused author questioned, scratching beneath his cap.

"I don't have to like it, Mr. Mallory; I just have to know if it will sell," Hunter insisted. "Send me a copy and I'll take a look at it. I will send you a contract next week." Hunter pulled a business card from his pocket. "Here's my cell number and e-mail."

Mr. Mallory took the card and gave Hunter a short smile. "All right, Mr. Donovan."

Chris stood to the side, turning red as Hunter took Mr. Malory's hand and gave it a firm shake.

"I like your style, Mr. Donovan," Mr. Mallory said with a lispy roll of his tongue. "I don't like the hard sell, myself. Just lay it on the line, and I'm fine with that."

Hunter gave his brother an indulgent side-glance. "Yeah, me too." Checking his watch, Hunter instantly felt the need to escape from beneath the condescending gaze of his brother. "Well, if you would excuse me, Mr. Mallory, I have another meeting. I look forward to reading your book."

Hunter left Mr. Mallory and his brother chatting on the floor of the convention center while he went in search of some much needed coffee. He did not understand why they had to meet the little man at such an early hour, but with his first appointment of the day out of the way, Hunter was glad to have some downtime before he had to once again play the role of the savvy book publisher.

"Savvy?" He snickered at the idea. "I'm about as savvy as a kid on his first day of kindergarten."

To the side of the convention center floor was a concession area serving breakfast, and a line of customers snaked around a metal checkout table. Bypassing the food, Hunter headed straight for the large silver coffee urn and grabbed the biggest cup he could find. As the dark liquid filled his paper cup and tantalized his nose, Hunter flashed back to his night with the leggy blonde whose name still eluded him.

She had been very attractive, looking for a publisher for her novel, and, from what he remembered, flexible as hell. He had left her that morning, promising to read her novel and follow up their tryst with an intimate dinner at a restaurant of her choice. But Hunter knew he had no intention of ever seeing the woman again. Second dates led to talking, which led to sharing of life stories, which for Hunter tolled the death knell for any relationship. One-night stands and brief interludes were better for him; there was less chance of things getting complicated, and one thing Hunter Donovan hated was complications.

Taking his desperately needed caffeine jolt to the checkout line, he felt better prepared to handle the rest of his tedious day. While standing in line, he discovered small packages of aspirin for sale and grabbed two of them. After leaving the concession area, he headed onto the convention floor, eager to walk, drink his coffee, and peruse the various exhibits in peace.

He had just downed two aspirin and a few gulps of his coffee when he was unexpectedly sideswiped by a short blonde, who sent splashes from his coffee cup onto his jacket sleeve. When she turned to him, the first thing Hunter noticed was the way her full, red-painted lips were heart-shaped like that of a doll. Over her round face she wore dark-tinted glasses that hid the color of her eyes. Her slim figure was more childlike than womanly, reminding Hunter of something he would find on a middle school playground and not walking the halls of the Book Expo.

"Oh, I'm so sorry," she professed in a lovely soft voice that instantly attracted him. She dabbed at his sleeve and clucked over the stain. "I'm so clumsy."

Hunter shook the coffee droplets from his hand and then wiped it on the side of his pants. "It was my fault. I should have been watching where I was going." He spied the ID badge around her neck with her name printed in bold black letters.

"Ms. Smut Slut?" he queried, raising his dark eyebrows.

The woman fingered her ID badge and then frowned. "It's my pseudonym. I'm a writer."

Hunter stood there for a second, taking in her black leather minidress that showed off her slender legs. "What do you write?"

"Erotica," she replied while shifting on her high black leather boots.

Hunter cracked a smile. "Really? Big market I hear."

"Very big." She angled over and read his ID badge, hanging about his neck. "Hunter Donovan of Donovan Books. I've heard of your company. You publish a lot of sweet little romances, don't you?"

"'Sweet little romances'?" he remarked in mocking tone.

"You know, soft sex, nothing hard core. And there's always a happily ever after in your romances. Not so much the case in erotica. Sex is the story for my genre, and happy endings aren't guaranteed."

"Yeah, well, we haven't ventured into the erotica market yet."

"Yet?" Her sarcastic grin taunted him. "What are you waiting for?"

He gave her an indulgent smile. "The right book, I guess."

Her cheerful giggle betrayed the dominatrix standing before him. She sounded sweet, homey, and like the kind of girl he would have taken to an afternoon at the zoo, and not bent over his knee and spanked with a riding crop.

"Your publishing company is based out of Atlanta, right?"

Hunter tried to peer through the tint in her glasses. "Yes, we are."

"I'm in Atlanta. I moved there after Katrina," she disclosed.

"Katrina? You're from New Orleans?"

"Yeah. All my books are based there; stories about love and lust in the French Quarter."

Intrigued, he took a step closer to her and then detected a whiff of some exotic, spicy perfume. He had been expecting something akin to cigarette smoke or well-oiled leather, but nothing like that.

"Who's your publisher?"

"MandiRay Books," she answered. "They handle a lot of erotica authors."

Hunter grinned. "Yes, I know."

A lapse of silence fell between them and Smut Slut took a step back. "Well, I should be going. I have a book signing in five minutes."

"Where?" Hunter inquired, never taking his eyes off her dark glasses.

She waved down the aisle. "At the MandiRay exhibit. I'll be signing my latest book."

"Care to tell me what it's about?"

"I'll save you a copy." She smiled for him, accentuating the curve of her full, red lips. "So stop by if you have the chance, Mr. Donovan."

He dipped his head politely. "I will make a point of it, Ms. Slut." He shook his head. "I never thought I would be saying that to a woman with a straight face."

Smut Slut leaned in a little closer, allowing him a glimpse of her cleavage. "Not all women like the gentlemanly approach, Mr. Donovan. Sometimes a woman likes it when a man lays it on the line."

"Is that an offer or a suggestion, Ms. Slut?"

Her smile deepened. "I hope to see you later, Mr. Donovan."

A tickle of excitement erupted in Hunter's gut. "I look forward to it."

When she turned away, Hunter was mesmerized by the way her small, leather-covered butt swayed down the aisle. Shaking his head at her bravado, Hunter wondered if perhaps he had been going to the wrong bars to meet women over the past few years. Every woman he met was perky, pretty, seemingly sweet, and a lot like the blonde he had spent last night with…boring. Very few had been half as self-assured as Smut Slut, or had elicited that sexual spark in him quite like she had done.

Gazing down into his coffee, he sighed. "You need to concentrate on business, Hunter." But when he caught sight of Smut Slut's black leather minidress disappearing around the end of the aisle, he smiled. "Yeah, right. To hell with business."

Following her down the aisle he took another sip of his coffee, suddenly feeling invigorated by the thrill of the hunt. This was much more fun than the blonde from the previous evening, who had laughed at all of his stupid jokes and practically jumped into his arms when he suggested they go back to her room. When he turned the corner at the end of the aisle where a large medical book publisher had set up shop, he spied the purple and gold banner of MandiRay Books. But what really took Hunter by surprise was the number of people gathered before the purple archways made out of fabric and wire that designated the entrance to the MandiRay Books exhibit.

A winding line of at least a hundred people, made up of women of all ages, was eagerly waiting before a table set up beneath a canopy of sheer purple fabric coming together to form a crown. Behind the table, and partially blocked by a pile of books, was the top of Smut Slut's blonde head, or at least he hoped it was her. Slowly approaching the table, Hunter was able to make out the woman's round face, darkly tinted glasses, and deep red lips.

"Our writers never pull in these numbers at the Expo," he mumbled as he took in the long line.

Deciding that perhaps this would be a good opportunity to do a little research, Hunter went to the end of the line of autograph seekers. He warmly greeted a few women waiting in front of him. They were mostly middle-aged, a little on the plump side, and had large canvas tote bags slung over each shoulder, crammed full of paperback books. Trim, toned, and six-foot-one, Hunter knew he cut an imposing figure, and wasn't too surprised when one or two of the women directed smiles his way. Taking full advantage of his angular features, deep green eyes, and alluring dimples, he inched closer to the women before him.

"Do you ladies read a lot from this author?" He nodded to an easel with a poster just ahead of them touting Smut Slut's appearance.

Light tittering broke out as the women's eyes darted to and fro.

"She's a rather guilty pleasure," a redhead next to Hunter confessed. "A friend turned me on to her. Now I can't get enough."

"What do you like about her books?" he persisted, easing in closer to the group.

"Everything," the redhead offered. "They're really good. You kind of get lost in them."

"Are there any particular publishers you follow, or is it just the authors?" he went on.

A round brunette wearing a casual blue cotton dress at the front of the group spoke up. "I like the authors, but I have some friends who follow certain publishing houses that put out a lot of erotica, or romances with erotica in them."

"And what is it about these books you ladies find so appealing?"

The nervous twittering rose to enthusiastic laughter as the women looked from one to the other.

"The sex of course. Why else would we read it?" the redhead professed. "I mean, honestly, if a book doesn't have sex in it, what's the point?"

"What about the story?" Hunter continued.

The smallest of the women pulled at the canvas tote bag on her shoulder. "Sure, the story is important. If it's a badly written book, no amount of sex is gonna help, but when it's a good story with smokin' love scenes…yeah, then that's somethin' I want to read again and again."

As the line moved along, Hunter sipped on his coffee and pumped the women for more information. By the time he had come within ten feet of Smut Slut's table, he knew the first names of all three women and that they worked at different jobs in the publishing industry.

Observing as each of the women bellied up to the table and interacted with the leather-clad blonde helped to harden Hunter's resolve. For years he had wanted to rev up the sex factor in the books published by his company, yet was afraid of introducing too much change and upsetting his father. But with profits beginning to slip and the market getting saturated with self-published books, Hunter reasoned he needed to implement those needed changes sooner than later. The only question was how?

"So, you came," Smut Slut declared when he stood before her table. "I'm impressed." She ran the tip of her tongue over her red lips.

Hunter set his coffee cup on her table. "I have to admit this has been quite an education, talking to your fans. I believe Donovan Books is missing out on a vital part of the market."

"Missing out on a hell of a lot of profit, too."

Hunter nodded. "Yeah, I was thinking the same thing."

Smut Slut pulled a book from the stack next to her. "You should read this." She slid the book across the table to him. "The best way to learn about a genre is to read the books."

Hunter inspected the cover. A woman wearing a red slinky dress was handcuffed to a brass bedpost as the shadow of a man stood before her. On her face was a come-hither smile.

"*The Ties That Bind,*" he said, reading the title. "And after I read it, will you be available for questions?"

"No." Smut Slut took the book from his hand and opened the cover. "But if you really want an education on erotica, this person can help. Her name is Cary Anderson and she's one of the best editors I know. All the top erotica authors work with her." She scribbled something inside the cover. "She also happens to be looking for a job at a publishing house." She held up the book to him. "Interested?"

Sporting a dubious frown, Hunter plucked the book from her hand. "If she is as good as you say, then why hasn't another house like this one," he waved to the MandiRay Books banner, "snatched her up?"

Smut Slut shrugged her shoulders. "They tried. But I think Cary isn't interested in becoming another in a long line of editors at a house that sees her more as a warm body and less like a vital contributor."

Hunter lifted the cover of the book and saw Cary Anderson's name and telephone number written inside. "But how can you be so sure your friend won't end up being just another 'warm body' at my company?"

Smut Slut's insidious grin stirred Hunter's desire. "Because you don't publish erotica, Mr. Donovan, and Cary would be able to open up a whole new world for you, instead of just blending in with your other editors. Plus, she lives in Atlanta and isn't interested in relocating. I think you're just what she needs."

Hunter shifted his weight and tilted closer to her table. "And what about you? What do you need, Ms. Slut?"

She shook her head and sat back in her chair, eyeing his figure. "I bet you're the kind of man who doesn't like it when women get clingy. One night, maybe two and you're done. Relationships are difficult, sometimes even painful for you, probably because you have had such a lousy time with them. Sex is a thrill, conversation is a bore, and you're getting to a point in your life where women are getting as predictable as the evening news." She rested her arms on her table, pushing up the cleavage peeking out from her low cut leather dress. "Am I right?"

Hunter collected his coffee from the table and cleared his throat. "Maybe I'm a really likable guy...merely misunderstood."

A light tinkling laugh escaped from her red lips, making Hunter's insides burn. "Grizzly bears that attack hikers are misunderstood, Mr. Donovan; men not so much. Let's just say men are sort of an occupational hazard for me. Just because I write what I do, dress to sell it, and speak my mind doesn't make me interested in a quick roll in the sack with you."

Hunter bowed his head. "I stand corrected."

She pointed to the book. "Call Cary. I think she'll be able to do a hell of a lot more for you than I can."

He tucked the book under his arm. "We will never know unless we try, Ms. Slut."

She waved to the next person in the line behind him. "I already know, Mr. Donovan." She gave him one last flirty smile. "Enjoy the book."

Hunter walked away from her table still grinning like a schoolboy. Why was it the interesting women, filled with the promise of something better, were always unattainable?

"Probably a lesbian," Hunter muttered, displeased that his charm had not melted her defenses.

The buzzing of the cell phone in his jacket pocket pulled his thoughts away from his encounter with Smut Slut. Juggling his cup of coffee and the book under his arm, he retrieved the iPhone. When he spied the text message from his brother, informing him that he was already late for their meeting with an independent bookstore owner, Hunter cursed.

He scowled as he put the phone back in his jacket pocket. "I should have listened to Mom and become a doctor."

Heading toward the front of the convention hall, Hunter took a few more fortifying sips of coffee and pulled out the book from under his arm. Finding a trash can, he dumped the almost empty paper cup and began flipping through the pages of Smut Slut's novel. As he walked along, he became entranced by the words on the page. Stopping in the middle of an aisle, he read for several minutes as people dodged around him. When his cell phone went off yet again, Hunter didn't even bother to check who was contacting him. He already knew.

"I don't get paid enough to put up with your shit, Chris," he softly vented as his long legs carried him along the busy aisle of the convention center and on to his next appointment.

Alexandrea Weis

Chapter 2

Hunter gazed out his third-story, arched window atop the offices of Donovan Books and yearned to escape to the small park across the street from his Georgian revival, red-bricked townhouse. The quaint park—whose name had always eluded Hunter—provided a needed sanctuary for the other businesses operating along his quiet street in the historic Fairlie-Poplar district of downtown Atlanta. As the cascading morning sun filtered down, Hunter yearned to spend a few moments luxuriating on the park's green grass before the weight of his duties at Donovan Books took precedence. Thoroughly disheartened by thoughts of another day reading other people's novels, Hunter turned from the window and sighed as his eyes gleaned the pile of manuscripts, invoices, legal contracts, and yellow message slips of paper that covered his oak desk. This wasn't what he had envisioned for himself after hitting forty. He had hoped to be firmly entrenched in his writing career, and spending his time polishing his manuscripts instead of hawking everyone else's.

Along the worn bamboo paneling on the walls were selected framed covers of the more successful books that had been published under his ten year tenure as head of Donovan

Books. The assorted titles were mostly romances; a few belonged to their former author, Monique Delome, but others were revered literary fiction novels that had won awards and gained Donovan Books a fair amount of prestige. In the far corner, stacked in a bookcase, was his father's collection of Alexander the Great statues that could not be thrown away on pain of death. Scattered about the two office chairs in front of his desk were more manuscripts waiting for his approval. The dingy yellow linoleum floor was worn, and desperately needed to be replaced. He had often vowed to renovate the office space, hoping to get inspired by a new look, but work had somehow managed to postpone the best of his intentions.

To the side of the desk, he glimpsed the book Smut Slut had given him in Los Angeles. He had read the book on and off in between meetings with his brother and other clients throughout that day. By the time he had finished the sexually compelling and well-written novel, Hunter was convinced that he had to bring Donovan Books into the twenty-first century, even without his father's approval. He had plotted ever since leaving Los Angeles to begin taking erotica manuscripts for possible publication, but he still did not know enough about the genre. Donovan Books needed someone well-versed in the virtual minefield of erotica fiction. That was when he decided to contact Cary Anderson.

Soon after arriving home from Los Angeles, he had called the editor, left a voice mail about the possibility of her working for Donovan Books, and asked her to get in touch. That had been three days ago, and the woman had never returned his call. Hunter was beginning to feel as if his plan to expand Donovan Books would die before it even got off the ground. He needed to find someone who could help him launch an erotica line without alerting his father and competing book publishers to his plans.

"Mr. Hunter?" A sweet-sounding voice came over the phone speaker, intruding into his thoughts.

Hunter hit the intercom button. "Yes, Julia," he said to the office receptionist on the first floor.

"I have a Ms. Cary Anderson here to see you."

Hunter stood back from his desk, amazed by the uncanny coincidence. *That is really creepy.* He eagerly pressed the intercom button on his phone. "Julia, send her up, will you?"

"Sure thing, Mr. Hunter."

Hunter went to one of the chairs in front of his desk and quickly began removing the manuscripts he had piled there. Racing to clear some of the clutter from his desk, he had just about enough time to run his hand through his curly hair and brush out the wrinkles in his white, button-down shirt when a shadow crossed his open office door.

Very petite, maybe five-foot-one, with a head of thick brown hair that was cut in a bob and sat just below her curved chin, Cary Anderson looked nothing like an expert in erotica. Big, chocolate brown eyes were seductively innocent, and peered out from her round face, reminding Hunter of a kindergarten teacher or librarian. Pink cheekbones flattered her creamy white skin, and a pair of full, heart-shaped, pink lips added to the sweet, doll-like image she presented. But the sudden thump the woman created in his gut was completely unexpected. It was almost as if he had been punched by some unseen hand.

"Mr. Donovan? I hope you don't mind the intrusion." She had a lilting voice that complimented her tiny figure.

Hunter went to the door, his hand outstretched. "Not at all, Ms. Anderson. I'm very glad you're here."

She took his hand and gave it a firm shake. Hunter instantly liked the feel of her hand in his; the softness of her skin and the warmth of her touch were strangely familiar.

"After hearing your message the other day, I thought I should meet you in person, and not have this discussion over the phone. If this isn't a good time, I could come back later when—"

"No," Hunter stopped her. "I was hoping to hear from you, but this is even better. I prefer meeting people face-to-face." He stood back from the doorway. "Please come in and have a seat."

"Thank you." She walked inside.

Hunter became distracted by how she moved. The feminine, yellow clingy sheath dress she had on offered a tantalizing glimpse of her slim figure. Despite her small stature, she had a confident grace that almost commanded attention, as if she were royalty making an appearance among the common folk.

"Ah, yes," he voiced, reining in his increasingly lurid thoughts. "When you didn't call me back, I began to think you weren't interested in my offer."

"Actually, Mr. Donovan, I've been thinking about your offer quite a bit; and that's one of the reasons I stopped by."

Hunter was spellbound by the way she glided to the empty chair in front of his desk. "Please call me, Hunter, Ms. Anderson." He quietly shut his office door.

"And I'm, Cary."

"Cary. Is that short for something?"

She shook her head, making her thick hair bounce about her face. "No, just plain Cary."

Hunter had a seat behind his desk and felt a tweak of embarrassment when his old chair squeaked with protest. "So, Cary, how do you feel about becoming part of the team at Donovan Books?"

"You cut right to the chase, Hunter, I like that." She placed her straw-colored purse in her lap and took a few seconds before she spoke. "I appreciate that you want your company to keep up with the changing desires of readers. I'm also flattered that you want me to be a part of that change as an editor for your erotica line." She paused and Hunter held his breath.

"But...," he inserted, anticipating this was not all going to be good.

"But what you're asking could take a long time, and I don't think I'm willing to commit long-term to any position. I do very well as a freelance editor."

"What if I offered you the position short-term...say one year? Enough to help me get my new erotica line started." He rested his elbows on his desk. "You could teach me what you know, help launch our first few books, and after that you could go back to your editing job."

"But what you describe goes beyond the job description of an editor. I can oversee the manuscripts, help build a brand for you in the erotica market, but you still have the marketing to bloggers, readers, and reviewers to do. How do you propose to get the word out about your books once you have published them?"

He motioned to her. "I had hoped you would help me with that, too. I got the impression from your client, Ms. Smut Slut, that you were very knowledgeable about the market, but you seem awfully young to be so well-informed."

The left corner of her mouth inched upward in a slight smile. "I am well-informed, Hunter, and I'm not that young. I'm thirty-one, and I've spent years setting up contacts in the industry."

"I know. I made a few phone calls to some editors I've worked with in the past. You come highly recommended."

"I have to admit I, too, did some research on Donovan Books. You've never delved into this aspect of the industry, and from what I can gather you need someone to build your brand from the ground up." The other corner of her mouth rose ever so slightly. "What you're describing, Hunter, is more like a division head who can take over the day-to-day running of your erotica line, and not just an editor."

Hunter momentarily scrutinized her brown eyes, attempting to uncover her intentions. "And you think you would be better as a division head rather than a chief editor for my erotica division?"

"I know what will make it work, but in order to build the successful line you want, I need more autonomy…and more money."

Hunter sat back in his chair with a slight thud. *Checkmate.* "So this comes down to money for you; is that it, Cary?"

Her smile remained intact. "If I'm going to spend day and night building a brand for you while neglecting my clients, losing money I could be making editing their manuscripts, then I want to make sure I'm compensated accordingly, and that I'm protected in case you feel you don't need me one day."

He folded his hands in his lap, trying to appear cool and collected. "Why would you think that?"

"It was my client, Smut Slut, who advocated the change in position. But she warned you had something of a short attention span, and figured a division head would be less likely to be disposed of than just an editor."

"Chief editor," he corrected.

"But still an editor, Hunter."

He paused, noting the way the light from his arched window shined on her face. Suddenly, she did not seem as sweet and innocent as he had first surmised.

"So you spoke to your client about me?"

She shifted in her chair. "I wanted her opinion of you."

"Her opinion?"

"Smut Slut is a very shrewd woman where men are concerned. She has a talent for breaking down a man in the first few minutes of meeting them."

Hunter shook his head. "Yeah, I noticed. Does your friend have a real name, or does everyone call her Smut Slut?"

Cary lightly laughed, filling Hunter's dingy office with the uplifting sound. "Yes, she has a real name, but I have been sworn to secrecy. You would be surprised at how normal she is…outside of her leather and wigs, of course."

He recalled the intriguing woman's blonde hair and felt a pang of regret that it may not have been her real hair color. Hunter loved blondes.

Standing from his chair, he considered Cary's offer. Bringing on another editor with the company would be easy enough to hide from his brother and father, but a division head would be something of a challenge.

"What if I were willing to offer you a division head position after we had launched our first book?" he proposed, peering out his window.

"That still does not give me a great deal of job security," Cary asserted. "What if you pull the plug after the first book?"

Hunter raised his eyebrows, agreeing with her as he turned from the window. "Then we'll have to make sure the first book we launch gets enough attention to keep your new division going."

"You would need a book from a well-established writer who is already known in the market," she countered.

He thoughtfully nodded. "If we could bring a known writer on board to launch our line, it would help assure our success."

She angled forward in her chair. "What if I could guarantee you a book that would bring in the numbers you need...would you give me the division head position then?"

He took a second or two to think about it. "It would have to be some book."

Cary glanced down at the purse in her lap. "Smut Slut has just finished her next novel, called *The Bondage Club*, and has been considering shopping it to another publishing house. She's not happy with MandiRay, but if you made it worth her while, she might be willing to come here. Especially if she knows I will be handling all of her promotion."

Hunter was floored by the suggestion. He remembered the line at the Book Expo and her popularity with readers. To corner such a writer for the debut of his erotica line would be a hell of a coup.

"Do you think she would do that?" He was almost shocked by the enthusiasm in his voice.

"I could talk to her. We go way back and she would listen to me if I suggested it. But you would have to offer her a better deal than she has with her current publisher."

Hunter took a step closer to Cary. "Absolutely. Let's get her on the phone right now."

"No, this needs to be handled delicately. If you call her, she will know I let it slip about her wanting a new publisher, and I can't jeopardize our professional relationship." Cary stood from her chair. "I'll call her later this morning and broach the subject. If she's interested, I will have her get in touch with you."

Hunter considered her offer for a moment. "If you get me Smut Slut's next book, you can have your division head position. I'll give you full control over the erotica line, including the advertising and marketing. Deal?" He held out his hand.

Cary came up to him and took his hand. "It's a deal, Hunter."

A flicker of electricity passed from her hand to his, making Hunter stifle a gasp. He studied the outline of her smooth jaw and upturned nose, and again felt that tug of familiarity pass between them. "Excuse me for asking, Cary, but have we met before?"

"No, we have never met before." Cary quickly backed away. "I should be going," she softly said, rushing to the door.

"Just let me know when you want to get started," Hunter called behind her.

Cary yanked open his office door. "Let me check my schedule and I'll call you later today with a start date." Then she hurried out of his office.

After she had left, Hunter detected the faintest trace of her floral perfume. He thought the fragrance oddly resembled her outwardly feminine appearance, but somehow he gathered what was on the inside of Cary Anderson was far from vulnerable and delicate.

Putting the woman out of his head, he returned to his desk with a renewed interest in the manuscripts and papers piled there. The idea of introducing a meatier genre of novels into the mix at Donovan Books almost made him giddy.

"The old man will have a heart attack when he finds out," Hunter said with a delighted grin. "This is going to be the best thing that ever happened to Donovan Books...and to me."

* * *

The veil of evening was reaching across his office window when Hunter's cell phone on the side of his desk rang. Checking the caller ID, he frowned when he saw that the number was blocked.

"This is Hunter Donovan," he barked into the phone.

"Do you always answer the phone in such a cheerful manner?" a sexy female voice reprimanded.

"That depends on who this is."

"Cary told me of your little meeting today, and your interest in my next book. You don't waste any time do you?"

Hunter's heart skipped a beat. "Well, well, Ms. Slut. Nice to hear your voice again. I hope your time at the Book Expo was worthwhile."

"You were the highlight of my trip, Mr. Donovan."

Hunter smiled as he sat back in his creaky desk chair. "I'm so glad. I was beginning to think you didn't like me."

"Have you ever met a woman who didn't like you?"

The question made Hunter chuckle. "Which answer will get me your next book, Ms. Slut?"

A high-pitched tinkling laugh came through the speaker of his iPhone, making Hunter's stomach flutter ever so lightly. "I like a man who doesn't waste time with sweet talk. Check your e-mail. I just sent you the manuscript. It's called *The Bondage Club*, and if you're interested, e-mail me a contract, and I will look it over."

"Can I ask what it's about? I mean, with a title like that I can guess, but...." His voice faded as his curiosity rose.

"There are many different kinds of bondage, Mr. Donovan, that don't involve ropes, chains, or even handcuffs."

Hunter gaped at his cell phone. "I don't get it."

"Love can be a form of bondage," she explained. "We can get tied to someone just as easily as we can be tied up by someone. The book is about bondage in all of its forms."

"Then I look forward to reading it." He paused as he thought of an idea. "But why not come to my office? We can discuss the details of the contract over lunch," he pursued with a hint of insistence in his voice.

"I don't think so. Lunch with you would be dangerous."

Hunter coyly smiled. "For which one of us, Ms. Slut?"

"I'm not your type, Mr. Donovan."

Hunter's body rippled with the hint of a challenge. "You never know; if Donovan Books handles your novel, we may grow on each other."

"I hope not. Getting involved with the man who publishes my book would complicate matters. I'm also a very demanding author. I might get on your nerves after a time."

"I have a lot of demanding authors. You would fit right in."

"Do you usually try and date your authors, or will I be the first?"

He fingered a corner of the manuscript on the desk before him as his imagination began to wander. "You would be the first. I never date clients."

"I heard a nasty little rumor to the contrary, about your brother and Monique Delome. They were engaged and then she up and married some Texas oil man. Lucky girl."

"Lucky to be rid of my brother," Hunter returned, pushing the manuscript in front of him to the side.

"Oh, do I detect a note of sibling rivalry, Mr. Donovan?"

He leaned back in his chair and turned his eyes to his arched window. "Rivalry, nah. More like deep-seated hatred. And if I'm going to bare my soul to you, you should start calling me, Hunter."

"Let me guess, Hunter." Her voice was throaty and delicious, spurring on his desire. "He stole your Legos when you were six and you have never forgiven him."

Hunter ran his hand over his face, feeling the conversation was getting a little too personal. "Never mind my brother. Let's talk about you."

"I make it a practice never to talk about myself. The less people know about me, the better."

"I don't agree, Ms. Slu…." Hunter crinkled his brow. "What else can I call you? Ms. Slut is too—"

"Call me Smuttie, if you like."

"Smuttie…don't you have a real name?"

"Smuttie is all you need to know." The sound of voices in the background broke in. "Let me know what you think of my manuscript, Hunter. I'll be waiting to hear from you." Then the line went dead.

Hunter stared at his phone for several seconds, trying to put the conversation into perspective. He figured most of what the woman was giving him was an act to help sell books, but there was something else about her that he found intensely appealing. He pictured her tight black leather minidress and high-heeled black boots, and wondered what she was hiding behind the costume.

His eyes swerved back to his desk and the pile of manuscripts waiting to be read. Reaching for his laptop, he hit his e-mail inbox. Scrolling through the e-mails, he spotted one sent from a Ms. S., and immediately opened it.

There was no introduction or note written, only the attached manuscript. Opening the work titled *The Bondage Club*, he sat back in his chair and decided to glance through a few pages. But one page made him hunger for the next, and soon he lost all interest in work and handed himself over to Smut Slut's whimsical writing.

Chapter 3

It was well after midnight by the time Hunter finished reading through Smut Slut's manuscript. *The Bondage Club* had been more than compelling. Set in the Midwest, it was the tale of an insecure woman who walked away from her high school sweetheart to find a life. Through a string of bondage-laden sexual affairs, she discovered that what she was looking for all along was love and not sex, and it had been right under her nose the entire time with her former sweetheart. The story had a happy ending, vital to the book's success, but the cynic in Hunter doubted a man such as the stalwart boyfriend in the book would have taken his former girlfriend back. Smut Slut may have known a few things about men, but she did not know their Achilles' heel; that overriding inability to share. Men were never willing to share anything, especially a woman with other men. It was the nature of the beast, and unlike women who were able to share clothes, makeup, and even secrets, men had a primal instinct to protect what they considered theirs.

Flipping down his laptop, Hunter grinned. Only a man would know such a detail, and that was probably why such novels never appealed to a male audience. Men needed raw stories filled with lust, power, and an occasional shoot out to keep them interested; women just needed romance and a happy ending. Oh, the pitfalls of estrogen.

Standing from his chair, Hunter stretched out his tired back and then retrieved the keys on his desk. Other than the misrepresentation of the male sex, Hunter knew the book was good. It would be a big seller and could make Donovan Books debut into the erotica genre a roaring success.

After slipping from his office, he made his way to the first floor of the building. Taking the stairs helped to push the cobwebs from his mind that the hours of reading had collected. Once he had set the alarm, Hunter locked the front entrance and headed down the darkened street to his waiting crimson red, Z4 28i BMW roadster.

As he turned over the ignition, his thoughts floated back to the book he had just read. He wondered if the story was a glimpse into Smut Slut's past. All writers drew from their experiences, and Hunter had been around enough of them to know that snippets of who they were and what they had been through seeped their way into each and every novel. Hell, he had even put pieces of his life into the pages of his book.

Cringing at the recollection of his novel, he reasoned that he had been too young to put pen to paper. Writing was an older man's game, or at least an experienced individual's calling. You had to first live life in order to be able to put a convincing interpretation of it in a book. Hunter figured starting a novel at twenty-six had been a futile effort from day one. But he had learned a lot since then, and had always, in the back of his mind, hoped to write again.

"Yeah, right," he clucked as the car sped along Walker Street to his loft residence in Castleberry Hill. "I'm too busy reading everyone else's crap to write my own."

Entering the garage of the ten-story, converted red-bricked building that housed his condo, Hunter doubted he would ever write again. Perhaps his brother had been right and he was better suited to publishing books instead of creating them. At least he still felt a part of the literary world, even if it wasn't very satisfying.

He pulled into one of his two reserved spots in the bricked garage and his heart fell to the pit of his stomach when he spied the spotless white Mercedes C250 Sport parked in the slot next to his.

"Shit," he cursed as he turned off the engine.

Climbing from his car, he glared at the Mercedes. Clutching the brown leather briefcase that he had stuffed with another manuscript, he headed to the garage elevators. Stepping into the elevator car, his thoughts raced ahead to the confrontation about to take place. He was tired and wanted nothing more than a hot shower, a shot of vodka, and to watch a little television before going to bed. He did not need another round of fighting with her, and as the elevator doors opened on the eighth floor, his impatience turned to anger.

As soon as he stepped from the silver and oak elevator car, he saw her standing beside his front door. Her long, silky brown hair was gathered around her right shoulder, accentuating the creaminess of her skin. With her tall, thin frame, long face, thin red lips, sunken cheekbones, and angled jaw, she could have easily been a model, but had always shunned her beauty. Wearing slim-fitting blue jeans and a soft brown cardigan, to Hunter she looked enticingly seductive, but his past experiences with the woman tempered his desire to take her to bed.

"What are you doing here, Kat?"

The smile she put on for him was absolutely radiant. "I was in the neighborhood and wanted to see you."

He went to the door and put his key in the lock. "In the neighborhood?" He snorted with disapproval. "Let me guess, you and Frank broke up."

Her deep-set brown eyes became a little rounder. "How did you know?"

"The only time you show up at my door is when you have broken up with your latest boyfriend." Shifting his briefcase from one hand to the other, Hunter angrily shoved the front door open.

"I was really in the neighborhood. I have a show starting later next week not far from here."

Exploring her curves with his tired eyes, he felt his aggravation with her quickly abate. "Business must be good."

"I'll send you an e-mail invite. You have to come to the opening party."

He sighed, knowing he would have to go to the party. It wasn't in him to disappoint her. "Have I ever missed an opening, Kat?"

"No. You've always been there for me, baby."

Hunter flipped the light switch by the front door. "You need to stop dropping by. We can't keep doing this."

She walked into the center of a shiny oak hardwood floor and stood next to a white breakfast bar with three chrome stools that marked the start of the recessed kitchen. Behind her, the adjoining living room was filled with a green sofa and plush, overstuffed wide chairs that stood before four tall windows set into the deep red-bricked wall. To the right of the door were the metal stairs that climbed the entire three stories of the condo. Left over from when the building had been a warehouse, the bricked walls and painted stairwell were the only reminders of the structure's historic past.

"I'm glad you bought this place. It suits you. Better than that ratty apartment we used to live in."

Hunter slammed the front door as his anger returned. "I bought this condo because I needed some place close to the office...and I liked that ratty apartment."

"Well, I like you better as a successful publisher rather than a struggling writer. You're better off this way."

Dropping his keys on the dark wooden table by the door, he let out a frustrated breath and then walked to the bar. "Why do you always show up on my doorstep, Kat?"

"We're friends, aren't we?" she questioned, slinking over to the breakfast bar.

"Every time you come over, we end up...." He ran his hand over his mouth, not wanting to upset her.

She had a seat on one of the chrome stools and peeled the cardigan from about her body. Hunter could feel his heart beating faster as he took in the swell of her breasts beneath her tight, white T-shirt.

Leaning against the bar, Kathleen traced her fingers along a swirl in the white-granite countertop that shone beneath the chrome dropped lights hanging from above. "Nothing has to happen this time, Hunter."

Hunter put his briefcase on the bar and turned for the built-in, wood-inlaid refrigerator behind him. "What happened with Frank?" He opened the refrigerator door. "When I saw you at your last opening several months back you were talking about marrying this one."

"He was already married," she admitted.

"Married? Did you know?" Hunter pulled a bottle of Gray Goose vodka from the fridge and went to a white-painted cabinet above the sink.

"He told me when we first started seeing each other about his wife. He said they were separated and were going to get a divorce."

Hunter smirked as he placed two glasses on the bar before her. "But he had no intention of leaving her, is that it?"

"He said she was going to want half of everything he had in a divorce and he could not afford it. So I told him marry me or else."

Hunter poured three-fingers of vodka in each of the glasses. "And he chose 'or else,' right?"

She picked up one of the glasses. "What's wrong with me, Hunter?"

"Nothing, Kat." He put the bottle on the bar as he took in her pouty pink lips. "You know you're beautiful, a great photographer with a very successful career, you're smart, and funny, and—"

"Why can't all the men I'm with see those things?" She lifted the glass to her lips and downed a quick gulp. Wincing, she put the glass back down on the bar. "You were the only man who really cared about me. I should have married you when you asked."

He grabbed for his glass as his heart stung at the mention of her refusal to marry him. "That was a long time ago. You said you needed space to pursue your career and you were right. Look at you now. You're one of the top photographers in Atlanta."

Her long fingers stroked the rim of her glass. "Yeah, I have my career, but not the husband and family I wanted. Why can't I have both?"

Hunter took a quick sip of the vodka, hoping to fortify his ability to resist her. "You can have both. Just stop dating married assholes."

She smiled and stood from her stool. "You're right. You were always right. That's what I could always depend on with you, Hunter. You told me the truth."

He set the glass on the bar as she cozied up to his side. "I'm your friend, Kat. When you moved out, we promised each other we would stay friends."

She ran her hands up his white shirt and began undoing the buttons. "We've stayed a hell of a lot more than friends."

Hunter let out a defeated sigh. All she had to do was touch him and his resolve to push her away melted. "Please don't. We've got to stop doing this." He held her hands.

Kathleen lifted his fingers to her lips. "Stop doing what?" she playfully teased, kissing his fingers.

She sucked on the tip of his index finger as her eyes carefully weighed his reaction.

Hungrily licking his lips, Hunter inched his mouth closer to hers. "Every time you break up with a boyfriend, you come here and we end up in bed together."

She lowered his hand from her mouth and placed it against her left breast, letting his fingers move back and forth over her erect nipple. "I need to know I'm still wanted. Do you want me, Hunter?" Her hand traveled to the crotch of his pants. "Do you?"

The blood was pounding through his veins and his debilitated defenses crumbled. Pulling her roughly into his arms, he cursed his weakness for her. Of all the women he had known, Kathleen was the only one who could continuously walk back into his life and make him want her just as much as the first day they had met.

When his lips came down on hers, there was no tenderness or emotion for Hunter. This was lust, pure and simple. He wanted to spend a few moments reliving the passion of his youth with the only woman he had ever loved. It may not have been healthy, but he knew it would sure be satisfying.

He stood back from her, took her hand, and led her to the metal staircase. Looking up, he hesitated as his eyes drifted up to the third floor of his loft.

She curled into his side. "What is it, baby?"

His gut filled with doubts as he brushed the long hair from her face. "Perhaps we should…not do this."

Laughing, Kathleen took his hand and pulled him toward the stairs. Hunter let her lead him up the metal steps, past the informal sitting room and exercise area he had on the second floor, to the third floor bedrooms. Passing up the small green and gold guest room that Hunter used as an office, she guided him into the master bedroom with its roof of skylights, and king-sized raised bed with a dark walnut cubicle headboard.

Kathleen went to the open master bath to the side of the room and peeked inside to the glass shower and white marble vanity. She smiled as she took in the clutter of aftershave, toothpaste, and other assorted toiletries that filled the vanity countertop. "Still a pig, I see."

Hunter crossed to the walk-in closet next to the bathroom. "Maid doesn't come until Friday."

Kathleen stepped from the bathroom. "Maid? Well, aren't you becoming quite the successful businessman? You never believed in maids."

"I could never afford a maid before, and working sixty plus hours a week makes housework impossible."

She pulled her T-shirt over her head and dropped it on the floor. "How about a girlfriend?"

Hunter had to concentrate on the question as his eyes homed in on her full breasts. "You know I don't need one of those."

Kathleen went to the bed and reclined over the gold bedspread. "Yes you do, Hunter."

He removed his shirt and tossed it aside, enamored by her glowing skin. "Let's not talk about that now."

Kathleen unzipped her jeans and wiggled out of them. "You're not happy, Hunter. You need a woman to make you happy." She let her jeans and underwear fall to the floor.

"You sound just like my mother when you talk that way, Kat." Angling over her naked body, he was fascinated by the curve of her narrow hips. She sat up and tugged at the zipper on his blue trousers.

Hunter kissed her neck as her hands worked his trousers and boxers over his firm, round butt. Once he had kicked the clothes to the side, he encircled his arms about her. The softness of her skin made him grow hard. He could smell the honeysuckle shampoo in her hair, and when he kissed her shoulder, she tasted sweet, like strawberries dipped in cream.

Kathleen's hands gripped his round butt. "I forgot how good your ass feels."

Nipping the nape of her neck, Hunter's hands eagerly roamed over her hips, squeezed her heart-shaped butt, and kneaded the long muscles in her back. When his fingers began to tease her left nipple, she wrapped her long legs about his hips. Desperate for him, Kathleen fondled his erection and then rubbed it against her wet folds.

"Patience, sweetheart," he moaned into her neck.

Depositing kisses down her chest, he kneeled between her legs, spreading her knees wide apart. When his lips hovered over her folds, Kathleen's fingers clutched his hair, anxious for his mouth to close in. Easing her delicate flesh open, he first flicked his tongue over her sensitive nub. Kathleen's grip tightened on his hair, and when he started sucking on her, her thighs quivered against his cheek.

"Yes," she cried out as his teeth grazed her flesh.

When she came, her orgasm threw her back against the bed and she let out one long, impassioned scream.

Hunter grinned and kissed her thigh. He loved that sound; the animal-like cry of a woman in ecstasy. "Now you're ready for me," he whispered against her flat stomach.

While Kathleen caught her breath, he slid his hands beneath her butt and angled her hips upward. Without warning, he dove into her, pushing as far as he could go. Kathleen sighed as he entered her. Pulling out, he thrust into her again, pressing her body into the bed. She raised her hips and held on to his shoulders.

"Do it harder," she commanded.

Wanting to please her, Hunter pounded into her with wild abandon. Soon, she was calling out his name as her body undulated beneath him. But Hunter wanted more. When she stilled, he withdrew and flipped her over. Positioning Kathleen on her knees, he forced her head down into the bed and then brutally entered her again. The act reminded him of something he had read in Smut Slut's manuscript. The heroine of the story had preferred to be entered ruthlessly from behind, and liked it when a man spanked her bottom as he penetrated her. Hunter ran his hand along the curve of Kathleen's small, round butt and was tempted to experiment. Lifting his hand, he gently tapped it against her ass.

Kathleen flinched. "You've never done that before."

Hunter paused, eager to discover her thoughts. "Did you like it?"

She backed her hips into him. "Do that again."

This time he did not hold back and slapped her ass, hard.

"Yes," Kathleen squealed.

He rammed into her as his hand spanked her bottom. Kathleen lowered her head and gripped the bedspread. With every deep and merciless thrust, he slapped her behind, until she began bucking beneath him and screaming with pleasure. The rough sex only heightened his desire, and he held off as long as he could before the urgency of his climax became unrelenting. Clasping his hands about her hips, he slammed into her with every ounce of strength he possessed. Sweat was beading on his forehead when that relieving tingle started to climb from his groin, up his back, and then explode throughout his body. Grunting loudly, he finally came and then collapsed on the bed, completely spent.

Listening to the sound of his rapid breathing, Hunter wiped the trickle of sweat from his brow. Kathleen turned to him and ran her hand along his muscular chest.

"Since when were you into the rough stuff?"

He let his hand flop down on the bed as his eyes went to the skylights above, taking in the twinkle of stars. "Never."

"You ever have fantasies about tying a woman up and having your way with her?"

"Nah. I was never into that. I just got the idea from a book I'm going to publish."

"Must be some book." She cuddled against him. "We might have to do it that way again."

"Again? We shouldn't have done it this time, Kat."

Her hands swept down to his groin as she placed her lips against his ear. "I liked being your bad little girl."

Hunter let out a long breath as a myriad of unhappy memories of their life together inundated him. "Yeah, I remember."

She giggled next to him. "But you liked it when I was bad, right?"

"Liked wondering where you were half the time? No, I didn't." Fuming, he pulled away from her. "You would just disappear and never tell me where you were going or who you were with. You made my life hell, Kat." Shaking his head, Hunter shimmied to the edge of the bed.

She sat up, gathering the sheets about her. "You knew how I was when we lived together. I needed my space sometimes. I never meant to hurt you. But I've changed. I want a life with someone now."

He stood from the bed. "Let's not do this again." He was about to turn to his bathroom when she stopped him.

"Where are you going?"

He pointed to his bathroom. "To take a shower."

"Do you want me to come with you?" She smiled suggestively.

He eyed her half-naked body and then thought about the work he needed to do. Inexplicably, the idea of work appealed to him more than a night of dealing with Kathleen's ego. "No. I have a lot of work to do tonight."

She scooted to the edge of the bed. "But I thought we weren't finished."

He was growing weary with her need for constant attention. "I'm just tired, Kat, and I don't feel like playing games with you."

"What games?"

"You know what I'm talking about." He waved his hand between them. "This. We do this every time you come over. We sleep together, start talking about us, and you begin hinting that you want to try again. Then, you sneak out in the middle of the night while I'm asleep and I never hear from you until the next guy dumps you."

"You asshole! You make me sound like some kind of pathetic...." She stood up. "I don't need this shit from you."

"Why are you getting mad at me? It's the truth, Kat."

She quickly began picking up her clothes from the floor. "You always were a heartless prick, Hunter."

"I'm heartless?" He pointed to his chest. "Kat, you were the one who ran away from everyone who tried to help you. You ran out on me and every other man you—"

"That's bullshit!" She struggled to pull her T-shirt over her head. "You're just jealous. I always knew what I wanted and went for it. I'm a renowned photographer, you said so yourself. I stuck with my dreams, but you're the one who ran away from yours. You gave up on your novel. You let your father and brother bully you into working in that crappy little publishing business." She shoved one of her legs through her jeans.

"If that's what you think, then why do you always come running back to me when your life turns to shit? You jump into my bed and then run off, making me feel like you just made the biggest mistake of your life. I'm sick of...whatever this is."

She zipped up her jeans and tossed back her long brown hair. "You can say what you want about me, but at least I'm living my dreams. What are you doing?"

She bolted from the bedroom, and Hunter listened as her feet furiously trotted down the stairs. When the front door finally closed with a loud bang, he leaned his shoulder against the entrance to the bathroom and ran his hand over his hair.

"Son of a bitch. I let her get to me again."

Turning for the bathroom, Hunter berated his inability to push his ex away. Every time he let Kathleen back into his life for the briefest instant, it always turned out badly. When would he learn his lesson? But as he flipped on the hot water in the shower, he recalled their interlude in bed and the way she had responded to his playful roughhousing. Things had always been pretty good with them between the sheets, but never quite like that. Shrugging off their fight, he decided that he had liked the change of pace in bed. Showing a woman who was boss appealed to him. Hunter questioned if that was why erotica books were so popular. It opened the reader to a new realm of possibilities; possibilities of pleasure that had only been whispered about but never indulged.

Smiling at the potential bankroll this could give Donovan Books, Hunter stepped below the rushing water. "I think I'm gonna like erotica. I think I'm gonna like it a whole lot."

Chapter 4

Hunter had been anxiously waiting for Cary Anderson's first day at Donovan Books. He wanted to get started on his new erotica line, especially after his experience with his ex. Ever since that night with Kathleen, he had been interested in learning more about the different forms of pleasure that Smut Slut had written about with detailed accuracy in *The Bondage Club*. After having purchased a few of his new client's e-books, he spent his nights with his Kindle in hand, eagerly reading her stories of love, sex, and bondage. By the time Cary walked into the offices of Donovan Books that Monday morning, Hunter was eager to learn all he could about the ins and outs of the erotica genre.

Waiting for Cary to arrive, he was at his desk, going through a stack of messages. Most were from writers wanting to hear if their manuscripts had made the grade for publication, some were from writers already signed by his house and curious about the current status of their books, and then there was one message from his father that had been left earlier that morning with the words Call Me written across the bottom of the yellow slip of paper and circled with red ink for emphasis. As Hunter was frowning at the message in his hand, Cary breezed in through his open office door.

"Good morning, Hunter," she said in a voice that instantly washed away the heavy atmosphere in the room.

Hunter briefly admired her green floral dress and the way her bobbed hair was swept to the side. "Well, hello and welcome." The air in his office filled with her floral perfume and Hunter stood from his desk, enraptured by the scent. "I hope parking wasn't too bad for you. We only have two allocated spots outside."

"No problem. I don't live too far from here. I walked from my apartment." She glanced back at the open door. "I hope it's all right, Julia told me to come straight up."

"Yeah." He cleared his throat, suddenly feeling nervous. "I need to get your key." He opened a drawer in his desk and pulled out a brass key on a key ring.

She was still standing by the office door, eyeing the array of Alexander the Great statues on the bookshelf. "Who's that? He looks familiar." She pointed to the collection.

"My father is a nut about the ancient Greek conqueror, Alexander. He collected statues of him. There are a lot more at his house."

"But why are they here?"

"This was my father's office and he likes for me to keep it as he did."

"But why?" she probed, furrowing her pale brow. "It's your office now, right?"

He rubbed his hand holding the key across his chin, trying to come up with an explanation. "Yes, it's my office, but my father is...a very long story." He held up the key, wanting to change the subject. "This opens the front door. I set the alarm after everyone has left for the night and Julia, the receptionist downstairs, is always the first one here in the morning, so you won't have to be bothered memorizing alarm codes." He handed her the key.

Her brown eyes scrunched together. "Are you always the last one out of here...every night?"

"Just about. But I'm the head of the business; that's what is expected of me."

Cary tilted her head slightly to the side, studying his features. "Is it? I would think you would want to be home, spending time with your family."

Hunter waved her to his office door. "I live alone. Don't even have time for a gerbil."

Cary stepped to the door, clutching the key. "I didn't realize the publishing business was so demanding."

"Neither did I until I took it over from my father ten years ago. Now I know why the man was never home when I was a kid."

Cary entered a short corridor with fluorescent lights above and white linoleum tile on the floor. "My family was just the opposite. My dad was always home. My mom was the one who was never around."

Hunter turned left down the hallway. "Where was your mom?"

"She's an attorney with a big firm back in New Orleans where I grew up. She was always out to prove herself, which meant being away a lot."

Surprised, he looked over at her. "You're from New Orleans?"

"I came here to go to Emory. I was going to go to law school when I got sidelined working for the school newspaper. During my second semester, I changed my major to journalism." She rolled her eyes. "My mother had a fit, but my father encouraged me to pursue it."

"Is that where you know Smut Slut from? She said she was from New Orleans, as well." He ushered her back down the hall.

"Believe it or not, we never knew each other in New Orleans. Smut Slut and I went to Emory together. We met in a writing class. Even then her stories were very sexually explicit. We became friends and she began letting me review her work. My reviews turned into editing and when she sold her first book, she asked me to be her editor. That was eight years ago."

"You ever write, or do you only edit other people's work?"

"I always had aspirations, but never the courage."

"Courage?" He drew his brows together. "Courage for what?"

"Courage to put my name on a book. The thought of owning up to what I write scares me. I see what other writers I edit for go through with readers and reviewers, and I'm not that brave. I make a better editor than a writer."

"I think you're wrong. If you want to write, you will." He stopped before a wooden door with a frosted glass top. "You just haven't found what you want to write about."

When he pushed the half-glass door open, two women sitting behind thick desks piled high with manila folders lifted their heads. One was a slender blonde with a very pretty face and alluring gray eyes. The other was a rather dowdy middle-aged brunette, wearing glasses.

"Sara and Amy," Hunter announced as he waved a hand to Cary. "This is Cary Anderson. She's going to be the division head for a new line we are starting. I need you guys to go over the accounting procedures with her, have her fill out her payroll paperwork, and bring her up to speed on how to submit requests for her budgets."

The two women stood from their chairs and came up to Cary. "Welcome to the family. I'm Sara Coe," the pretty blonde greeted.

"And I'm Amy Wallace," the round brunette said, removing her glasses.

"Great meeting you ladies," Cary returned with a warm smile.

"Take good care of her," Hunter instructed. He nodded to Cary. "Come back to my office after you're done here and we'll start hacking out the particulars."

Cary turned to him. "Yes, Hunter."

The sunlight from the large window beyond the two cluttered desks reflected off her hair, momentarily captivating Hunter.

"Is there anything else?" Cary questioned.

He shook himself from his stupor. "No." Hunter hastily departed the room.

After returning to his office, Hunter went back to the pile of messages on his desk, eager for a distraction. Pulling the one from his father out from the pile, he picked up his office phone and dialed the number.

"Took you long enough to call me back," a deep, commanding voice barked. "I called you two hours ago, Hunter; where have you been?"

Hunter sighed before answering. "Working, Dad. Where else would I be."

"I figured you were still lounging around in bed with some bimbo. Your brother told me about the Expo. He said you were busy chasing blondes and not drumming up business."

Hunter sank back in his creaky chair and felt as if he were five years old again. "Chris is just being...Chris. I was right by his side for every meeting. We added a few new authors and I even got some ideas for a new line."

"No new lines," his father loudly protested. "I told you and your brother the day you two took over Donovan Books to keep to the formula. Alexander always maintained that 'Victory over one's enemies is only perfected when you avoid taking on their vices.' We can't be like every other publisher and introduce new lines all the time. We have to be better than the rest."

"Dad, this isn't some ancient war against Persia; it's book publishing."

"Might as well be war," Jim Donovan huffed. "We've been selling the same kind of books for over thirty years and it still works. We're pulling in over ten million in sales annually. That's how you could afford that fancy condo of yours. And how your idiot brother can afford to live in that ostentatious penthouse he has in the city. I swear you boys never learned a damn thing from your mother and me. We taught you two to be frugal and—"

"Dad," Hunter interrupted. "Can we save the lecture for the holiday dinner? I've got to get back to work."

"Jesus, you're such a smartass." Jim Donovan paused and let a hissing sigh out through his teeth. "I was calling to remind you to send your mother flowers. Her anniversary is coming up and I want to make sure you and your brother pay your respects."

Hunter closed his eyes and fought back the ache in his chest. "Dad, she's been gone for ten years. Maybe Chris and I should do something else, like take you out for lunch. All you do is sit around in that big house every day and—"

"Never mind about me. You see to my Gracie. Remind your brother to send flowers and visit her at the cemetery. Neither of you boys should be forgetting her."

Hunter crumpled the message from his father in his hand. "We can never forget about her."

An edgy silence filled the phone line. "Well, I just wanted to remind you…and no changes to my company, Hunter. You keep my publishing house like it has always been. That's what works. Don't be jumping on all these new book fads. I know the e-book thing has gotten big just like you predicted, and I agreed with converting the company to the whole paperless nonsense, but that is technology and not entertainment. Our books have always been bestsellers."

"But readers are changing."

"Yeah, I know. Your brother told me of your desire to put more sex in our books. But that is not the kind of publisher we are. We don't publish porn. You want to publish crap like that, then fine, do it when I'm dead and buried next to your mother. But while I'm breathing, Donovan Books will stay as it is."

Hunter could tell by the tone of his father's voice that the discussion was finished. It was the way he had always been. What Jim Donovan said was law around the Donovan household. His mother had been the only person ever able to change his father's mind. Gracie Donovan could flash her pretty smile, bat her green eyes, and all of Jim Donovan's ultimatums and shouting would go out the window.

Thinking it best to avoid further argument, Hunter decided to agree with his father...for now. "All right, Dad. Donovan Books will stay as you envisioned."

"Good boy. Don't forget to speak to your brother about the anniversary."

"I won't, Dad." Hunter tossed the crumpled yellow paper in his hand to his trash can. "I'll call you soon." He quickly hung up.

"Is our old man on your ass again?" a painfully familiar voice spoke out from the doorway.

Hunter felt his misery complete when he spotted his brother. Decked out in a fitted double-breasted blue suit that showed off his blue eyes, Chris Donovan strutted in the door, making Hunter's stomach recoil.

"He called me this morning, too, but I never got back to him," Chris admitted, eyeing the collection of statues on the bookshelf. "Are you ever going to get rid of that stuff?"

"No," Hunter replied. "You know how he feels about those statues."

Chris shook his head. "Old man was always obsessed with that guy."

"He wants us to take flowers to Mom's grave. The anniversary of her death is coming up."

"So it is. I forgot about that." Chris arched a graying eyebrow. "I'll have something delivered to her grave from both of us."

Hunter shook his head, disgusted with his brother's casual disregard. "He wants us to visit her, not just send flowers, Chris."

"Why? East View Cemetery is an hour away, and neither one of us have time for that kind of drive." Chris strolled up to his desk. "I'll just tell him we went over there and he won't know the difference."

"You lie to Dad with such ease." Hunter folded his arms over her chest. "I always wondered how you could do that."

"Don't start, Hunter. You get that holier than thou attitude like you were the good son and I was the bad one, when you know damn well it was the other way around."

"Don't give me that horseshit, Chris. You know I wasn't the one who came home every—"

"Excuse me?" a female voice called from the doorway.

Hunter turned to see Cary's eyes volleying between the two men.

"I'm sorry to interrupt, but I had a question."

Chris momentarily leered at Cary. "Well, hello. You're a new face around here."

Hunter's gut twisted with disgust. He knew Cary was just Chris's type: petite, and more like a little girl than a woman. Hunter had seen that same quality in Monique Delome, and he knew Chris had recognized it in Cary.

"I'm Cary Anderson." She came into the office with her hand extended.

Chris hastily moved across the office, and then eagerly took her hand firmly in his. "I'm Chris Donovan. Co-owner of the company." Chris held on to her hand for a few seconds longer than necessary before she pulled away.

"Co-owner? Since when?" Hunter's eyes swerved to Cary. "My brother manages most of our authors. He sets up their book tours, arranges media appearances, and is their all-around gopher."

Chris's blue eyes glared at his brother. "I am not a gopher." He pivoted to Cary. "I manage the PR for the authors at Donovan Books, which means I have a very important job. Unlike my brother, I have to be out in the public, selling our authors to media outlets, talk shows, and reviewers."

Cary gave him a tolerant smile. "How nice for you."

Hunter hid his amused grin. He was beginning to like this woman.

"My brother never told me he hired anyone new," Chris went on, not seeming to notice her slight. "What will you be doing for our esteemed publishing house?"

"Cary is our new chief editor," Hunter jumped in. His eyes pleaded with her to go along with him. "She will be overseeing all the lines."

"Chief editor?" Chris leaned in closer to her, appearing smug. "That is something. My brother never wanted to hire a chief editor before because he likes to micromanage everything." Chris's eyes drifted up and down her slender figure. "I'm surprised he's relinquishing control to you. Where will your office be?"

"Why are you so interested, Chris?" Hunter snapped.

Chris spun around to his brother. "Just wondering where you were going to put her, since the office you have for our other editors is rather cramped."

"I have a place in mind," Hunter coolly returned.

Chris faced Cary, wearing a synthetic smile. "Just make sure you're happy with your new office. If not, let me know and I will pull some strings."

She curiously eyed Hunter, standing behind his brother. "I appreciate that, but I'm sure it will be fine. I think I'll be too busy doing my job to be concerned about my office space. I have a lot of ideas for Donovan Books."

Chris gingerly placed his hand beneath her elbow. "Really? I would love to hear about your ideas. Perhaps we could get together for drinks sometime and discuss them."

Cary's eyes rotated back to Hunter's scowl. "I would like that, Mr. Donovan."

"Chris, please," he insisted. "We don't stand on formality at Donovan Books."

As Chris escorted Cary to the door, Hunter recognized the hint of lust in his brother's blue orbs. At the door, Chris let go of her arm. "I will see you again, Cary, since I spend a great deal of time here."

"You do?" Hunter blurted out. "That's news to me."

Chris gave him a contemptuous sneer and once again turned back to Cary. "It was a pleasure meeting you, Cary." Without looking back at Hunter, Chris waved his hand and walked through Hunter's office door. "I'll talk to you later, Hunts," he called over his shoulder.

After his brother had left, Hunter's body sagged with relief. Sometimes he did not know who was worse, his brother or his father.

Cary thumbed the doorway. "Is he really your brother?"

"Yeah, older brother by eight years." Hunter took a step closer to her. "I apologize for his...I think our mother dropped him on his head a lot when he was small."

She let out an adorable short giggle. "Are there any more Donavan's working here?"

"First of all, my brother does not work here, and no, it's just the two of us, which according to my mother was plenty."

"That must have made for an interesting home life."

"Uncomfortable, aggravating, even infuriating at times, but it was never interesting. We're not the closest of families."

"Yeah, I noticed," she added with a grin.

Now it was Hunter's turn to laugh. "Was it that obvious how much we hate each other?"

She pinched her thumb and forefinger together. "Just a smidge."

Hunter combed his hand through his curly hair, feeling a tickle rising in his gut. "Chris was always very competitive, so everything between us was a contest growing up. Still is."

"Why does he get to manage the authors while you're left to run the company?"

"He never wanted the day-to-day grind of my job. Chris always wanted lots of attention when we were growing up, and that's why he likes living in the limelight of the writers he manages."

Cary leveled her brown eyes on him. "Why didn't you want to tell him about my real job?"

He frowned and went to his office window. Peering out to the small patch of green grass across the street, he tried to find a way to explain his situation to her.

"My father was pretty adamant when I took over that I never change anything about the business. He's still that way, and unfortunately my brother agrees with him. They both feel we need to stay with that wholesome, sweet image we have, but I want to upend that image." He faced her. "Donovan Books needs to get edgier to attract a brand new type of writer like your friend, Smut Slut. I read her new manuscript and thought it was pretty graphic, but it was also very well-written and the story was timely and exactly what we need. I just don't want to say anything to either of them yet, until I get this first book out there. If we can make *The Bondage Club* hit some really high sales numbers, then I know my brother and father will change their minds."

Cary stood before his desk with her arms folded over her chest, carefully weighing his words. "You sound pretty passionate about this new line."

He stood for a moment, dazed by her comment. No one had ever called him passionate about anything. Remembering why the woman was in his office, Hunter tried to regain his businesslike composure. "Was there something you needed to see me about?" he questioned.

"Yeah, I was just wondering what you wanted me to call the new division, I mean besides erotica. Most publishing houses give their line a name."

Hunter clasped his hands behind his back. "What would you suggest?"

"I always liked the name 'Hot Nights' for an erotica line."

He pondered the name, and a slew of advertising possibilities rushed to the forefront of his thoughts. "Hot

Nights by Donovan Books. I like it. There's a lot of potential there."

She gave him a warm smile that caused his belly to ignite. "Hot Nights it is."

He waited as she sailed out of the room, her green dress flowing behind her. Heading behind his desk, he plopped down with a dull thud into his chair. As he contemplated working side-by-side with Cary for hours on end, he also recalled the way his brother had drooled over her. Hunter may have found Cary attractive, but he was damn sure his brother had already set his sinister sights on the woman. And when Chris Donovan wanted a woman, he was ruthless in getting her.

Irritation stirred in Hunter's belly as he thought of Chris pawing his new employee and eventually getting what he desired out of her. Usually he would stand aside and let his brother do whatever he pleased with a woman, but this time Hunter wasn't going to remain passive. He had to safeguard his company's future, and if Cary Anderson was going to be an integral part of that future, Hunter needed to keep her away from his lecherous brother.

Struck by an idea, Hunter hit the intercom button on his office phone. "Julia, call Bryan at our storage facility. Tell him I've a job for him to do."

* * *

After lunch, Hunter was at his oak desk, going through the slew of e-mails he received every day when Cary knocked on his open office door.

"I've finished up with the ladies in accounting. If you just tell me where my office is, I will get settled in."

Hunter pointed to a dark wooden desk in the corner of his office. "You're going to be in here with me."

Cary eyed the desk. "That wasn't there before."

"No, I had it brought from our storage facility while you were in accounting." He stood from his chair. "I figured since we will be working so closely together on this new line, it might be better for us to share an office in the beginning."

She went to the desk and ran her hand lovingly over the smooth surface. "Sure I won't cramp your style?"

Hypnotized by the way her hand caressed the wood, Hunter inched closer to her side. "For you to learn the workings of this place, and for me to learn everything I can about erotica, we need to be together," he told her as she went behind the desk. "Once we have launched our Hot Nights line, I can have a new office prepared for you. Until then, I honestly don't have any other place to put you." Hunter waited as she opened the drawers and inspected the black leather desk chair. "Your computer will be installed tomorrow. Your phone line the day after that. If you need additional room, let me know and I can have a bookcase and file cabinet brought over for you."

She shook her head and dropped her black purse in an open drawer. "No, all I need is a desk and a computer."

He leaned his hip against her desk. "I sent your friend, Smut Slut, a contract for her latest book, *The Bondage Club*, but I haven't heard back from her. You're sure she wants us to represent it?"

"Not to worry. She's been out of town at a conference. She'll be home tonight."

Hunter slid his hip up on her desk as he crossed his arms over his chest. "What conference? I wasn't aware of any going on right now."

Cary lowered her eyes to her desk. "I, um, I'm not sure. It could have been something else. She is always on the go. I can't keep up.

"Are you two close?"

"Pretty close." She nodded. "We share a lot of things."

"Share what things? Like clothes?" He pictured Cary wearing Smut Slut's black leather minidress and tried not to grin.

"God no." She softly laughed. "Her taste in clothing is far different from mine. But we do share the same love for Chinese food, white wine, jazz music, books, the list goes on." Cary rested her arms on the desk. "So tell me...what did you think of Smut Slut's new book?"

"I liked it, very much. But I can't help but wonder...." He stood up, shaking his head. "Never mind."

"What is it, Hunter?"

He gazed down at her, unsure of how to phrase his question. "How does she get such details in her books...I mean, she seems to know an awful lot about bondage and other kinds of... pleasurable pursuits. You're her friend...is she into that stuff? Is that why she writes about it?"

A devilish smile crept across Cary's lips. "I get that question a lot."

"Why do you get that question?"

Her smile fell. "I mean, people want to know if the writers who write about bondage and S&M actually do that stuff. Like Smut Slut. To make any story believable they do have to do a good bit of research."

"What kind of research?"

Cary sat back in her chair, studying Hunter's face. "Do you really want to learn about this genre? And I'm not talking about from the publishing angle; I'm talking about from the real life angle."

Hunter inched his hip back onto the desk. "A real life angle? I don't understand."

"If you're going to learn everything that erotica writers write about, you really need a crash course in the underground culture that revolves around such alternative sexual preferences."

"And do you know about this underground culture?"

Cary leaned forward, grinning. "An editor needs to be as well-informed as their client."

Hunter's hearty chuckle permeated the office. "I would never have imagined you to be…." He paused when an idea came to him. "Can you teach me about this underground world?"

"I'm not sure you will like it. Some parts are…I always stay away from the hardcore bondage geeks. But I guess I can show you some of the less uncomfortable elements."

Hunter eagerly rubbed his hands together. "Great. When do we begin?"

"Are you free this evening around seven?"

"Seven?" He nodded. "Sure."

Her engaging smile brightened. "Great. The club meets at seven thirty."

"What club?"

"The bondage club."

Chapter 5

Hunter was standing outside of an eight-story glass building on an outlet of the Georgia State University campus located in downtown Atlanta. The structure seemed better suited as an office building instead of a university setting, but Georgia State University was often called "the concrete campus" because it was considered an integral part of the central business district of Atlanta.

Checking his stainless watch, he was anxious to make sure he had the right time when he saw Cary coming toward him. Wearing a pair of slim fitting jeans and a casual top, she looked good…damn good. Her slender hips swayed beneath the fabric of her jeans, making Hunter instantly regret agreeing to see her after hours. The stirring in his belly he had felt in the offices of Donovan Books whenever she was near instantly resurfaced. He just hoped he had the self-control to handle this.

"Why did you want me to meet you here?" Hunter asked as she halted in front of him. "I thought you said we were going to a bondage club."

"We are," she assured him. She made a move toward the glass front door, but Hunter jumped in front of her and held it open. "Thank you," she added with a smile.

"But this is part of the GSU campus," he pointed out as they walked into a pale gray lobby. On the wall between the main elevators was painted the blue and white panther mascot of the school.

At the main elevators, she pressed the call button. "College campuses are the fastest growing places for bondage clubs. It's not like it used to be where you go to some out of the way bar on the bad side of town to find like-minded individuals. Thanks to *Fifty Shades of Gray* bondage has gone mainstream, and several major college campuses now have these kinds of clubs."

"I'm shocked to hear that, and a little mad that it wasn't available when I was in college," Hunter admitted.

An elevator opened to their left and Cary stepped inside. "We're going to the club that meets here every month. It's a small group of about twenty core members, but there are a lot that come just to see what it's about. The group encourages people to talk about their experiences, exchange ideas, and basically accept whatever lifestyle a person believes in as long as it's consensual."

"How long have you been coming to this group?" Hunter remarked as the elevator rose upward.

"About four years, on and off. I come to listen mostly, learn about trends, and get a better understanding of the people that participate in bondage."

"And what kind of person does this?"

"Every person does this, Hunter. There are no stereotypes when it comes to bondage. I've met doctors, lawyers, rich, poor, high school dropouts, and a nuclear physicist at these things. I would have to classify it more as a mood than a lifestyle."

On the fourth floor, the elevator doors opened and Hunter followed her along a gray-carpeted hallway. "What do you mean by 'a mood'?"

"Sex is a mood. Like hate or love, we have to be in the mood for sex. Bondage is a mood, too. A person has to be in the mood to be either the person who maintains control, called the top partner, or the person who rescinds control, called the bottom partner." She examined the large oak doors lining the hallway, and carefully read the numbers painted in black on them.

"I thought bondage was about tying someone up and spanking them with a riding crop or something."

Cary halted before a door with 433 painted in black across the top. She placed her hand on the silver doorknob and turned to him.

"Bondage isn't about tying someone up, it's about control. Giving it and taking it. Wait...." She turned the handle. "You'll get a better idea of what I'm talking about."

Hunter was expecting to see a circus of people dressed in black leather and tying each other into a series of complicated knots meant to make the human body resemble something that should be roasted on a spit. But the stark white classroom that greeted him was far from extraordinary.

A bearded gentleman with glasses, jeans, and a casual shirt was standing at a wooden podium at the head of the room with a long whiteboard behind him.

"Welcome everyone. For some new faces with us tonight, let me introduce myself. I'm Wayne Coleman, professor of sociology here at GSU. I oversee several support groups on campus for a variety of student issues, but I started this monthly bondage club because of my personal interest in the subject. I have been participating in bondage play for over twenty years, and my goal for these meetings is to make bondage discussions open and comfortable for participants." He turned to the board behind him, and picking up a marker, he wrote out the word Safety. "Tonight we are going to discuss safety when using different bondage techniques," Wayne Coleman added.

Hunter browsed the assorted desks scattered about the white linoleum floor. Most of those in attendance must have been college students, with only a few older faces mixed in. He was eyeing a young Asian couple with numerous body piercings at the front of the class when Cary tugged at his arm and pointed to two desks at the back of the room.

"Bondage should take place between sober, trusted partners who are fully aware of the risks involved and the precautions necessary to ensure safety," Dr. Coleman continued. "When performing acts of bondage, it's important to trust your partner and for your partner to trust you. If you can't, then I would suggest you find a partner you can trust."

A gangly young man with green overalls and sandals on his feet raised his hand. "What if you have more than one partner? Like a group thing?"

"That's a good point." Wayne Coleman nodded to the man. "Make sure acts are performed in a supervised location, or with a group of trusted friends. If you don't know strangers introduced to your group, then rely on your trusted partners to protect you from harm. There is a growing subculture of people who seek out others interested in bondage and pursue such activities with people who they don't know. I have personally heard some upsetting stories from other club members, so be careful who you play with."

"I had a friend who suffered nerve damage from a black sheet party," a tall woman with frizzy red hair called out next to Hunter. "She was tied too tight and left for hours by a group she had never played with before. Turned her off completely."

Hunter leaned over to Cary in the desk next to his. "Black sheet party?"

"BDSM orgy," she told him. "What toga parties were to the eighties, black sheet parties are to the current college generation."

"I think I'd prefer the toga party," Hunter quipped.

"That brings me to my next safety suggestion, the safeword," Wayne Coleman broke in. "There should be some clear way for any partner to indicate distress and a wish to discontinue or temporarily stop activities of the play. Safewords can be anything, but should be decided on prior to any play. If the subject has been gagged or can otherwise not verbally communicate, a different form of the safeword is needed. For instance, they may hum a tune, or move their hands or toes repeatedly. It is also very important never to leave a bound person alone." He pointed to the woman with the red frizzy hair. "Like your friend. She should have had a partner she could trust to check on her." Dr. Coleman came out from behind the podium. "Avoid positions or restraints which may cause a person to black out due to lack of oxygen or impaired breathing. If you plan on leaving a partner confined for any period of time, then make sure to change their position at least once an hour to avoid circulatory problems. Make a point to frequently talk to your partner to ask if they are all right." He paused and tossed up his hand in the air. "Sometimes we do get rather into our role playing, but it's best to always make sure that your partner can be released quickly in case of an emergency. I always keep a pair of scissors close by, or something that can cut through rope. And please, remain sober. Alcohol and drugs should always be avoided. Don't participate in any form of bondage play if you are incapacitated in any way."

"But a lot of groups we have been hanging with serve alcohol," the young Asian man with the body piercings spoke out. "What do we do, not go? I kinda thought getting a little wasted made it better."

Dr. Coleman gave an indulgent sigh. "Unfortunately, bondage groups usually do use alcohol to increase the arousal factor. But alcohol does not arouse, it impairs, and you need to always consider your partner's safety first. You might find that by staying sober, your experience is much more pleasurable."

"But where can I learn to tie some of those really complicated ties?" a pale blond man in the second row from the front demanded. He had on a ripped blue jean jacket and wore thick black leather boots. "You know, like the Japanese bondage stuff. I've seen those pictures and me and my girlfriend want to try it."

"That's a good question and I wanted to address the issue of trying to replicate scenes depicted in bondage photographs or videos," Dr. Coleman responded. "Visual stimulation can add to the fantasy value of an interaction. But sometimes these positions are dangerous or cannot be maintained for more than a few minutes. It takes a great deal of skill and practice to get to some of this high level inverted bondage, or suspension from the wrists and ankles. Especially in highly artistic Japanese bondage like you mentioned, years of experience with bondage are required to avoid the risks." Wayne Coleman's brown eyes took a turn of the room. "Let me briefly mention self-bondage. It is extremely risky, particularly because it violates an important principle of bondage safety; never leave a bound person alone. Without someone to release them in the event of an emergency or medical crisis, self-bondage can lead to severe and permanent physical damage. Especially in combination with asphyxiation, self-bondage can be lethal."

A general rustling could be heard from a few members of the audience as Dr. Coleman went back behind his podium.

"Now why don't we take a break and let everyone chat and get to know each other before we get into the hands-on portion of our meeting."

Hunter turned his panic-stricken eyes to Cary. "Hands-on?"

"The part of the meeting where they practice different kinds of bondage ties."

Hunter abruptly stood up. "Perhaps we should skip that part."

"Have you ever been tied up in bed, Hunter?"

"Of course not," he barked.

Cary slowly stood from her desk. "Ever wanted to be tied up? Handcuffed to a bed? Had a woman make you her sex slave?"

The blush on his cheeks burned his skin. "I've never needed any of that to...." He ran his hand over his mouth, controlling the uncomfortable feeling her eyes were creating in his belly. "I do just fine without all of that."

"So you like vanilla sex?"

He came alongside her, keeping his voice low. "What is that supposed to mean?"

She retrieved her purse from the floor. "Vanilla means you've never tried anything like bondage in bed, but perhaps you should."

His green eyes traveled the round curves of her face. "You ever try it?"

She shifted her gaze to the front of the classroom. "Perhaps I have."

"Cary," Dr. Wayne Coleman greeted as he approached from across the room. "I thought that was you." He held out his hand to her. "It's been a while since I've seen you here."

"Professor, it's good to see you again," Cary said, taking his hand. "I've been busy with work, but I wanted to bring my friend here tonight. Professor Coleman, this is Hunter Donovan. He owns a publishing company that is going to start a new erotica line, and he wanted to learn more about what he will be putting into print."

Dr. Coleman extended his hand to Hunter. "Great to meet you, Hunter. And we can always do with more books that explore the pleasurable side of bondage."

"Dr. Coleman has always been a great reference for anything related to bondage," Cary informed Hunter.

"Yes, I've been studying the entire culture since my college days. I was always fascinated with the dominant-submissive mindset. I got so into it that I ended up being a convert. Twenty years later here I am, teaching it in my classes, studying it for my research, and offering groups like this to the public to hopefully improve the safety."

Hunter glanced about the classroom. "Have you seen an uptick in the number of people attending your meetings?"

"You mean since *Fifty Shades of Gray* hit the market?" Dr. Coleman laughed. "Yeah, I get a lot more curiosity seekers in here since that book came out. Mostly young girls, thinking they will meet a billionaire with a bungee cord fetish, but they soon learn that's not the reality of what goes on in bondage groups. Some stay, but most go back to their vanilla sex."

Hunter gave Cary a smug side-glance. "Yes, vanilla sex does have its drawbacks."

"Are you a partaker of the bondage lifestyle, Hunter?" Dr. Coleman exuberantly inquired.

Hunter returned his gaze to Dr. Coleman. "Oh, I've been letting women tie me up in knots for years." He took Cary's hand. "I hope you don't mind, Dr. Coleman, if we sneak out of the class early, but we have dinner reservations."

Dr. Coleman smiled through his thick beard. "Not to worry. Come back anytime. Cary knows our schedule. Next month I will be having a talk on the erotic benefits of animal play."

Hunter tried not to laugh while staring into Dr. Coleman's puppy-like brown eyes. "Animal play?"

"Where the subservient partner acts and dresses up like an animal. You know, a pig, cat, dog, or cow."

Hunter tugged at Cary's hand. "I'll definitely have to come back for that one."

After he had all but yanked her from the classroom, Hunter made a beeline for the elevator.

"What's the rush?" Cary demanded, jogging behind him as his long legs charged down the hallway.

"Animal play?" He gaped over his shoulder to Cary. "Was he serious?"

When they reached the elevator, he let go of her hand and hit the call button.

"It's just role playing, Hunter. Every couple does it. When you take a woman to bed, don't you fantasize about her being someone else? Sex is about the fantasy."

"Sex is about sex," he insisted. "Fantasy has nothing to do with what goes on between a man and a woman."

"Man and woman, man and man, woman and woman, it doesn't make any difference. Sex is about the mind, not the body."

The elevator doors opened. "Last time I checked, the body had a hell of a lot to do with it." He rushed into the elevator.

"You're uncomfortable talking about this, aren't you, Hunter?"

"No, I'm not." He waved her inside the elevator. "I'm very comfortable talking about sex."

She walked into the elevator and touched his brow. "You're sweating."

He tilted closer to her. "I'm hot."

"If you can't admit that you're insecure about your sex life then I—"

"I am not insecure!" he argued.

The elevator doors closed while Cary continued to scrutinize him. "Answer one question for me."

He frowned at her. "I don't think I want to."

She turned to the elevator doors. "Fine. Where are we going for dinner?"

"Dinner?"

"You told Dr. Coleman we had a dinner reservation. So where are we going?"

The elevator slowed as it came to the lobby. "Do you like sushi?"

She nodded. "Yes, I do."

When the elevator doors opened, he guided her into the lobby. "I know just the place. Come on, I'll drive."

* * *

Thrive was a downtown restaurant that offered a mix of American food with sushi not too far from Donovan Books' offices. As Hunter escorted Cary through the lounge-like dining room with white plush chairs and couches set against chrome tables, she noted the modern décor and the hip crowd of sharply dressed businessmen and women milling around the shiny chrome sushi bar.

After they slid onto a white bench next to the glass and chrome table, a willowy young woman with arms no bigger than twigs handed them long black menus and gave a gaunt smile. Hunter grinned warmly at the hostess.

"How often do you come here?" Cary interrogated, after their hostess had stepped away.

"Every now and then," he confessed, opening his menu.

"Do you like the people in here?"

He lowered his menu. "The people?"

"You know, the trendy crowd; the kind who like to look good and expect all their friends to look good, too. Personally, I think they lead vacuous lives and realize when they hit forty that they never did anything worthwhile."

Hunter cringed. "That's kind of harsh, Cary."

"Is it?"

"It's just a restaurant. It's not a social statement."

"But places like this are a statement, just like having the right kind of car or house." She paused as her dark eyes explored his face. "Have you ever looked at people, Hunter? I would have thought at some point you would have noticed the people around you."

He put his menu down on the glass table. "What is wrong with you? You're fine in a room full of deviants who like tying each other up, but go to a public restaurant to eat dinner like a normal person and you're the one breaking out in a sweat."

"I just don't do well in places like this. I always feel...." Her voice dropped as her eyes scanned the dining room.

"Feel what?" He waited, but she said nothing. "Come on. I told you how I felt about your little bondage club. Now you tell me how you feel about this place."

Cary's eyes came together, the irritation apparent on her face. "I don't belong here, all right? Happy?" she stated in a sullen tone.

Hunter smiled, entertained by her sour countenance. "That's silly, Cary. Of course you belong here."

"Maybe I'm not good with people." She shrugged and snapped up her menu. "I'm not like you. I can't walk into a room and feel like I own it."

Hunter burst into a hearty belly laugh. "I assure you that is not me. That sounds more like my brother." He picked up his menu. "You're just like anyone else in here."

She shook her head. "No, I'm not. I'm different. There are two kinds of people in the world: those who see other people, and those who see only themselves. In this room, there are only those who see themselves."

Hunter took a moment to absorb what she said and observed how she nervously tapped her fingers on the table. "And that makes you different, because you see other people who don't see you?"

She gleaned over her menu. "I've felt different all my life. I've always been one of those people you look over and not at. Like you with the hostess who seated us. You thought she was pretty, didn't you?"

He casually nodded his head. "Yes, she was. Thin, but pretty. So?"

Cary lowered her menu and glared at him. "If I had brought you a menu, you would never have noticed me."

"That's not true," he objected. "You're an attractive woman. I'm sure you have had lots of men tell you that."

"This isn't about looks, Hunter. It's about perception. You saw the hostess, because that's what you want in a woman. You would never have seen me. I'm not what you want."

He snickered at her comment. "But you're sure what my brother wants."

"I'm what your brother sees in a woman. An object he can possess. Just like you see someone you can sleep with."

"I do not." Hunter gaped at her. "I see women as they are."

"We both know that's not true." She raised her menu again. "You're like most men. What you need in a woman is what you perceive them to be."

Hunter reclined in his seat, holding his menu. "I didn't realize editing erotica made you a guru on men."

"It doesn't. I just think if you would stop looking from the outside in and shift your perspective to the inside out, you would be more successful in relationships."

Hunter bristled at the comment. "I don't see you with a wedding ring, Cary. What makes you any more successful with relationships than me?"

Her eyes never wavered from her menu. "I never said I was successful. I'm just offering an opinion on why perhaps you keep yourself from having what you want in life."

"I have what I want," he loudly refuted, instantly regretting losing his cool.

Cary's dark eyes peered over her menu at him. "If you say so."

A young woman donned in black pants and a black T-shirt came to their booth. "Welcome to Thrive. What can I get you two to drink?"

Hunter slapped his menu down on the table. "Vodka and soda, and make it a double."

Cary's eyebrows went up and then turned to their waitress. "I'll just have iced tea."

"I'll come back with your drinks and get your order," the server added with a smile and then left their table.

Cary placed her menu to the side. "You all right, Hunter?"

"Fine," he grumbled. "Everything is just fine."

* * *

After two double vodkas, Hunter was having a hard time pulling his keys from the pocket of his jeans as he and Cary walked out of Thrive.

"You can't drive," Cary told him, grabbing for his keys. "I'll take you home."

Hunter tried to snatch the keys from her hand, but was too slow. "No, I'll drive you back to your car."

"My car will be fine where it is." She moved ahead on the sidewalk. "I can pick you up in the morning and you can drop me at my car before going to the office. You can't drive home drunk, Hunter."

"I'm not drunk," he insisted, following her.

"Oh, you're drunk, all right. You didn't touch your sushi, and would have probably ordered a third round of drinks if I hadn't told you I wanted to leave."

He came alongside her. "But my car has a stick shift. Can you even drive a stick?"

She confidently smiled up at him. "I'll manage."

"Manage?" He shook his head, knowing he had no other choice, and then waved down the street. "Fine. You can drive me home."

She glimpsed his crimson red roadster parked along the curb. "Glad to see you're not too far beyond reason."

When she hit the remote lock on his key ring, Hunter went to the passenger side of the car and opened the door. "Be careful with my car. If you wreck it, I will have to fire you."

She grinned at him over the top of the car. "Yes, boss."

As they drove to his place in Castleberry Hill, Hunter kept his head turned to the open window, hoping the cool night air would help sober him up. He hated to admit it, but Cary had been right, he was drunk. Her words back at the restaurant had made him drink more than usual. There was nothing worse than having someone else show you how wrong you were about yourself. Such moments tended to anger Hunter because he hated seeing his life through the eyes of another. It only made him feel like a bigger failure than he already was.

"The big one up on the right," he said to her as they came to his building on Walker Street.

"There's a garage entrance just up ahead."

After pulling into his designated spot in the garage, Hunter swiped at the keys still in the ignition. "I have to get my front door key."

Cary switched off the engine and snapped up the keys. "I'd better take you up to your place to make sure you don't fall flat on your face."

"I'm not that drunk, Cary."

She stepped from the car, ignoring him.

In the elevator, Hunter kept clenching his jaw, holding back his irritation at being treated like a child by his employee. He knew she was only looking out for his interests, but it still goaded him when anyone tried to tell him what to do. When the elevator doors opened, he stumbled out and headed to his front door at the end of the short hallway.

He was at his polished oak door, rummaging through his pockets for his keys when he remembered that Cary still had them.

"Searching for these?" She held up his keys as she came toward the door.

Hunter nabbed the keys from her hand. After fumbling with the lock, he pushed the door open and hurried inside. He flipped on the lights and headed across the shiny hardwood floor to the kitchen. Opening the refrigerator, he searched for something to drink. After finding a bottle of water, he turned and saw Cary standing in the doorway, holding the keys that he had forgotten in the door.

"Nice place." Her eyes explored the open stairwell that offered an unencumbered view all the way to the third floor.

He gulped back the water, wanting to quell his sudden dry mouth. "Thanks."

"How long have you lived here?" She pocketed his keys and shut the front door.

When the door closed with a loud thud, Hunter became edgy. "Ah, about ten years. I bought it after I took over Donovan Books." He set his bottle down on the white granite countertop on the bar, silently praying she would turn around and leave.

Cary ventured further into his home. "Fancy sports car, upscale home…you enjoy your success, don't you, Hunter?"

"What is it with you? Are all people who happen to look good and have nice things on your shit list?"

"No, I just don't see you here. I would have pictured you in something a little…simpler."

His anger ignited, and he went around the bar to confront her. "I like to live well."

"No, you like to show people you're doing well, but liking it?" She shook her head. "That's not what I see."

He lowered his head to her, taking in the cool condescension in her eyes. "You remind me of my brother. He always likes to tell me what a failure I am."

"I'm not saying that, Hunter. I'm trying to tell you that this," she waved her hand about the first floor, "isn't you."

Annoyed with her smug attitude, he edged toward her. "You don't know me, Cary."

"You're wrong, I do know you." She tilted her head slightly to the side as her eyes drank in his features. "We're exactly alike, Hunter. We're both trying to be something we're not."

Distracted by her full, red mouth, his hostility quickly retreated. "And what are you trying to be?" he whispered.

Her red lips lifted into a half-grin. "What do you want me to be, Hunter?"

He did not know if it was her lips, or the way her face looked in the pale light from his kitchen, but there was something so alluring about her in that instant. Before he could register what he was doing, Hunter inched forward and gently kissed her.

When he realized what he had done, it was too late. The softness of her lips was too tantalizing to refuse. He was committed, and as he wrapped her tiny body in his arms, he felt her kissing him back. His mind kept screaming at him to stop, reminding him that this was an employee and something like this could only end badly for both of them. But instead of heeding the advice, he pulled her closer.

What was happening to him? He had considered her an adorable girl who was feminine, smart, funny, but never his type. Now in his arms, she had become the passionate, captivating woman he had always longed for but could never find. How could one kiss change everything?

Opening her mouth, she yielded to him, and the act made Hunter grow hard. His kisses became more insistent. His tongue darted in and out, tempting her. And when Cary moaned, it took everything he had not to lift her from the floor and carry her up the stairs to his bedroom.

Cary was the first to pull away. Her lips were red and puffy, her eyes wide with disbelief, and her breath was coming hard and fast as she stood in front of him. Lowering her head to the floor, she placed her hand over her mouth, as if comprehending the magnitude of what they had just done.

"Shit." He took in a breath and passed his hand over his hair. "I shouldn't have...I was out of line."

"Ah...I should go." Spinning away from him, she dashed to the door.

"Don't go," he implored.

But she never stopped, and after wrenching the door open, she rushed down the hall to the elevator.

Hunter knew he should go after her, but his feet never left his spot in front of the breakfast bar. As she disappeared behind the closing elevator doors, he figured perhaps this was for the best. He could claim he was drunk, laugh it off as one of those awkward moments in life he would always regret, and then start their working relationship anew. But in his gut, he knew it would not be that easy for either one of them. He had liked kissing her; liked the taste of her lips and the feel of her against him, so much so that he did not want it to end. The funny thing was he had felt the same sensation from her. She had wanted him, and Hunter knew that kind of want was going to be dangerous for both of them. That was the problem with desire; if you didn't pursue it, you ached, and if you did indulge, you eventually spent the rest of your life wondering when everything had gone so horribly wrong.

Chapter 6

When Hunter awoke the next morning, the pounding in his temples felt like a five-year-old had been using his head as a drum. His mouth was parched, his body throbbed, but his mind was instantly flooded with visions of Cary. After she had run out the door, he went to the refrigerator and tried to blot out the memory of their kiss with gulps of vodka. But that did not help to quell the burning in his gut for her. It was as if her kiss had ignited something in him, a sudden need he had never realized he possessed.

Climbing from the bed, he groaned at the change in altitude and spied the wrinkled blue jeans and the half-opened, button-down shirt he had slept in. Taking in a few deep breaths, he stood up and wobbled for a moment before catching his balance. Pointing his body in the direction of his bathroom, he willed his feet forward, anxious to wash the crummy feeling from his bones.

After a hot shower and two very black cups of coffee, he felt somewhat better, but far from normal. He was running around his first floor living room, frantically searching for his keys, when he remembered that Cary had taken his car and his keys with her last night. Flopping down on his sofa, he dreaded calling her, but then recalled the spare set of keys to his condo that he kept in his kitchen drawer. Figuring he could catch a cab to work and settle things with her after his head had cleared, Hunter was comforted by the fact that he could postpone their eventual confrontation about that dreaded kiss.

By the time he caught the elevator, he was already coming up with explanations to give Cary about the previous evening. While hitting the button for the main lobby, Hunter decided he would admit he was drunk, profusely apologize, and give her the opportunity to quit her position. He hoped she would feel the same way and want to leave Donovan Books. The idea of working closely with her every day on his new book line scared the hell out of him, and if he couldn't make the launch of the new line work, then he would hire someone else who could. How hard could it be? Everyone was replaceable, right?

"Hey, there, Hunter." George Lansky from the floor below his stepped into the elevator. "Off to work?"

Hunter eyed George's pressed suit and shiny dress shoes, feeling blessed that he didn't have to don such attire for work.

"Yeah, heading to the office," Hunter remarked as George hit the button for the garage right above the main lobby button on the console.

"How is the publishing world?" George inquired, switching his black briefcase from one hand to the other.

"Fine, George, fine."

"Got any more *Fifty Shades of Gray* hitting the bookstores soon? My wife loved that book." He winked at Hunter. "I loved it, too, if you know what I mean."

Hunter suppressed his desire to cringe at the older man's suggestion. "Ah, no. I think that was a one-time fluke."

When the elevator stopped on the garage floor, George stepped out the doors. As Hunter waited for the doors to close again, he saw George turn to him.

"You're not driving in?"

Hunter held the elevator doors. "No, ah, my car isn't here. I left it somewhere—"

"What are you talking about?" George butted in. He pointed to Hunter's parking spot by the elevators. "It's right there."

Hunter burst through the open doors. Sitting in his reserved spot was his red roadster.

"Son of a bitch."

"Must have been a hell of a night if you can't even remember driving home, Hunter." George walked up to him and patted his shoulder. "Take a bit of advice from this old attorney, next time take a cab."

As George ambled to his blue Jaguar in a spot close by, Hunter headed toward his car. He tried the door handle, and to his surprise, the car door opened. He slid inside and spied his leather briefcase in the back seat. Looking around, he quickly found his keys in the ignition.

He was astounded. She had not taken his car last night. But then as he considered the consequences, he became angry. How did she get home? Was she safe? Questions one after the other barraged his mind. Turning the ignition, he revved the engine and all but peeled out of his parking spot, anxious to get to work. He became consumed with images of Cary making her way alone on the downtown streets of Atlanta late at night.

Racing out of the garage, he muttered, "If anything has happened to her, I'll never forgive myself."

* * *

Hunter had not even closed the glass doors that marked the front entrance to the offices of Donovan Books when he viewed Julia's silver and white art deco desk. His long legs strode across the pearl gray and silver reception area that he had spent a small fortune on during a much regretted renovation until he stood glaring into Julia's beady blue eyes. The round, middle-aged receptionist with the perky personality and affinity for cats stared at Hunter, appearing completely confounded by the look on his face.

"Are you all right, Mr. Hunter? You look like crap."

"Is she here yet?" Hunter blurted out.

"Who?" Julia came back, furrowing her wrinkled brow.

"Cary Anderson, the new girl. Did she come in yet?"

Julia nodded. "A few minutes ago." She picked up a paper cup of coffee on her desk with the familiar green and white logo. "She got Starbucks for me. Is there a problem?"

Hunter shook his head, letting out a relieved breath. "No, it's...never mind."

He left his receptionist and went to the gray painted door to the stairwell, not wanting to wait for the old, slow elevator that serviced the building. Taking the steps two at a time he climbed to the third floor and flung open the plain wooden door that led to the hallway outside of his office. The pounding in his head was made worse by his jaunt up the steps, and when he finally stood before his open office door, he eagerly peered inside. But Cary was nowhere to be seen.

Rushing to his desk, he slammed his briefcase down on top of the ever-present pile of manuscripts and cursed.

"What's your problem?" a high-pitched voice asked behind him.

When he whirled around, Cary was standing in the office doorway with a tall Starbuck's coffee cup in her hand.

"How in the hell did you get home last night?" He barreled across the room to her side. "You want to explain what you were doing traipsing around downtown Atlanta in the middle of the night?"

Cary's deep chocolate eyes twinkled. She did not say a word, but turned to the office door and quietly shut it. Then, she walked over to her desk and put down her cup of coffee.

"I took a cab from your place to GSU and got my car. I can assure you, at no time during the evening was I 'traipsing around downtown Atlanta.'"

"You could have left me a note or something. When I found my car in the garage, I about had a heart attack worrying that you—" He shut his mouth, afraid to go on.

She folded her arms over her pretty pink blouse. "Perhaps we should talk about last night. Get it out of the way so we can get back to work."

Hunter momentarily lost his capacity for speech. He didn't know what to say or how to say it without sounding like an idiot.

"I think what happened last night was the vodka and not you," she assured him.

A trickle of relief snaked through him. "Yeah, I was rather lit. It was a stupid thing to do. I apologize and completely understand if you don't want to work here anymore."

Her girlish laughter wafted about the office. "I'm not going to quit over a kiss, Hunter. It's not like we slept together. It was just a kiss." She went around her desk.

Perhaps he had underestimated her desire. He had sworn that she had kissed him back, but maybe he had been too drunk to discern what was real and what was imagination. He feigned a weak smile.

"You're right, it was a silly mistake. I'm glad you're not upset."

"It's already forgotten, Hunter."

Her words jarred him like a tow truck hitting a golf cart. He had always prized himself on his kissing prowess. Women had complimented his skill in the past, and he hoped the alcohol had not impaired his ability. Questions about how good a kiss it had been began to plague him. Perhaps he wasn't up to his usual level of performance. Maybe he needed to reassure her that he was a really good kisser. *What in the hell am I thinking?*

He took a seat behind his desk and flipped open his laptop. While he waited for the computer to warm up, he purposefully kept his eyes from her pink top that clung to her small breasts. The room began to stir with the smell of coffee mixed with her floral perfume. Hunter's hands began to sweat and his heart raced a little faster as he became acutely aware of her presence. The way she had felt against him during their kiss haunted him. Unable to stand the antsy sensation in his legs, he stood from his desk.

"I think I'll get some coffee," he uttered and bolted for the office door.

"Julia just made a fresh pot in the employee's lounge," she told him.

Hunter placed his hand on the doorknob. "Thanks," he got out before he shoved the door open and entered the hall.

He was halfway to the employee's lounge on the second floor when his heartbeat finally slowed down. Gulping in a few breaths of air, he rounded the doorway to the lounge and the smell of freshly brewed coffee hit his nose.

The rectangular lounge housed a full service kitchen with a working gas stove, microwave, refrigerator, sink, and coffeemaker on the white Formica countertop. Painted a pale shade of green with framed pictures of tropical getaways on the walls, the room calmed Hunter's frazzled nerves.

"I must be more hung over than I thought," he remarked as he stretched for the coffee pot.

After filling a mug with the company's gold star logo imprinted on it, Hunter leaned against the counter and took several sips from his coffee until that uneasy feeling left his body. Before heading back to his office, he refilled his mug. Now he was assured he would be better able to handle another encounter with Cary.

Taking the elevator from the second floor, he slowly neared his open office door and paused when he heard a man's deep voice coming from inside.

"Say yes," the familiar voice urged. "It's a really hot ticket in town. I promise you will enjoy it. I'll take you to dinner before at this little Italian place I know."

When Hunter stepped into his office, all his efforts to calm his anxiety went out the window when he saw Chris sitting on Cary's desk, leering down at her.

"What are you doing here?" Hunter growled from the doorway.

Chris turned to him. "Ah, there you are." He stood and wiped his hand over the trousers of his fitted black suit. "I came to get you."

Hunter scowled at him. "Get me for what?"

"Breakfast. We have a meeting with my client and yours, Scott Tursdale. We're going to talk to him about the PR tour for his upcoming book." Hunter gave him a blank stare. "You set this up three weeks ago."

Hunter had been so distracted by his night with Cary that all thoughts of business had been completely swept from his mind. "Yeah, I remember." He went over to his desk, invigorated at the opportunity to get out of the office for a few hours. As he placed his mug of coffee on his desk, he spied Chris still smiling at a blushing Cary.

Picking up a pad of paper and a pen, Hunter tossed the items into his briefcase. He shut the briefcase and stepped over to his brother's side.

"Ready?"

Chris gaped at him as if he were insane. "What in the hell is wrong with you?"

"Nothing is wrong. Why?"

"You look like shit." Chris rolled his eyes. "Let me guess, you didn't get this one's name either. Jesus, Hunter." With one last glance to Cary, Chris went to the office door.

Hunter turned to her. "I'll be back in a while."

She smiled, appearing amused. "I'll be here."

As he walked from the office, he could feel Cary's eyes on him. The sensation was disturbing and yet…exciting. Perhaps he had been wrong about their kiss and she had been turned on. Maybe Cary Anderson was a woman who found the thrill of the chase a lot more appealing than the climax of the hunt. After all, Hunter reasoned, most women liked the game; it was the men who were only interested in the prize.

* * *

Breakfast with the science fiction writer who was building a following among tech geeks was at a downtown coffee house. The short man with the unibrow and chubby cheeks, who spoke with an annoying nasal whine, promised to commit to a four week publicity tour to promote his upcoming book release, and after several minutes of fiery refusal, finally agreed to three television appearances on some heavily viewed syndicated morning shows. Despite Scott Tursdale's repeated reference to his deep-seated stage fright, the author had relented and done exactly what Chris had wanted. After forty-five minutes in the dingy, diner-like coffeehouse with its vast collection of decorative mugs cluttering the walls, Chris declared he had to hurry to another appointment. Hunter paid the tab for the coffee and assorted breakfast pastries, encouraged his author to get back to his final edits, and then rushed with Chris out the door.

On the drive back to the office in Chris's black Land Rover, the effects of Hunter's hangover were leveling off after putting some food in his stomach and downing two more cups of strong coffee. With the office just ahead, Hunter's apprehension about being alone with Cary began to consume him.

"Before I drop you off, I want to talk to you about the new girl, Cary," Chris said as the car slowed for a red light.

Hunter snorted with disgust, knowing where this conversation was going. "Leave her alone, Chris. She's too young, too smart, and way too independent for you."

"That's not the impression I got," Chris returned with a wanton grin.

Hunter recalled what Cary had told him the previous evening about perceptions. "Like I said, she's too damn smart for you."

"I'm not out to marry her, Hunter. Is she involved with anyone?"

"How would I know?" Hunter indignantly replied.

"She works for you. Has she mentioned a boyfriend?"

"Christ, Chris. I don't ask about those kinds of things."

Chris traced his fingers over the black leather steering wheel. "So you don't have a problem if I take her out?"

"Yeah, I do. She's an employee of the company. It looks bad."

"I could give a shit if it looks bad. I'm only asking if you mind. Like if you're interested in her for yourself?"

Hunter's anger erupted from his gut. "I don't date employees, Chris, and neither should you. Cary is a nice girl and she doesn't need your bullshit."

"My bullshit?" Chris chuckled as the light turned green. "That's rich coming from you. I figured it was only a matter of days before you tried to bed her. Let's face it, Hunts, if it has got a skirt, you chase it."

"Don't call me that," Hunter roared as the car zoomed ahead. "I hate it when you call me Hunts. And leave Cary alone. I don't need you pulling your macho crap with her."

"What macho crap?"

"Come on, Chris. The same crap you pulled with Monique. You damn near smothered that woman to death. No wonder she ran off with the other guy."

Chris waved his hand at his brother. "You don't know anything about Monique Delome or our relationship. And that has got nothing to do with your new girl. All I'm asking is for you to put in a good word for me."

"What?" Hunter shouted. "I'm not going to help you get her in bed by telling her a bunch of lies about you."

Chris rolled his eyes. "Oh, all right. I'll pass on Cary, if it upsets you so much."

"It doesn't upset me. I just think it's a bad idea."

Chris parked the car in front of the three-story, red-bricked townhouse of Donovan Books. "Get back to work, little brother, and forget I mentioned it."

Hunter opened the car door and grabbed for his leather briefcase. "You're still an asshole."

"Asshole?" Chris shook his head. "At least I know their names the next morning."

Hunter grunted when Julia greeted him as he walked in the glass doors of the building. Climbing the stairs to the third floor, his rage ate away at him as he pictured Cary spending an evening with his brother. By the time he made it to his office door, he was ready to punch a hole in the wall. But when he saw Cary at her desk, typing away on her new black laptop computer, he tried to curtail his anger.

"Hey," she called when she spotted him in the doorway. "Look what I got. Your computer guy, Jesse, just finished getting me hooked into your Wi-Fi network here."

"That's great," he mumbled as he shot across the room.

Cary's cheerful demeanor fell. "Did you have a bad meeting?"

He banged his briefcase down on his desk. "No, I had a very good meeting." He went behind his desk and took his chair. "But I think you should stay away from my brother."

Cary sat back in her chair. "Stay away? I don't understand."

"Chris is interested in you and I don't think you should be encouraging him."

The atmosphere in the office became thick with apprehension. "Are you saying you don't want me to go out with him?" she finally questioned.

"No." He took a calming breath, tempering his desire to slam his fist into his desk. "I'm just saying you need to be careful with him."

"So you don't mind if I do go out with him?"

"I didn't say that," he argued.

"You either want me to go out with him or you don't, Hunter."

"You're an employee of Donovan Books, Cary, and he is a part owner. It might look—"

"Aw, come on." She slapped her hand on her desk and the sound made Hunter flinch. "This has got nothing to do with Donovan Books. This is about last night. I thought you said that kiss was a mistake. Was it a mistake, or was there something more?"

Hunter was stunned into silence. He couldn't tell her that the kiss had done something to him, and that he desperately did not want her going out with his brother.

"There was nothing more." He turned to his laptop. "Forget I brought it up."

She stood from her desk chair. "Are you sure you don't want to talk about this?"

He punched a few keys on his laptop and opened his e-mail. "No." Keeping his eyes glued to his inbox, he scanned the unread e-mails until he saw something he had been waiting for.

After reading the e-mail, he grinned, enjoying the first glimmer of hope he had entertained all morning. "We'd better get rolling on this new erotica line," he called to Cary.

"Why, what is it?"

He raised his eyes from his computer. "Smut Slut, just sent me her approval for the contract. Looks like we have *The Bondage Club* to launch as the first novel in our line."

Cary's face sobered. "First order of business needs to be the book cover. She will want to see it as soon as possible. She's pretty particular about her covers."

"Sounds good," he agreed. "Any ideas?"

She came around to the front of her desk. "I know what she likes. I can come up with something and send it on to her."

"We have a graphic designer named Jesse Hart in the basement. He handles all of our computer problems, phone problems, and online problems, too."

"Yeah, we've met. I just told you he set up my computer for me." She paused, letting her eyes wander over his face. "Are you okay?"

"I'm fine...just tired." He brushed off her concern. "Why don't you get with him and come up with a few cover designs? Send her a selection. Once we have a cover, then you and I can work on a launch date." Cary was heading to the door when he stopped her. "We will need to set up a meeting with her soon to go over the details of the launch."

"That might be hard to do. Smut Slut is rather a recluse, and is always working on the next book." She glanced back at him. "And she isn't a big fan of meetings, especially with publishers."

"Talk her into it," he ordered.

"I'll try, but I make no guarantees." Cary quickly walked through the open office door.

When Hunter returned to his e-mails, his stomach clenched when he saw the one with Kathleen's name attached to it.

"Son of a bitch," he mumbled, opening the e-mail.

You were right, and I was wrong. I'm an ass and I'm sorry. Please come tonight. It's at the Marcia Wood Gallery at eight. You've never missed an opening.
Kat

At the bottom of the e-mail was an address of an art gallery in the SoNo part of downtown.

Hunter debated if he should go. He had known Kathleen almost twenty years, and in that time he had seen her rise to the top of her field. It was true he had never missed an opening of any of her shows, but he wondered if the time had come to cut those ties. They had continued their malingering relationship for too long to be considered healthy, and his feelings for her had become almost maddening. Maybe he could consider tonight his last good-bye, wish her luck, and then walk away. Perhaps the time had come to find someone who built him up instead of ripping him apart.

Closing her e-mail, he once again read Smut Slut's response to his contract offer. A sense of power invigorated him. His plans were beginning to take shape, and the most important step had been locked into place. Now if he could just keep his relationship with Cary Anderson platonic, everything would be perfect. The future of his company was at stake and he needed to concentrate on that and not her. But as he thought of their kiss, his determination wavered.

Why her? Why now?

The monotony of his job took a turn toward the interesting as he thought of the days they would have to spend together getting his new erotica division up and running. As he flipped through a few more e-mails his mind returned to his conversation with his brother, and Chris's desire to take Cary out on a date.

"If she wants to get involved with your brother, then don't say a word. It's her life…stay out of it," he reasoned, trying to temper his reservations and his attraction to the woman. "Think of the new line, Hunter. Think only of that, and to hell with everything else."

* * *

It was late in the afternoon when Cary returned to the office. Hunter was in the middle of a phone call with one of their distributors.

"Elliot, I understand that the tracking number was lost," Hunter said as Cary had a seat at her desk. For some reason the sight of the woman coming into his office immediately made him forget what he was saying. "No…what was that?" he asked, rubbing his hand over his face. "I needed to know when another box of books could be sent out. We've already missed the debut date and that has cost me sales, Elliot." Out of the corner of his eye he saw her open her laptop. "Yes, send out another shipment and...look, let me call you back. Just get the shipment out today so I can tell the bookstores something." She was twirling a lock of her hair about her finger, causing his stomach to flip. "Just handle it, Elliot," he barked and then abruptly hung up the phone.

When he pivoted his eyes across the office, she was intently reading something on her laptop. For a fleeting moment Hunter was lost in the way the light from the window behind his desk lit up her face.

I've got to stop this.

"Did you get the cover done?" He struggled to make his voice sound a little deeper and more dictatorial than usual.

"We've got three potential covers for her to choose from."

He got up from his desk. "Let me take a look."

When he went to her side of the office, the aroma of her perfume hit him, inciting that insidious tingle in his belly. He came around to the back of her desk and pointed to her laptop. "Show me what you've got."

Cary hit a few buttons on her keyboard and pulled up three possible covers, lined up side to side.

Angling over her desk, Hunter's eyes scanned the images. Three mock covers, each with a scantily clad woman in handcuffs and a beefed up man in the shadows, were displayed on the computer screen. The covers were provocative and alluded to the story, but they lacked something Hunter could not quite put his finger on.

"Maybe that one." He pointed to the middle picture of a leggy blonde leaning against a man with bulky muscles bulging beneath his dark suit. "But it needs more polish," he insisted.

Cary patted the computer screen. "I think these are good. She'll like them."

"We need something stellar to launch this book. You should work on them some more."

Cary flopped back in her chair. "What? Now?"

He returned to his desk; the sensation in his belly was becoming unbearable. "Why not now?"

"Well, I wanted to leave a little early," she disclosed.

Hunter flung his body into his chair and winced when his butt hit the hard seat. "Why do you want to leave early?"

"I, ah…have plans."

His eyes swerved to her. "Plans?"

"Yeah, with…a friend."

Hunter's skin crawled with dread. "What friend?"

"Well, it's actually kind of a date."

Hunter sat back in his chair, gritting his teeth. "A date? I see." He ran his hand over his mouth as his gut twisted. "You go on then. We can hit it first thing in the morning."

She gave him a radiant smile, adding to his displeasure. "Thanks." Reaching for a drawer in her desk, she added, "I hope you don't mind."

Sitting back, Hunter saw the glint of excitement in her eyes and was crestfallen that it wasn't for him. "Is this a boyfriend?"

Her body sagged slightly. "Not a boyfriend, no," she answered, avoiding his gaze.

When she pulled a drawer out from the bottom of her desk, Hunter bubbled with questions about the man. What did he do? Where did he come from? Would he keep his hands off her during their evening together? Feeling like a high school boy with a crush, he choked back his interrogation and focused his attention on his computer.

"I'd better head on home." She slung the strap of her purse over her shoulder. "You know how us girls need time to get ready," she joked.

But Hunter wasn't laughing. The idea of Cary getting ready to go out with another man was disturbing him more than he could understand.

She stopped at the doorway and turned back to him. "See you in the morning."

"Sure," Hunter mumbled. "See you then."

After she had gone, Hunter sat at his desk, staring at his computer screen and seething. He knew he should not even be considering a relationship with his employee, but the kiss they had shared still lingered with him. And the concept that she could so easily kiss him and move on to another man the next day only added to his outrage. Maybe he should have spoken up, talked her out of her date. But then he visualized that confrontation, and the awkward emotions it generated instantly made him regret the idea.

He rested his elbows on his desk and placed his face in his hands as his curiosity gnawed at him. *I have got to get a grip. Find some way to distract myself this evening.* He placed his hand on the keyboard of his laptop and scrolled down his e-mails until he came to Kathleen's. Eyeing the invitation, his lips slowly curled into a devious grin.

"Yeah," he whispered. "That sounds like just what I need."

Alexandrea Weis

Chapter 7

After knocking back two shots of vodka, Hunter decided it would be better to walk in the chilly night air than drive to the gallery. Located a few blocks down Walker Street from his building, he figured he could just take a casual tour about the gallery, say hello to Kathleen, and then return home for the night and bury his restless mind in another manuscript.

As he strolled along the cracked pavement toward the gallery, his thoughts kept migrating back to Cary. He considered what it was about the woman that was driving him mad. Sure she was adorable, had a sparkling personality, and if she had not been his employee, he might have considered taking her out. Though she was a far cry from his usual type—long legs, blonde hair, and a vacuous personality—he could not narrow his attraction to her down to one specific thing. If he had met her in a bar, he would have probably passed her over for another. But ever since the day she had walked into his office, he had felt something different for her. Never before had he felt so possessive of a woman he barely knew.

"I'm turning into my brother," he softly grumbled as the gray, one story building of the Marcia Wood Gallery loomed just ahead.

He reached a small group of people gathered outside of the entrance who were eagerly puffing away on cigarettes, making him hold his breath as he walked through the cloud of smoke.

Inside, the gallery smelled of stale air-conditioning, sweaty people, and a faint trace of chemicals. Attired in everything from black dresses to blue jeans, the gallery was already thick with guests. The main showroom was composed of four white walls, covered with black and white framed photographs. The hardwood floors shined beneath the overhead spotlights placed strategically about the room. Doorways to the right and left led deeper into the gallery. Hunter searched the sea of faces but saw no one he knew. He progressed to the side of the room and glimpsed the photographs on the wall.

Most were shots of various sites around Atlanta, but contrasting against the shiny steel high rises or bright lights of Five Corners were the images of homeless people. The photos were meant to show the contrast between wealth and poverty, with the gleaming structures of downtown setting the backdrop for intimate portraits of the homeless problem that plagued many big cities.

Hunter shook his head, recalling how Kathleen had first become interested in taking pictures of homeless people. They had been living in a crappy apartment where vagrants were an everyday obstacle one needed to walk over to get to the entrance of their building. Kathleen had snapped several pictures, hoping that a photograph with a homeless person in it would attract attention. Since then, she had made a fortune taking pictures of the homeless in cities across America. What bugged Hunter was that Kathleen had never meant to help the plight of the homeless, but merely to capitalize on their misfortune. For Kathleen, it was never about doing what was good; it was about doing what netted her the most money.

His mind drifted back to the fights about bills, the heated arguments about getting more allowance from his father, and the too numerous references she had made to his family's wealth. But when his father finally ordered him to work for Donovan Books, Kathleen had been less than thrilled. By the time he had signed the papers on his trendy new condo, she had moved in with a well-known plastic surgeon from Decatur who had promised to make Kathleen his wife. Hunter had been hurt, but not surprised by her sudden departure. Somehow he had always known that she would leave him.

"You made it," a woman's velvety voice said, intruding on his memories.

Hunter spun around to see Kathleen, carrying a flute of champagne in her hand and sporting a tight black dress that cut across her slender thighs and accentuated her long legs. Her brown hair was teased and swept into a trendy coif. Her brown eyes were already shining from too much alcohol, and her red lipstick was smeared about her lips; a sure sign of all the kisses she had been depositing on the cheeks of her many friends.

"Hello, Kat." He kissed her cheek. "Everything looks great."

She held up her champagne glass. "Another smash, so Frank tells me. Haven't gotten the reviews yet, but he assures me it will go over well."

Hunter glanced about the room. "Where is your boyfriend?"

She held out her left hand. "Fiancé now."

Hunter inspected the large diamond ring on the third finger of her left hand. "When did this happen?"

Kathleen took another sip of her champagne. "After the other night, when I left your place. I was really pissed at you, and he called me wondering where I was. So I told him the truth. I told him I had slept with you." She tossed her head back, laughing. "He was always jealous as shit of you, but that sent him over the edge. The next morning he showed up at my door and gave me this." She flaunted the ring in his face. "Told his wife it was over and filed for divorce the same day."

Hunter skeptically eyed the ring. "He has said that to you before."

"Well, this time he means it. His wife moved out of their downtown condo this morning and went to their house in Dunwoody. He told me I can move in whenever I want." She admired the ring on her hand. "I have you to thank for it. If you hadn't got me so mad, I might never have told him about us."

"Glad I could help," he jested, shaking his head. The remark was just what he would have expected from her. "If he is what you want, Kat, then I'm happy for you," he added.

"What I want?" She let out a cold snicker. "It's more like what I need, Hunter. Someone who wants to build my career, that's what I need. Frank will do that. Right now he is in the back with a guy from a gallery in New York. He's trying to get me a gig there." She squealed with delight. "Can you imagine? My pictures being shown in New York?" She thoughtfully cocked her head to the side. "I've gone as far as I can go in Atlanta, but to really make it you have to be in New York. Frank promised he would get me there."

"That's great, Kat."

Her face softened and she patted the sleeve of his blue jacket. "Thanks, baby. That means a lot. It means a lot that you came, too. It wouldn't be an opening without you,

Hunter." She laughed, spilling a drop or two of champagne from her glass onto the brightly polished floor. "I was just telling Chris how we used to always—"

"Chris is here?" Hunter interrupted.

"Yeah. I thought you knew." She pointed to the doorway on her left. "He's here with a date. Some mousy thing. But then again, your brother always liked them small and helpless."

He turned to the doorway as an uncomfortable burning rose in his stomach. "I'll be back, Kat." Without another word, Hunter made his way across the room.

Standing at the entrance to the second showroom, his eyes scoured the crowd for his brother. It did not take long to find him. Dressed in a black suit, he was standing in a corner and admiring a photograph on the wall in front of him. There was a woman next to him with her back to Hunter. She had short brown hair and was wearing a tight black cocktail dress with high black heels. Inching his way into the room, he kept his eyes on his brother, hoping to get a glimpse of his date. Then, just as he was a few feet away, the woman turned. Her brown eyes flickered when she saw him, and then shot to the ground.

"Cary?" Hunter's voice cracked when he stood before her.

"Hey, Hunts," Chris taunted. "I see you found us."

Hunter's eyes never left Cary. "Chris is your date?"

She fidgeted with the black clutch purse in her hand. "I didn't want to say anything to you before."

"You son of a bitch," Hunter raised his voice to his brother. "I thought you said you weren't going to ask her out."

"I never said that." Chris placed a protective arm about Cary's shoulders. "I explained to Cary that you weren't happy about the arrangement and asked her not to say anything. I knew it would only piss you off." He held up the old-fashioned glass in his hand. "And I was right." Chris sipped from his drink.

Hunter scrutinized his brother's flushed cheeks and glassy eyes. "Are you drunk?"

Chris grinned. "Of course not."

Hunter turned to Cary. "How many has he had?"

"Hunter, please," Cary begged. "Lower your voice."

"You're not getting in a car with him, Cary," Hunter affirmed.

Chris snorted. "To hell she isn't."

Hunter inched closer to his brother. "You brought her here knowing I would show up, didn't you?"

Chris pushed him back. "Get out of my face."

Cary forced her way between the two men. "Stop it, both of you." She took in the people around them. "You're attracting too much attention."

Chris lifted his glass to his brother. "Oh, Hunts just loves attention. He's been fighting for it all of our lives."

"Shut up," Hunter snarled.

Cary grabbed Chris's arm. "Let's get out of here."

But Chris refused to budge and pushed her hand away. "No, I think you need to hear my little brother's life story. He's quite the failure, did you know that?" Chris swung back around to Hunter. "Ever since we were kids, he's failed at everything he has ever tried. He even failed our mother. He couldn't take care of her when she needed him most."

"That's enough," Cary snapped.

"Hey, what's going on?" Kathleen demanded, coming up to them. "I could hear you two shouting from the other room."

"There's his biggest failure." Chris flourished a hand over Kathleen's figure. "Did you know my brother blew it with this fine creature? Didn't even put up a fight when she ran off with another guy."

"What is wrong with you?" Kathleen said to Chris.

Hunter stood next to her. "He's drunk."

"I'm not drunk," Chris argued.

Kathleen pointed at Chris. "Get him out of here. I can't afford a scene; especially with the guy from New York here."

Chris laughed out loud, making a few heads in the room turn his way. "Finally shooting for the big time. Lord knows you've been at it long enough, Kat."

Kathleen's brown eyes tore into Hunter.

"All right." Hunter yanked on Chris's arm. "We're going."

"No, we're not," Chris bellowed.

The entire room around them went quiet. Kathleen's eyes darted about the guests and she hooked her hand about Chris's arm. "Time to go, Chris," she declared, urging him toward the doorway to the main showroom.

Chris gave in to Kathleen and allowed her to escort him across the room. Hunter took a firm hold of Cary's elbow and followed right behind Kathleen and Chris.

"We'll get Chris a cab, and then I'm taking you home," Hunter whispered in her ear.

"Leave me, alone." Cary shirked off his hand and walked ahead of him.

In the main showroom, Kathleen said something in Chris's ear. His brother straightened up, and immediately went to the main entrance. Cary followed Chris outside while Hunter went up to Kathleen.

"Sorry about that," he told her. "You know how he gets when he drinks."

Kathleen shook her head, appearing more disgusted than mad. "No, this is how he gets when he's around you. You two could never stand to be in the same room together. Just make sure he doesn't drive home, Hunter."

Hunter kissed her cheek. "Thanks, Kat."

The displeasure retreated from her eyes and she patted the sleeve of his blue jacket. "I like the spunky brunette. But I get the feeling she's more your type than your brother's."

He brushed off her comment. "She's my employee, Kat," he defended in a curt tone.

"She's more than that, Hunter. I saw the way you were looking at her. You only get that flicker of interest in your eyes when something or someone turns you on." Kathleen viewed the entrance. "Better see to Chris before he makes a bigger ass of himself."

Hunter wanted to tell her that she was wrong about Cary, but instead of debating the point, he walked away. What Kathleen believed no longer mattered to him, and that realization took him by surprise. She had always been the reason for the hole in his heart that no amount of long-legged blondes could fill. Now the hole was gone, satiated by another, but instead of being appeased, he was terrified. Then, a more compelling notion hit him. If Kathleen was aware of his feelings for Cary, he wondered if Chris had noticed, too.

And do you think Cary knows? The question cut through his heart like an executioner's sword.

Clenching his fists, he ignored the aggravating voice in his head. He had bigger things to worry about.

Outside of the gallery, he found Cary dragging Chris through the throng of smokers to the sidewalk. As he approached Cary's side, he noted the way Chris's arm was slung over her shoulders, causing his jealousy to bubble to the surface.

"Chris, I'm getting you a cab," Hunter growled.

"I don't need a cab, little brother. I can drive."

"No, you're not driving, especially not with my employee." Hunter looked down the street. "Where are you parked?"

Appearing a bit unsteady on his feet, Chris waved off his concern. "Forget it, Hunter." He began stumbling down the sidewalk, dragging Cary by the hand. "Let's get out of here."

Hunter ripped Cary away from Chris. "You always do this when you drink, Chris. You get belligerent and become obnoxious."

As Hunter was pulling Cary back to his side, Chris wheeled around and took a swipe at his brother. The blow landed squarely on Hunter's left jaw, knocking him backwards.

"Son of a bitch!" Hunter yelled, grabbing at his jaw.

Cary rushed to Hunter, who was wobbling on his feet. "Are you all right?"

"Hey, I didn't mean it, Hunter." Chris came up to him, patting Hunter's shoulder. "You never were very good at getting out of my way."

Hunter stood up and immediately punched his brother on the side of his left cheek. Chris's head snapped back just as Cary's short shriek cut through the air. The pain that shot through Hunter's hand when his fist connected with Chris's face hurt more than his throbbing jaw. When he stumbled away from his brother, Hunter was shaking out his hand and cursing under his breath.

"What is it with the two of you?" Cary screeched.

"What in the hell did you do that for?" Chris screamed, clutching his cheek.

Holding his sore right hand, Hunter howled, "Because I felt like it, asshole."

Chris took a few shaky steps backward, appearing as if he was going to fall to the ground. "You were always such a stupid jerk, Hunter." He gestured for Cary to join him. "Come on, I'll take you home."

"Are you kidding me?" She shook her head, pointing at him. "I'm not getting in a car with you."

Chris had his hand to his cheek and his glazed over eyes were burning into Cary. "Find your own way home then," Chris grumbled and staggered away.

Cary went after him, but Hunter seized her arm. "Let him go."

"You can't be serious?" She broke free of his grip. "He can't drive. Aren't you going to stop him?"

"No." Hunter held up his left hand, and jingled the keys he had in them. "I swiped his keys from his jacket pocket when I punched him. Stupid bastard is so drunk he didn't even notice."

"You swiped his keys?" she tittered, grinning.

"I used to pick the keys from his pocket all the time when he came home from college and then take his car at night. I got pretty good at it. It used to really piss him off." Hunter wanted to roar with delight. He could not remember when he had ever felt such satisfaction in his brother's anger.

Cary took his right hand and examined his red, swollen knuckles. "You need to ice this." Her fingertips grazed his left jaw, sending a spark through his groin. "You need to ice that, too."

Steadying his defenses, he eased her hand away from his face. "I'll take care of it later." Gazing about the street, he declared, "Right now I need to get you a cab."

"You're not going to find a cab down here at this hour." She wrapped her arm about his. "I'll call for one from your place."

"My place?" A sudden feeling of dread rose up his spine.

"You took a pretty good hit, and I would feel better knowing you got home all right."

He waved down the street. "Perhaps you should see to my brother. He's the one in need of a babysitter, not me."

She tucked the small black purse under her arm. "But I would rather go home with you."

"You're not going home with me, Cary."

Her dark eyes traveled the contours of his face. "Do you honestly think I could leave my boss traipsing around downtown Atlanta in the middle of the night?"

In the half-light from the streetlight above, he tried to gauge the depth of her concern. He had always considered himself very astute at figuring out women, but for the first time he was absolutely befuddled by one. Hunter was intrigued, but at the same time petrified by the thoughts gathering behind those intoxicating dark eyes.

"All right, you win, Cary."

A teasing smile blossomed on her lips. "I always do, Hunter."

With a puzzled look on his face, Hunter let Cary lead him away from the lights surrounding the gallery and into the dark shadows that lined Walker Street. He may not have wanted Cary to go home with him, but stronger than his determination to keep the relationship strictly business was his desire to appease her. It had been a long time since he had felt that way about anyone, but Cary Anderson was quickly becoming the one person he wanted to get to know from the inside out.

* * *

Switching on the lights as they walked in the front door of his home, Hunter went to pull the keys from his lock when Cary beat him to it. The hint of electricity that flowed from her hand when she passed him the keys made him swallow hard. He could not understand why, but he was nervous. Usually he was the one who was cool and confident when bringing a woman home. Suddenly, he felt as if he were a sixteen-year-old virgin without a clue of what to do with a woman.

"I'll get the ice," she said, moving toward the kitchen.

Stepping behind the breakfast bar, she went to the built-in refrigerator.

"There's a bottle of vodka in there. Bring it with you." He shut the front door and tossed his keys to the dark wooden table by the entrance.

"The last thing you need is a drink," she chided. "What if you have a concussion? Alcohol would be the worst thing in the world for you."

He shrugged off his blue jacket, wincing slightly as it went over his sore hand. "I got punched, not knocked out."

She removed an ice tray from the freezer. "Don't have to be knocked out to have a mild concussion, Hunter."

He slung his jacket over one of the barstools. "What are you, a nurse?"

She laughed as she brought the ice tray to the counter. "Believe it or not, that's what I wanted to be when I was a little girl."

"What changed your mind?" He came around the bar to her side.

"When I got into high school, those dreams were pushed to the wayside by my writing."

He raised his dark eyebrows. "So you do write."

"I wasn't very good. What I was good with was helping others to find their voice. Even in high school, editing sort of became my calling." She twisted the plastic tray and a few cubes of ice fell onto the white granite countertop.

"Maybe you should consider taking up writing again."

She gazed about the kitchen. "Where are the plastic bags?"

He pointed to a drawer beneath the bar.

She pulled out the drawer. "I have been so into editing—reading how good everyone else is—that I know enough to not even attempt writing." She filled a plastic bag with the cubes that were scattered about the countertop.

"But you have to attempt it first before you can decide that, Cary. And you never know; your voice may come with time. It takes time and experience to be a writer."

"You sound like you know something about being a writer." She placed the bag on his hand.

He winced slightly as the cold bag hit his skin. "Yeah, a little. When I finished graduate school, I tried to write the great American novel, but with no luck." He removed the bag from his hand. "I think we all dream of being a writer, but only a few of us are really talented enough to be able to do it."

"How far did you get with your novel?"

He dropped the bag of ice on the countertop. "Over halfway."

"What's the story?"

He went around the bar and had a seat on a stool. "Good question. I was trying to write about a man coming to terms with life changes and the decisions he had made, but it fell short."

"Did you have a title?"

He briefly nodded. "*The Other Side of Me.*"

"Good title." She slipped around the bar and edged closer, her brown eyes intently focused on him. "Can I read it?"

He vehemently shook his head. "Hell no."

"Oh, come on. I'm a professional editor, able to spot what is good and what isn't. You wouldn't have hired me if you didn't believe in my ability."

"That was for erotica, not this."

"A good story is a good story, Hunter." She placed the bag of ice against his left jaw. "It doesn't matter the genre, it matters how the story is told."

He removed the ice and slapped it on the counter. "Well, I'm a pretty shitty storyteller." He stood from his stool and went to the refrigerator.

"Why don't you let me be the judge of that?" she told him.

Opening the refrigerator, he removed a bottle of vodka. "Forget it, Cary. My writing days are behind me."

Her fingers lazily traced circles over the white granite countertop while her eyes glared disapprovingly at the bottle in his hand. "If that's the case, then what harm will it do if I read your manuscript?"

He stood there as her fingers skirted the countertop. The gesture was driving him crazy.

"Fine." He unscrewed the cap on the vodka, desperate for a drink. "I'll let you read it." He took a swig from the bottle. "But I was really young and stupid when I wrote it. I believed in dreams coming true then. Now, I have a more practical viewpoint."

"Dreams come true, Hunter. You just have to allow them to manifest, and not block them at every turn."

Coming alongside her, he banged the bottle down on the bar. "Nice philosophy, but not very realistic. And don't worry about telling me that it's crap. I'm a big boy, I can handle it." He turned away and walked into the adjacent living room.

He went to a wall of white bookshelves stuffed with a selection of paperbacks and hardcover novels. Interspersed throughout the books were occasional knickknacks; models of sailboats and small lighthouses.

Cary followed behind him, taking in the seaside tokens. "You into boats?"

He pulled a spiral-bound book from the third shelf from the floor. "My mother collected them. She loved sailboats and lighthouses. Her dream was always to live by the ocean. When she died…I took all of her mementos with me." Hunter made his way back to her, carrying the book in his hand.

"When did your mother die?"

"Ten years ago." Anxious to change the subject, he shoved the book toward her.

"You had it bound?" She took the book from him.

"No, my girlfriend did. She wanted to make sure I kept it preserved, in case I ever returned to it."

Cary gleaned the plain white cover with the words *The Other Side of Me* typed across it. "What happened to her? Your girlfriend?"

He hurried to the breakfast bar. "You met her tonight. Kathleen Marx and I lived together for almost four years." He collected the bottle of vodka from the bar.

"That's why she was so friendly with you and Chris?"

Hunter lifted the bottle to his lips. "That's why."

Carrying the book in her hand, Cary moved closer to the bar. "What happened to the two of you?"

He took a hearty swig of vodka. "What usually happens in relationships? We got bored with each other."

Cary dropped the book on the white granite countertop. "Did she get bored or did you get bored first?"

"I think it was pretty much mutual." He pointed to the book. "Take it home with you if you like."

She pulled out a stool from the bar. "I'll stay here and read a little."

"Suit yourself. I'm going to bed." He went to the silver-painted metal stairway next to the front door. "Just lock up on your way out," he said over his shoulder and started up the steps.

Once on the third floor, he took another long pull from the vodka. The burning of the liquid in his throat helped to ease the throbbing in his jaw. He had barely kicked off his shoes when he flopped down on his bed. Putting the bottle on the floor, he closed his eyes, eager to put the whole troubling evening behind him.

Chapter 8

Hunter awoke with a start from a nightmare about being chased by a pack of blue-eyed wolves. Sitting up, his eyes did a turn of his bedroom, and then he fell back on his gold bedspread. Wiping his hands over his face, he let out a long, shaky breath. As he lay there, the events of the previous evening came back to him, and then the throbbing started in his jaw.

Clasping his jaw, he sat up on the edge of the bed. He was still wearing his light blue, button-down shirt and khaki pants from the night before. Standing from the bed he unbuttoned his shirt, and then the pain in his hand made him bend over. Shaking out his hand, he headed to the bathroom in search of painkillers.

After digging through his medicine cabinet, Hunter was disappointed to only find a bottle of Maalox and a couple of packages of condoms. Shutting the mirrored door above his vanity, he recalled the bottle of Advil he had stashed in the kitchen after catching the flu last year. Removing his shirt, he tossed it to the floor and then retrieved the bottle of vodka still sitting by his bed. Vodka in hand, he descended the steps to the first floor. From outside, he could barely detect the whine of a police siren. He remembered that the keys he had picked from Chris's pocket were still sitting by his front door. Hunter smiled as he stepped on the first floor landing, wondering what his idiot brother ended up doing once he had recovered from his drunken stupor.

"Stupid bastard deserved it."

He crossed the entryway beyond the front door to the kitchen and turned on the chrome lights above the bar. Spying the clock on the microwave, he could not believe that he had been out for over five hours. Most people in the world were dead asleep at three in the morning, but not him.

Rummaging through the spice rack next to the stove—where he thought he had put the Advil—he was wondering if he would ever get back to sleep, when out of the corner of his eye he saw something moving in his living room. He careened his head around and caught sight of a small form curled up on his green sofa. Stepping around the breakfast bar, he headed toward the darkened living room. As he drew closer, he could just make out a black cocktail dress draped over the back of the sofa and a pair of black high heels on the floor beside the glass coffee table. Brown tufts of hair were peeking out from beneath a light blanket decorated with sailboats that he always kept on the sofa. When he stood next to the sofa, the figure began to stir.

"What time is it?" Cary asked.

"A little after three. Why are you still here?"

She shoved the blanket aside, and then he saw her black lace bra standing out against her creamy white skin. A flash of heat tore through him.

"I got so caught up in reading your book that by the time I finished it, I was too tired to wait for a cab. So, I decided to crash here." Wrapping the blanket around her body, she sat up on the sofa.

"You finished it?"

She patted the cushion next to her. "We should talk about your book."

"Now? Perhaps I should take you home."

"You don't want to talk about your book?"

He scratched his head. "No, not particularly."

She pulled the blanket closer around her shoulders. "I don't know why you feel that way. It was good, Hunter, really good."

"Thanks, but I think...." Running his hand over the back of his neck, he sat down next to her. "Well, it doesn't matter."

"Have you ever let anyone read your manuscript? I mean a professional, someone in the business?"

"Other than me...." He let out a sigh. "No."

"I can't understand why you stopped. You have a wonderful way with words, with transporting the reader inside the pages. I was really disappointed when it just abruptly ended. Also, I was a little sad. I wanted to know how it ended. Did the character, Stone, ever find happiness? He felt so lost." She pensively shook her head. "You should be discovering your voice as a writer and not helping others find theirs as a publisher. Your inner demons have to come out on the page, Hunter, otherwise you'll never feel satisfied."

He became acutely aware of the black bra strap angled against her white shoulder. "It seems my inner demons aren't meant for the page. I was never able to come up with an ending. I got...distracted."

"That's not the impression I got. It almost felt like you lost your inspiration near the end."

"Maybe I did." He flopped back against the sofa. "I stopped writing right after my mother died."

She leaned back against the sofa next to him. "How did she die?"

"Car accident." He rubbed his hand over a long white scar on his left, upper chest. "She drove off the road and into a ravine. My father lost it, and Chris had to take over all the duties at Donavan Books. But he couldn't handle it."

"Is that why you two don't get along? Because of what happened to your mother?"

He arched back his shoulders as he rested his head against the sofa. "No, Chris and I have never gotten along, but things got worse between us after I got strong-armed into taking over the publishing house."

"Strong-armed?" She sat up. "What do you mean?"

"My father had been footing the bill for me to discover myself as a writer. That was while Kathleen and I had been living together. My father cut me off and told me to take over the publishing house. I didn't have a choice; I needed the money, and a master's degree in English wasn't exactly going to get me a job."

"We've all got to work, Hunter. Before my editing business started taking off, I worked a ton of odd jobs. Even waited tables in this nightclub...well, it wasn't really a nightclub, not the kind where the girls on stage kept their clothes on, if you know what I mean."

Hunter looked at her anew. "You worked in a strip club?"

The blanket fell away from her shoulders, revealing the lacy edge of her bra. "Only as a waitress. I had a pair of really short shorts and a tank top, but I kept my clothes on."

"I would never have pictured you...." He stopped when he realized he had never pictured himself running his father's business, but here he was. "I think it's great you had such an...adventure," he softly added.

"It really wasn't that bad. I learned a lot about people, and erotica." She brushed the hair from her face. "It was funny, but in that business, it wasn't considered weird or different to tie each other up or live out some wild sexual fantasies. It was just…normal."

"Sort of the way you and Dr. Coleman see it, huh?" He chuckled and sat up.

She shook her head, frowning. "It's fiction to me, just fiction. It isn't any kind of lifestyle."

"Really? You're not hiding a dominatrix under that little girl exterior of yours?" He pointed to her blanket.

"What little girl exterior?"

"Well, you look," he waved his hand down her figure, "like a little girl so much of the time. All sweet and innocent."

Her loud laughter reverberated about the living room. "I'm hardly sweet and innocent, Hunter."

He took a moment to examine her eyes, trying to determine how much of what she was telling him was the truth or a lie. "I don't see it. There's no steamy vixen behind all that…cuteness."

"Cuteness?" Her mouth fell open. "I promise you I can be just as vixenish as the next woman."

"Vixenish isn't a word, Cary."

"No word is a word until a writer gives it life," she proudly insisted. "Writers are like Dr. Frankenstein, in a way. We can create life simply by putting words on a page."

"We?" He grinned at her. "I thought you said you weren't a writer."

"I just meant…." She lowered her eyes to the hardwood floor. "I told you, I was never any good at it."

"Could have fooled me." He paused, taking in the slight blush on her cheeks. "You know, a lot of guys like it when a woman acts like a little girl."

"Like your brother?" She tugged her blanket closer. "He made it pretty clear what he wanted at dinner earlier this evening when he ordered for me and tried to feed me from his plate."

Hunter's face sobered at the mention of his brother. "You were the one who agreed to go out with him, Cary."

"Well, I had to do something to shake you up." The blanket slipped a little from her shoulders, revealing even more of her black bra.

His eyes were immediately drawn to her lacy lingerie. "What are you talking about?"

"You know how sometimes when a man sees a woman he wants with another man, he does something about it." Her eyes narrowed on him. "I decided that if I went out with Chris, you would—"

"Wait a minute?" He jumped up from the sofa. "You planned all of this?"

She giggled at his reaction. "Not this particular moment, no."

He peered down at her. "Do you mind telling me why you went to all of this trouble?"

She tilted her head, smirking. "You know why. I wanted to find out if you felt the same about me as I do about you." She stood from the sofa and touched his sore jaw. "But I never imagined you and your brother would come to blows over me."

He tipped his head away from her fingers. "So you did plan this."

"No, I planned on showing you how you would feel if I went out with another man. That the other man happened to be your brother was just a matter of convenience."

"Convenience?" He gawked at her. "Look, I don't know what you are trying to do, but this," he motioned his hand between them, "is not going to go anywhere."

"Why not? You're attracted to me, I'm attracted to you. It seems there is only one logical conclusion."

He threw his hand up. "Cary, you're my employee."

She let the blanket dip about her shoulders. "Then why did you kiss me?"

"That was...." He wiped his hand over his damp forehead. "It was just vodka and the heat of the moment. I never intended...." Feeling naked without a shirt, he shimmied a little further away from her. "I need to take you home."

She smiled, looking more menacing than adorable. Hunter's insides roared to life with an all-consuming fire. "Hunter, you need to stop thinking of me as an employee. Especially after that kiss."

"Now I'm definitely taking you home. Get dressed."

He was about to turn away when she dropped the blanket to the floor.

"I think it's time you and I came to an understanding." Cary leaned forward and placed her hands on his chest.

Hunter's eyes were riveted to her small, perky breasts covered by the sheer black material of her bra, and then he spied her black lace thong panties.

"I think you're wrong about that kiss," she murmured, raising her head to him.

"Wrong?" he thought he heard himself saying.

"Yeah." She stood on her toes. "I think we should do it again, just to make sure."

When her lips met his, the heat from them caught Hunter off guard. Her kiss was electric and nothing at all like the last time. Swept up in the intensity of the moment, his arms flew about her, crushing her body to his chest. All thoughts of pushing her away fled from his mind. He wanted her, badly, and as his hands moved from the curve of her back to her small round butt, his desire for her raged out of control.

"What are you doing to me?" he sighed against her skin.

She nibbled on his neck. "Seducing you."

He rocked his head back, summoning his self-control. "We can't do this."

She kissed the scar on his chest. "We need to do this, so we can stop wanting each other. Then we can be friends. What do you think?"

"That is the dumbest...." The heat from her body was blocking out all rational thought. Unable to hold back any longer, he lifted her in his arms and lowered her to the sofa. "Perhaps, just this once." Hunter gently climbed on top of her.

"What do you like?" she whispered to him. "What do you want me to do?"

He kissed her shoulder. "Just be you, Cary."

"Me? But you don't know who that is, Hunter."

His hand traveled down to the valley between her legs. "I know you've been driving me crazy since the day we met." He slipped his hand inside her underwear and ran his fingers along her wet folds. "Damn, you feel good."

Cary rocked her head back as he bit her neck. "I thought you didn't like me when we first met." She stroked his round butt. "You were so businesslike. Not at all the way Smut Slut described you."

Jolted by the memory of the blonde he had met at the Book Expo, he sat up. "What did she say about me?"

Cary appeared a bit bewildered. "Ah...that you were very friendly. A little too friendly, according to her."

He sat back on the sofa. "She said that?"

Cary rested on her elbows. "Yeah. She said you hit on her."

Hunter dragged his fingers across his brow. "Hit on her may be a bit strong."

Cary sat up next to him. "I don't think so. Admit it, you liked her. Or at least liked what she represented."

He knitted his brow. "What?"

She moved her mouth closer to his. "A woman who takes charge. That's what she was to you; someone who was up front with her sexuality. With her there was only going to be sex and no...games."

"You're exaggerating, Cary."

He went to kiss her lips, but she placed her hand on his naked chest, stopping his advance. "No, I'm not." Her eyes steadily gazed into his. "That's what you're into, isn't it? You want a woman to be in charge."

Before he could resist, she had flipped him over on his back and straddled his hips. "What are you doing?" he half-laughed.

Grinding her hips against him, she softly said, "Giving you what you want."

Hunter sat up, balancing her hips in his lap, and went to wrap his arms about her. "I don't think I—"

She stayed his hands. "No, let me please you." Reaching behind her, she snapped off her bra.

Hunter stretched for her small, perky breasts, but she grabbed his hands, shoving them behind his back. "I said I was in charge."

He winced as she tightly tied his hands together at the wrists with her bra. "You're kidding, right?" He halfheartedly struggled against the bra. "I'm an injured man."

Angling over him, Cary dangled her left breast over his mouth. "Do you trust me, Hunter?"

After a few tries, he caught her pink nipple. When he pulled on her flesh with his teeth, she sucked in an excited breath.

"I'll go along only if I get my way with you later," he asserted.

Her fingernails raked down his chest as she pushed him back on the sofa. "Once I'm done with you, I doubt you'll have the strength for later." She wrestled his boxers and trousers down his hips and then positioned them on his thighs, forcing his legs together.

"I can't believe you're doing this," he laughed.

"If you want to learn about erotica…." She eased down his legs, placing her mouth over his erection. "Then you need to experience it."

When her tongue swirled around his tip, Hunter moaned.

"You know the best thing about being in charge?" She kissed his ripped abdomen. "I get to go as fast or as slow as I want."

He raised his head, scowling up at her. "Then go fast, because my sore hand is beginning to throb."

Cary shook her head, clucking at him. "You shouldn't have said anything." Standing at the side of the sofa, she slowly eased her underwear from her hips. "Let's see how hot I can get you," she added, dropping her panties to the floor.

Hunter's green eyes went wide. "What does that mean?"

She turned from the sofa and walked toward the kitchen.

"Where are you going?" he called out.

She opened the freezer side door. "Just getting a little something to add to the fire."

When she returned to the sofa, she was holding an ice cube between her teeth. She straddled his thighs, and taking the ice cube in her hand, she lowered her mouth over his erection. Then, she began to rub the ice cube up and down the base of his shaft.

Hunter arched against the sofa as his pleasure skyrocketed. The combination of the heat and cold was dizzying. Her lips urged him on, sending him tumbling toward climax. His blood was bounding in his veins, his arms were pulling against the material of her bra, his legs squirming beneath her weight, but he let her take control. Just as the rush of his orgasm was climbing from his groin, she stopped and bit his tip, making him yelp.

"What in the hell are you doing, Cary?"

"Just wait. You'll love it." She dropped the ice cube on his stomach.

"Christ, and here I thought you were a nice girl."

She pinched his left nipple, making him flinch. "I am a nice girl, but that is during the day." Her hands fondled his swollen member. "This is what I like to do at night."

She skillfully aroused him with her lips, sending him hurtling toward climax once more, and when she stopped again, he fought harder against his restraints. Surprised to find the bra to be pretty resilient, he tried shifting his hips, but to no avail.

For what seemed like hours, she kept toying with him, teasing him with her mouth. She would bring him closer and closer to coming, only to pull away moments before. He screamed when she shifted on top of him; his arms were going numb, and his body ached for release.

Cary wiped the sweat from his brow and then took something out of her shoe next to the sofa. "I think you've had enough," she cooed.

Taking his erection in her hand, she skillfully slipped a condom over him and then gently guided him inside her. Her flesh molded perfectly around him. She felt so good, and as she started riding him he uttered a contented sigh. Her pale skin began to glow and her perky breasts moved up and down before him. He yearned to put his mouth on her pink nipples, and tried to thrust his hips upward, but he could not find the strength. Soon, that insistent tingle began to creep up his spine, creating tension as it went, until he was overcome by a wave of white hot bliss. Arching back, he attempted to drive into her with one last powerful thrust.

"Yes," Cary cried out above him, and then flopped down on his chest.

Breathing hard and drenched in a light sweat, Hunter relaxed against the sofa, then the pain in his hands quickly roused him.

"Cary, my hands," he hoarsely entreated.

She popped up from his chest, helped him sit up, and went for the bra tied behind his back. But after several seconds, Hunter was still not free.

"You pulled on it and made the knot too tight," she fussed, tugging at his hands.

"Then get a knife from the kitchen."

"This is a fifty dollar bra, Hunter."

"I don't care!" He tried to sit up. "Just get me out of this."

Cary stood from the sofa and jogged to the kitchen. Despite the pain in his hands, Hunter did enjoy watching her round butt jiggle as she ran. He thought of several things he would like to do to that fine white ass as soon as he was free.

She returned to the sofa carrying a kitchen knife. Leaning over him, she carefully sawed the knife back and forth over the bra. "I really liked this bra, too."

"Well, then maybe you shouldn't have tied me up with it," he scolded.

"How come this never happens in the movies?"

"The movies aren't real life. In real life, we have to live with our mistakes. In the movies, mistakes are simply cut away."

The bra finally loosened, and then fell away completely. Hunter let out a loud sigh and rubbed his wrists.

"You sound like a man with regrets," she commented, dropping the knife on the coffee table.

He sat up on the sofa and removed the condom. "Everyone has regrets, Cary." He wriggled his underwear and khakis up his hips. "Like I'm beginning to regret ever hiring you as my chief editor."

"I thought I was a division head?" She sat down on the sofa with a thud, pouting.

His eyes drank in her naked body. "Right now you're neither." Unable to resist, he wrapped her in his arms. "Where in the hell did you learn to do that? And where did that condom come from?"

She nestled against him. "I had it in my shoe."

His fingertips gently ran down her back. "Your shoe? Are you kidding me?"

"You read enough erotica, you pick things up, like where to keep condoms."

He arched away from her. "Do you make a habit of attacking men like this?"

She tilted her head to the side, pretending to think. "No, of course not. And I didn't attack you."

"You could have fooled me. I'm almost afraid to ask how many other men you have been with."

"I'm not some kind of...." She eased out of his embrace. "If it makes you feel any better, the last man I was with was my fiancé, Winter."

"Fiancé?" His arms dropped to his sides.

"He was working on his fellowship in cardiology at Emory when we met. It lasted about two years before he asked me to marry him." She sat back against the sofa, examining the scar on his right chest. "How did that happen?" She fingered his scar.

"Never mind that." He rested back against the sofa next to her. "What happened to Winter?"

"He found someone else." She stood from the sofa and snapped up her underwear. "She was a fellow in thoracic surgery. They married a few months after we broke up." She frowned at the remnants of her bra, and then nabbed her dress from the back of the sofa.

"What are you doing?" He stood up next to her.

She stepped into the dress and then showed him her back. "Going home. Isn't that what I'm supposed to do?"

Hunter turned her around, ignoring her zipper. "No. You're supposed to come upstairs with me, crawl under the covers, and in the morning…," he kissed her nose, "you can make me breakfast."

"I don't think that's a good idea." She took a step away from him. "Having sex with you is one thing; a relationship…that's something else."

"Does that mean no breakfast?"

She slipped on her shoes. "I think it's better this way."

"You're not serious." He gaped at her as she walked toward the front door, struggling with her zipper. "It's after three in the morning. You don't have a car. You'll never get a cab. Cary, be reasonable."

She retrieved her black clutch from the table by the door. "Don't worry about me, Hunter. I'll be fine." She opened his front door and then waved back to his living room. "You really should give that manuscript another go. You're a very good writer." She walked through the doorway.

He raced to the door in time to see her hurrying down the hall to the elevator. "You're going to leave, just like that?" he called behind her.

"Just like that," she replied, without glancing back. Raising her hand in the air, she waved good-bye and then disappeared into the open elevator car.

Astonished by her speedy getaway, he waited as the elevator doors closed and still stood in his open doorway as he listened to the old car descend.

"Shit," he shouted and slammed his door closed.

Usually after a night of great sex—he had to admit that despite the discomfort, it had been pretty damn good—he was the one in a hurry to rush out the door. But he had wanted Cary to stay with him, looked forward to waking up next to her and having breakfast together. Never before had a woman turned down his invitation to stay the night. The few he had asked, he remembered being pretty damn thrilled about it, but not Cary.

He reflected on their heated encounter on the sofa, how she had tied him up, held him down, and tantalized him with her mouth. But something had been missing during the steamy interlude. It was almost as if she had become the man, and he the woman, taking what she wanted from him and then walking away. As he thought more about it, he realized that it had lacked the passion he had wanted from her. Sure it had been sexy as hell, and turned him on, but it had just been sex, right? Could there be anything more?

"I can't believe I'm thinking this way."

Walking back to the living room, he spied his manuscript on the coffee table. He picked up the bound copy of his one-time effort at being a writer and returned it to the bookshelf. Sliding the spiral-bound book back into its hiding spot, he felt his vulnerability slowly receding. Hunter had shown her a part of himself he rarely showed others. The intimacy of his words on the page had been more revealing than his nudity. After all, baring the soul begins with revelation and works its way toward truth. Opening up to others was never easy, but required when starting relationships.

The thought gave him pause. *Relationship? Was that what this was becoming?* It had lasted longer than his other encounters, and because of their professional circumstance she could not disappear from his life. Perhaps he had made a mistake, and should have insisted on staying friends. But he knew that wasn't what he wanted from her.

Climbing the steps to his bedroom, he thought over all the things she had told him.

"Winter? Who in the hell would want to have the same name as such a crummy season?"

As his footfalls echoed on the metal steps, he wondered what other secrets Cary had hidden from him. At least he was assured of one thing…getting to know Cary Anderson was going to be a hell of a lot of fun.

Chapter 9

The next morning Hunter rose from bed feeling enthused about work for the first time ever. Usually facing a day of reading manuscripts, fighting with writers, and generally shouting until his voice gave out wasn't his idea of fun, but today was different. He willed himself not to believe Cary was the reason for his excitement, but as his Z4 BMW pulled into his usual spot in front of the red-bricked townhouse, he could not deny his feelings for her were changing.

Yawning, he grabbed his briefcase and climbed from the car. Exhausted and stiff from being tied up the night before, his impatience to see her spurred him on. He had spent most of the early morning hours worrying about her, especially after two calls to her cell phone had gone right to voicemail. But he had refrained from leaving a message, fearing he would appear overprotective and possessive like his brother. Vowing to keep it "business as usual" with Cary, Hunter turned the brass handle on the door to the building he frequently referred to as his "hell away from home."

"Good morning, Mr. Hunter," the always effervescent Julia greeted as he neared her reception desk. "I have your first appointment of the day already waiting in your office."

He picked through a few pieces of mail sitting atop her desk. "What appointment?"

Julie's sassy blue eyes zeroed in on him. "The pretty blonde. A Ms. S? She wouldn't give me anything more than that." She tugged a stray brunette hair behind her ear. "What happened to your face?" She pointed to his still swollen cheek.

"Ah, nothing." Hunter dropped the mail on her desk and rubbed his sore jaw. "When did Ms. S. get here?"

Julie gave a slight shake of her head. "About ten minutes ago."

He eyed the fancy silver clock on the pearl gray wall of the reception area. "Where's Cary?"

"Not in yet," Julia told him.

"Why isn't she here yet? It's after nine."

"I don't know," she offered with a shrug.

"Well…tell her when she gets in that our new client, Ms. S., is here." Hunter ran his hand over his untidy hair and patted his wrinkled yellow, button-down shirt as images of Smut Slut pushed Cary from his mind.

"She's a client?" Julia questioned with an arched eyebrow. "And she doesn't have a name?"

"She doesn't need one," he replied. "Why do you ask?"

Julia grinned, but he could tell by the facetious glint in her eyes that she wasn't buying his explanation. "No reason. Just most people have names, especially writers."

"Not all writers, Julia."

Hunter turned for the stairway entrance when he thought he heard Julia mumble, "Looked more like a hooker than a client to me."

Ignoring her comment, he took the stairs two at a time until he came to the entrance to the third floor and once again combed his hand through his hair. As he pushed the stairwell door open, he felt a nervous twitch in his belly. Then, a shot of guilt cut through him. Here he was, getting excited about seeing Smut Slut when he had just slept with Cary. *Where in the hell did that come from?* That was a new sensation for him; guilt. Usually hopping from one woman to another had never been a big deal, but this time it felt...wrong.

He took a moment in front of his closed office door, gathering his wits about him before confronting the compelling woman inside. He thought it funny how he had spent years bedding dull, lifeless women, and in the space of days found two women who not only attracted him physically, but challenged him mentally. Briefly thinking of Cary and her soft, white skin, he opened his office door.

She was standing by his arched window, gazing out over the bit of green space across the street. The sun was dancing in her blonde hair, or wig, he wasn't sure, and she was dressed in a tight, short red leather skirt and lacy red camisole. Black high heels with ankle straps added to her provocative attire.

"I'm surprised you're here," he said, closing the office door. "Cary gave me the impression you were something of a hermit."

When she turned, he was disappointed to see the same big, dark sunglasses she'd worn at the Expo were still in place, hiding most of her round face.

"I am a hermit. But we need to talk about my book before we both get buried in pre-launch details." She moved away from the window. "Cary tells me she's very happy with the new job. I'm glad. She's a good person and deserves to be treated well."

He took his briefcase to his desk. "Is that a warning, Smuttie?"

"No doubt she told you that we go way back. I care for her like a sister and I would be very angry if I was to hear she was hurt in any way."

"She has become invaluable to me." He put his briefcase down and perused the pile of yellow message slips on his desk. "I can assure you that I have no intention of hurting her…or you."

She pointed to his face. "Did you get the name of the person who did that to you?"

He touched his swollen jaw. "A silly accident. It looks worse than it feels." He waited as she stepped closer to his desk. "Would you like some coffee?" he suggested.

"No, thank you," she curtly stated. "I went over the cover samples Cary sent me yesterday and chose one I think best reflects the storyline of the book. I'm also putting together a synopsis and other related info you will need for the launch. Cary says you want to hurry this book to publication."

He fought to concentrate on business and not her face. "Ah, yes…I want to get it out for early fall."

Her red lips turned downward, appearing unhappy with his plan. "Fall is only a few months away."

"Is that going to be a problem, Smuttie?"

She came around to the front of his desk, appearing lost in thought. "It shouldn't be. Cary and I can go through the edits pretty quickly, since she knows my style. The brunt of the prep will be on your end. My schedule is pretty open, so I can fit in whatever conventions or book signing tours you get lined up."

He sat down on the corner of his desk, taking in her legs. "I figure we can get you into Atlanta bookstores the week of the launch. I have a call into a connection at Barnes and Nobles to schedule a few signings at some of their stores, then there are the big fall book conventions I want to get into. I'll also have Cary set up interviews for magazines, and see if we can get you some radio and TV time."

"I'm impressed." She nodded her head with approval. "With MandiRay Books all I got was some blog tours, the Book Expo gig, and a book signing here and there at a few independent bookstores."

He folded his arms over his chest, pleased with her reaction. "We have to make this debut big. I want to really hit it hard to announce our newest line and introduce your book." His eyes settled over her face. "I think the time has come for you to take off those glasses."

The edges of her red-painted lips curved into a taunting smile. "And let you see the real me?" She took a wary step back from the desk. "I think not."

He stood from the desk. "You like to play games with men, don't you?"

"With men, naturally." Her smile deepened. "With publishers, never. With my publisher, I'm always transparent…metaphorically speaking."

He laughed, shaking his head. "Somehow I don't think you have ever been transparent, Smuttie."

"Then let me turn over a new leaf, right now." She tugged at the five gallon black handbag hanging from her shoulder, and her playful smile vanished. "The reason I came here today wasn't really to talk about the new book or the launch. There's something else I want from you."

Intrigued, but at the same time cautious, Hunter leaned back against his desk. "I'm listening."

"I think the time has come for me to change things up and delve into a different genre. MandiRay Books was not a publishing house that was open to any new ideas from me. One of the reasons I wanted to leave." She took in a deep breath, appearing apprehensive. "I want to start writing some contemporary romances, not erotica, just simple stories of love. And there could be no association with Smut Slut books. I want this new venture to be separate from my erotica line, under another name of course."

Hunter angled slightly forward, carefully considering the proposition. "You would have to be sold as a new artist. Create a whole new fan base which could take time, and cost money." He wiped his hand across his chin as he thought of a way to make it worth his while. "If I had a guarantee from you, perhaps for two other erotica books in addition to the one we're publishing, I might consider it."

She tipped her head to the side. The gesture reminded him of someone, but he could not place who at that moment.

"I can promise you two more Smut Slut books, if you agree to publish three contemporary romance novels under my pseudonym."

"Which will be what?"

She waved her hand dismissively. "Something I have yet to decide on. Are you interested?"

"I'm very interested, but I only have one question." He paused dramatically, eyeing her dark glasses. "Why?" he softly demanded.

Her shoulders sagged forward as if the question required more effort than a simple sentence. "You're an author. You know that after a while you crave different kinds of stories, with new characters facing different life choices. I want to also find out if I can make it as a romance author, to discover if I can write outside of erotica. Become something other than…Smut Slut."

A kick of concern hit his gut. "How did you know I was a writer? I never told you that."

For a spilt second she hesitated, and then bit her lower lip. "Cary let it slip that you wrote a manuscript. She said you were a very good writer."

He pushed away from the desk. "When did she tell you this?"

She raised her head, and her cool demeanor returned. "This morning. I called her on my way here. I told her I wanted to meet with the two of you to discuss my proposal."

I knew I shouldn't have shown her that stupid book, he silently lamented. "Cary should never have mentioned my novel," he voiced to Smut Slut. "It was a very lackluster attempt to be something I am not."

"If Cary thinks you have talent, Hunter, then you have talent. You should pursue your talent. To waste a gift is to shirk one's destiny. For who you are is what you are meant to be."

His irritation with Cary subsided as he chuckled at Smut Slut's advice. "Did you get that from some sex manual, Smuttie?"

"The answer might surprise you." She took a step closer to him. "We are at our most vulnerable when we're lying naked with another. All the masks we hide behind are stripped away during sex. You can learn a lot about a man by taking him to bed."

Hunter inwardly scoffed at her girlish notions. He had bedded a long list of women through the years, but none had managed to make him feel vulnerable...until Cary. He pushed her soft brown eyes from his mind. "Perhaps you should be writing a sex book for men, instead of romance novels for women," he stated, keeping the sarcasm from his voice. "I think we could make a hell of a lot more money."

"Nobody writes for the money, Hunter. We write to be heard." She leaned over to him, letting him get a glimpse of her cleavage. "Are you willing to publish my new romance novels, or should I take my books elsewhere?"

He let out a long breath, hoping he wasn't going to regret his decision. "If you can guarantee me two more erotica novels over the next two years, I will publish three romance novels from you over the next two years, under a pseudonym." He held out his hand to her.

Smut Slut took his hand and gave it a firm, businesslike shake. "We have a deal."

"I'll put a contract together and e-mail it to you later in the day." He squeezed her hand, hoping for more.

She quickly let go of his hand and stepped back from him. "That sounds fine."

Hunter wasn't so easily deterred. "Perhaps we should celebrate. How about dinner?"

The sound of someone clearing their throat from the office doorway made them both turn around. Hunter's stomach clenched when he saw the elderly gentleman standing there.

Leaning on a wooden cane and wearing a blue Braves baseball cap, jeans, and a loud Hawaiian shirt, the deep blue eyes of the older man were glued on the couple before him.

"Am I interrupting?" he asked, waving his cane at Hunter and Smut Slut.

"Dad?" Hunter took a step back from Smut Slut, his mind scrambling for explanations. "No, ah, come in." He nervously motioned to Smut Slut. "Dad, this is one of our authors, Ms....Simms."

"Simms?" Jim Donovan's booming voice filled the small office. "I don't recall an author named Simms on the booklist."

Hunter turned to Smut Slut; her confused expression forced him to do some quick thinking. "Ms. Simms is new to us. Her first book will be coming out in the early fall. It's a sweet little romance, the kind we are known for publishing." He smiled at her, praying she understood his veiled meaning. "You'll have to forgive my father, Ms. Simms. He doesn't do well with new people...or new ideas."

"What does that mean, new ideas? You're not still going on about that new book line you wanted," Jim Donavan complained. "We've already discussed this, Hunter. No new lines."

The knowing smile that erupted on Smut Slut's lips assuaged Hunter's anxiety. She swayed up to his father, holding out her hand. He was grateful that she could put all that sex appeal to good use.

"Mr. Donovan," Smut Slut purred. "It's a pleasure to finally meet the man who founded this publishing house. Hunter has told me a great deal about you."

Jim Donovan's beady blue eyes devoured the woman's figure. "The pleasure is all mine, Ms. Simms." He greedily took her hand. "I must admit I'm jealous of my son. Being surrounded by such lovely talent makes me almost want to come back and resume control over my business."

"Our business," Hunter quickly corrected. "You left it to Chris and me several years ago, Dad."

Jim Donovan's stern features soured. "But I still own twenty percent of the shares."

"Mr. Donovan," Smut Slut sweetly broke in. "You must be very proud of your sons. They have both done a fine job with your company."

Distracted by the woman's pretty smile, Jim Donovan's features once again lifted. "Have they? That is open for debate, Ms. Simms."

Hunter's stomach rolled with disgust that his efforts over the years could be so quickly discounted. "Let me see Ms.

Simms out, Dad, and then we can talk." Hunter took Smut Slut's elbow and gently nudged her toward the door.

"Mr. Donovan, I hope we meet again," she imparted with a wistful grin.

"It was a pleasure, Ms. Simms, and I look forward to reading your book," Jim Donovan called as Hunter walked her out of the office.

Escorting her down the hall to the elevators, Hunter leaned over to her. "Thank you for not saying anything back there. If my father knew I was branching out into erotica, he would have a heart attack."

She stopped at the elevator doors and turned to him, frowning. "But you won't be able to hide the fact from him forever, Hunter. What are you going to do when my book comes out?"

Pushing the elevator call light, his stomach tightened as visions of his father's fury came to mind. "By then it will be out and all he can do is scream, tell me what a disappointment I am, and then go back to his life in Decatur."

"You think you're a disappointment?"

"No, I know I am. My father has turned haranguing into something of a national pastime. All my life I was constantly reminded of what a failure I'd turned into."

"Then why are you here, running his company?"

He peered into her dark glasses and yearned to get to know the woman behind them. "That explanation is best suited for dinner conversation." The elevator doors opened and he stepped closer to her. "How about tonight?" he whispered.

Smut Slut smirked and entered the elevator. "That would be a bad idea." She tugged her wide purse higher up her shoulder, her face once again serious. "We'll talk again, Hunter."

The elevator doors were about to close when he stuck his arm out, blocking them. "Why is it a bad idea?"

She lowered his arm from the door, pouting at him. "I think we should stick to daylight encounters. That way we both can be on our best behavior."

His eyes lingered on her lips. "What if I don't want to be on my best behavior with you?"

"Good-bye, Hunter," she spoke out right before the elevator doors closed.

Banging his head against the closed silver doors, Hunter cursed his luck. As if on cue, images of Cary rocketed across his mind. There was another woman he found fascinating, but in a different way from Smut Slut. With Cary there was the promise of a relationship; with Smut Slut, there was the promise of some really nasty sex.

Turning from the elevator doors, he trudged back to his office, dreading the conversation ahead with his father.

"Interesting woman," Jim Donovan voiced when Hunter re-entered his office. "What's with the glasses?"

Hunter closed the door. "She writes under a pseudonym and likes to keep her identity hidden."

"Why? Everybody and their mother are killing themselves for fifteen seconds of fame, and you've got a writer who wants to protect her anonymity?"

"Not every writer wants to let it all hang out there," Hunter insisted, setting out for his desk. "Some have jobs and careers they don't want to jeopardize with their writing. Everyone has got to eat, Dad."

"Then they need to write books that won't threaten those careers. Good, clean, wholesome stories can never hurt anyone."

Hunter went around his desk and had a seat in his creaky chair, his patience waning. "Why are you here?"

Jim Donovan flopped down in a chair before Hunter's desk, and then rested his cane against the side. "Your brother called me this morning. He said you two had an altercation in front of some art gallery over a woman. By the look of you, I'd say he landed the first punch." The perpetual scowl Hunter remembered from childhood emerged on the older man's face. "Want to tell me what happened?"

Hunter sat back in his chair, dumbfounded. "Since when do you give a shit if Chris and I pummel each other?"

He shook his finger at his son. "You know your mother never tolerated such language."

"You cursed more than any of us at home, Dad, and Mom never told you to keep it down."

Jim Donovan's eyes dropped to the linoleum floor. "That's because my Gracie was a lady. She never told me how to live my life, she just supported me. She always supported me." When his blue eyes returned to Hunter's face they were once again hard and determined. "That's why I came down here, for her. You know how she hated it when the two of you fought, and God knows I should have stepped in more to break up your fights, but now I feel I have to say something. He's your brother, Hunter, and even if he is a bit of an ass, he's still blood." He paused and rested his hand on the curve of his cane. "And you also have to think about the repercussions for the business. What if you had been spotted by some media type? Remember what Alexander said, 'Upon the conduct of each depends the fate of all.'"

Sick of listening to his father's quotes, Hunter shook his head. "Yeah, well, he didn't have a raving lunatic for a brother."

Jim Donovan let go a disgusted chortle. "Just the answer I expect from you. You were always the wisecracker and your brother the peacock." He sat back in his chair. "Chris told me this fight was about a girl; a girl who is working for you. Says she's your new editor."

An uncomfortable knot formed in Hunter's stomach. "Her name is Cary Anderson, and Chris was hitting on her from the moment she walked in the door."

"And probably so were you. You and your brother always had the same taste in women."

"We do not," Hunter balked. "Chris is the one who likes them...." He let his voice drift away, not wanting to have such a discussion with his father. The less said the better.

"I agree your brother is an idiot where women are concerned. Lord knows the business was sent into a tailspin with that whole Monique Delome situation. But that is in the past and I'm here to make sure neither of you screw up like that again. I told Chris to stay away from your employee, and I'm going to tell you the same thing. Keep it professional, Hunter. If you want to publish wholesome books, then you had better run a wholesome business."

Enraged at his father's antiquated viewpoint, Hunter slapped his hand on his desk. "Dad, no one cares about wholesome values anymore, unless you're running for political office, and even then a good scandal is probably worth more media attention than a candidate with no scandal. Let's face it, sex sells, and the juicier the story, the more press you can play off it. You ever think that maybe it's time we changed a few things around here?"

"Never." Jim Donovan grabbed his cane and stood from his chair. "Just because everyone else in the world has lost their mind and their morals doesn't mean we have to."

"What are morals, anyway, but the dictates of others telling you how to live your life? Laws we have to abide by, but morals can be left open to a hell of a lot of interpretation."

"Where is this coming from?" Jim Donovan barked. "I never raised you to be disrespectful of others, and your mother certainly never tolerated such talk. She was a good, God-fearing woman who—"

"Who lived a miserable existence because she was too afraid to tell you exactly how she felt," Hunter jumped in.

"You bastard!" Jim Donovan angrily stamped his cane on the floor. "Where do you get off telling me—"

"Come on, Dad. Someone needed to say it. That night when she came to the office and—"

"I will not have you discussing that night," Jim Donovan shouted.

"Why? You don't want to face the fact that you killed her, do you? I was there and I saw—"

"Excuse me," Cary interrupted from the doorway. "But I thought...." She lowered her voice when she spotted Jim Donovan. "I'm sorry. I'll come back later." She turned to go.

"No, Cary, wait," Hunter called to her. "My father was just leaving."

She nervously slipped in the door, wearing a lavender silk dress that hugged her curves and made her brown orbs appear tinged with blue. Hunter strained to pull his eyes away from her and focus on his father's deep scowl.

"Dad, this is Cary Anderson," Hunter announced, waving to Cary.

"Mr. Donovan." Cary came toward him with an extended hand. "It's a pleasure."

An amused grin crossed his father's lips, and Hunter found the feature somewhat disturbing. Jim Donovan never grinned.

"Ms. Anderson?" He shook her hand. "It is interesting to meet you." He examined her dress and slender figure. "I get the impression we've met before," he added, his elusive grin growing wider.

Cary shook her head, a little confused. "I'm afraid we haven't, Mr. Donovan."

Jim Donovan dipped his head. "Forgive me. I'm just getting old and my eyes are not what they used to be."

"Men never get old, Mr. Donovan. They just get...more experienced."

Jim Donovan let go a tremendous cackle. "A delight, Ms. Anderson." He turned to his son, and the scowl instantly returned. "We'll talk again, Hunter. I'll leave you and Ms. Anderson to get back to work."

His father started for the door, tapping his cane on the linoleum floor as he went. At the bookcase housing his collection of Alexander the Great statues, he halted. "Don't forget to dust my boys there." He pointed his cane at the bookcase. "And ice your face before you scare the hell out of a client."

Hunter ran his hand behind his neck as his stomach churned. "Sure, Dad."

Jim Donovan tipped his baseball cap to Cary. "You have a good morning, Ms. Anderson."

She gave him a flirty smile. "Good morning, Mr. Donovan. I hope we see each other again."

Jim Donovan pointed his cane at Hunter. "Make sure he brings you to see me one day. I have a feeling we have a lot to talk about." He pulled the office door open and stepped into the hall.

Once he was gone, Hunter rushed to the door and firmly shut it. He stood with his back to Cary, taking a moment to summon the courage to face her. Sucking in a fortifying breath, he turned around.

"Quite a character, your old man. I see where you and Chris get it from." Cary proceeded to her desk.

"Get what from?" he questioned, following her to the corner of the room.

She opened a drawer in her desk and dropped her small black handbag inside. "Your arrogance," she proclaimed, and then slammed the drawer closed. "Last night gave me a pretty good snapshot of how you and your brother really are." She pointed to his face. "He was right about the ice. You look like the other guy won."

"Cary, about last night...."

"No." She held up her hand. "There's nothing to say. What happened is behind us. I think we both needed to get that out of our system. We wanted to know how we would be together and now...well, we can get back to the business of putting out books. Right?"

Hunter didn't want to tell her that he was both relieved and confused by her statement. He was under the impression that last night was the beginning of something between them, not the end. Hunter wondered what approach to take, whether to challenge her viewpoint or reassure her conviction. Deciding such a conversation was probably best broached after business hours, he simply nodded his head.

"Yeah, you're right. We needed to get that out of our system."

The smile she gave him lacked her usual warmth. In fact, if he didn't know her better, he could have sworn he detected a tinge of disappointment in her doe-like eyes. "Great," she affirmed, standing behind her desk. "I ran into Smut Slut outside and she told me you two had a quick meeting before your dad showed up. She also had a few questions for me about what exactly was going on with your father. You want to tell me why you introduced her as your new romance author to your father?"

He stood before her desk, scowling. "You know why. I can't exactly tell my father about the new line, yet."

"When are you going to say something?"

"I figured I would send him a copy of *The Bondage Club* when it comes out; by then he won't be able to shut it down."

Her eyes grew wide. "Shut it down? Could he do that?"

Drenched with worry over his plans for the new line, Hunter strode across the room to his arched office window. Gazing out to the green grass across the street, he thought of what to tell her. "Dad saw to it that Chris and I split the ownership of the company with forty percent a piece, with him having the deciding twenty percent in case there was a problem," he explained. "If he and Chris got together against me, then yes, they could shut down the new line."

"Do you think they would really do that?"

Afraid to see her reaction, Hunter never turned from the window. "I honestly don't know."

"No wonder Chris kept asking me about the business."

He spun around. "When was this?"

"At dinner before we went to the gallery, he kept asking me questions about my job, and how you were running things."

Incensed, he pivoted away from the window. "Selfish son of a bitch would love to see me fall flat on my face. He's always hated me."

Cary moved out from behind her desk. "I'm sure he doesn't hate you, Hunter."

"Forget about him." He pushed his animosity for his brother aside and marched behind his desk. "Did Smut Slut tell you she offered to give the company two more books in addition to *The Bondage Club*?"

"Plus, you have agreed to publish her contemporary romances under a pseudonym over the next two years. Yeah, I heard. She was pretty excited about that. She has wanted to get away from erotica for a while."

He took a seat in his old desk chair, filling the room with a short stint of creaking. "You should have been here to talk with her."

She folded her arms and proceeded across the office to his desk. "Well, next time I'll make sure I get to bed before four in the morning."

He opened his briefcase, avoiding her eyes. "How did you get home?"

"I called a friend." She rested her hip on his desk.

"A friend?" Hunter eyed the curve of her dress along her hip, and for an instant he was back on his sofa, feeling her riding him and...

"Yes, a friend." Cary's voice interrupted his flashback. "Handy to have. Perhaps you should try having a few."

He ignored her. "You need to get started on PR for the book. I want to set up the launch for the beginning of September."

"September? But we still have to edit, proof, get it to printing, not to mention setting it up on—"

"Can you do it?" he cut in.

"What's the rush?"

"The sooner we get out there, the better." He flipped up his laptop. "Once we get rolling on the PR, I'm not going to be able to keep it a secret from my father or Chris. I'm just hoping we'll be too committed by that point for them to want to shut everything down."

"I'll get started on the marketing right away. I was thinking we'll also need an author photo for the back cover. I wanted to show Smut Slut in her element, like in a club or something." She tilted her head to the side, thinking. "There's a bondage club in the city. They have a lot of atmosphere. I can talk to the manager there, and see if I can arrange a shoot. Is that all right with you?"

"Sounds good. We can go together, tonight, after work."

Cary's face fell. "I can't tonight, I have plans." She hurried to her desk.

"Plans?" He eased back in his chair, carefully observing her. "What kind of plans?"

She sat behind her desk. "Dinner plans," was all she volunteered.

Visions of her with another man tormented him, and then he got ahold of his emotions. "How about tomorrow night? I'll pick you up."

She lowered her eyes to her computer. "That'll be fine."

As he watched her typing on her laptop, Hunter thought of the woman she had been the night before. All the decorum and reserved demeanor she now exhibited was a total contrast to the girl she had been, making him wonder which one was the real Cary. Chalking up the change in mood to the fluctuating tide of female emotions, he reasoned there was no point in trying to understand the woman. In his experience, navigating the treacherous caverns of a woman's emotions was akin to predicting when a volcano was going to erupt. All a man could do was pray for some warning, and have an escape plan for the exact moment when all hell broke loose.

Chapter 10

It was well after eight that evening when Hunter parked his car in the appointed slot of his building garage. Exhausted and mentally drained from a long day of phone calls, he wanted nothing more than a quiet evening alone with his favorite vodka.

Pushing his front door open, he relished the peace of his home. There were no ringing phones, no nervous writers hanging about, no staff asking a lot of questions, and no Cary. Of all the things he had endured that day, her discerning eyes glancing over at him from across the office had been the most disturbing.

Dumping his leather briefcase on his kitchen bar, he went to the refrigerator to retrieve his bottle of Gray Goose vodka. Anxious to feel the burn of the alcohol, he eagerly snapped the cap off the bottle and carried it to the living room. Before taking a seat on his sofa, his mind raced with thoughts of his night with Cary. How she had been aggressive in taking what she wanted from him, how she had relentlessly tortured him with her mouth, and then the final moment when he had found satisfaction in her warm, wet….

Shaking his head, he sat down on the plush fabric. He wished she was with him now, kneeling before him, but then he recalled her mentioning dinner. Did she have a date? Was it someone new or a man from her past? What kind of man would she prefer to date? As his head swirled with questions, he became convinced that no ordinary man would keep Cary interested for long. She was too smart, too bold, and way too assertive for most men. But somehow Hunter felt sure he was just what she needed.

Taking another long swallow from the bottle, he squelched his desire for her. Desperate to distract his libido, he focused on the bookcase on the wall across from him. Perusing the many titles of books he had published during his time as head of Donovan Books, he thought he should feel a surge of pride, but instead he only felt remorse. They were not the kinds of books he had wanted to publish; they had only been something he had done to pay the bills. When his eyes lighted on the red spiral binding of his half-finished novel, he tilted his head to the side, remembering what Cary had said to him. Putting the bottle on the glass coffee table before him, he stood from the sofa and walked toward the bookcase. Tugging the spiral-bound book free, he felt the weight of it in his hand and then opened the front cover.

It had been years since he had read the work, too afraid to discover just how bad of a writer he had been. But as he pored over the first few paragraphs, a strange sensation flowed through him. It was a mixture of surprise and awe that he had actually written the words on the page. But by the third paragraph, he found mistakes with his style, flaws in his ability to succinctly deliver the essence of his meaning. Instead of being disgusted with his futile attempt, his mind began to come up with new ways he could change the wording and rearrange the paragraph to make sense. Wanting to jot down some notes, he went to the kitchen and searched the drawers for a pen. When he found one, he returned to the sofa and began making notations in the margins of the first page.

He read on, scribbling suggestions as he went, and when Hunter finally glanced up from the manuscript to the clock on the microwave, he discovered two hours had elapsed since the moment he sat down to make his notes. Shutting the cover of the book, he seized the bottle of vodka on the coffee table. Swallowing back a long pull of the liquor, he felt gratified. For the first time in ages, he had accomplished something that evening. In all the years he had been running Donovan Books, he had never felt quite the same sense of satisfaction as he did after working on his book. Smiling, he realized that Cary had been right. He had been stifling his creative voice to help others to be heard. Maybe it was time to rediscover his muse, and allow all of those inner demons he had been ignoring to come crawling back onto the page.

* * *

Walking into his office the next morning, Hunter was immediately hit by the smell of coffee. On his desk was a tall paper cup from Starbucks, while in the background the clatter of typing filled the air.

"I got you an espresso roast with a shot of dark chocolate," Cary chirped from her desk. "You could use a treat this morning, instead of the usual boring coffee in the employee's break room."

He turned to her and was unnerved by her pale peach top and the way it complemented her creamy complexion. Quickly returning his eyes to the coffee cup on his desk, he wanted to chug back a few swift gulps to make his tired eyes stay open. But instead of giving in to his impulse, he lugged the always heavy briefcase in his hand onto his desk and removed his blue suit jacket.

"Thanks for the coffee." Patting down the wrinkles in his white shirt, he added, "I can use it this morning."

"Your face looks better today," she offered from her desk.

"Yeah, it's better." Itching to know how her evening went, he asked, "Did you have a nice dinner?"

"Yes," she conceded, without elaborating any further.

"Where did you go?" He tried to sound casual.

"We ate at the hotel where he was staying. Nothing fancy."

His curiosity was getting the better of him. "Hotel?"

"Yeah, Lionel is in town for a restaurant supplier's convention. He wanted to check up on me." She kept typing on her computer as she talked.

He sat back in his chair, a little aggravated. "Who's Lionel?"

"My brother. He came in from New Orleans yesterday."

He sank in his chair with relief, and then he became concerned that he felt that way in the first place. "You never mentioned you had a brother."

"I have three of them, actually. I'm the youngest, and according to my brothers the most spoiled. Lionel is the closest to me. We are only three years apart. My oldest brother, Frank, is ten years older than me, then there's Andrew, he's five years older, but he lives in Spain, so I don't get to see him very often."

"What's he doing in Spain?"

"He works for an international bank. He's been the lucky one, travelling around the world. He's lived in Singapore, Hong Kong, Berlin, London, and now Barcelona."

He shook his head, feeling a stab of envy. "Sounds like a great life."

"You ever want to travel?"

With a slight grin, he clasped the tall cup of coffee on his desk. "Yeah, when I was younger. There were cities I wanted to see, to run away to, actually." He removed the white lid from his cup. "San Francisco, New York, Denver, Miami, New Orleans; I was particularly interested in New Orleans."

She stopped typing. "You wanted to go to New Orleans?"

"Nah, I wanted to live there. You know, in the French Quarter in one of those quaint little cottages. Write books like Tennessee Williams, drink coffee and chicory, hang out in the bars, and walk among the tourists. I guess that all seems kind of cliché to you."

"It's just not the New Orleans I know. I mean, sure it exists if you live in the Quarter, which also happens to be the noisiest place on earth, so writing would be practically impossible. But I can see that kind of romanticized view of the city. It's just that there is so much more to it."

He held the warm coffee in his hands, mulling over the regard he heard in her voice when she spoke about her hometown. "Why didn't you go back to New Orleans after college?"

"I thought about it, then Katrina happened. I wanted to go and help my father rebuild the family business, but he insisted I stay in Atlanta."

Interested in learning more, Hunter sat up in his chair. "What family business?"

"My dad started a restaurant supply business before I was born. Now it is the biggest in the city. Frank and Lionel help him run it."

"You ever consider moving back home?"

"Oh yeah, one day. I miss it too much to stay away forever." She hesitated and her eyes glistened, enthralling Hunter. "It's hard to explain to someone not from there what that city does to you. New Orleans has a way of staying with you. You carry it around inside of you…always. The traditions, the holidays, the food, the people, the places, I miss it all. But for now, my life is here."

"I really hope you get back there some day. It sounds like you belong there."

"Maybe you'll get there one day, too. I think in New Orleans you could be the kind of writer I know you can be. You have the talent, Hunter. Just not the will."

He frowned at her. "I thought you said I lacked inspiration."

"They're the same thing. What drives a writer to write is something that comes from within. I call it will, some call it passion, you call it inspiration. But it's whatever motivates you to sit there and get the words out." She picked up the tall Starbucks cup sitting next to her computer. "Don't give up on your writing. That story you wrote was…." She peered into her coffee. "Well, it made me green with envy that I will never be able to express my thoughts quite so…eloquently."

He took a deep sip from his coffee, wanting to banish all thoughts of his book. "Thank you for the encouragement, but in the meantime…where do we stand on the new release?"

She sat up in her chair and motioned to her computer. "I've put together a press release to send out to bloggers and reviewers I know. After we check out that club tonight, I was going to get with Smut Slut for possible dates to do the cover shoot. You sure you still want to go with me?"

"Of course. Why wouldn't I?"

She put her coffee down on her desk. "Hunter, these places can be pretty…they may take some getting used to. Unlike the class the other night, this kind of bondage club will be more…uncomfortable. Are you sure you are ready for that?"

He flashed back to how she'd tied him up on his sofa and suppressed an urge to laugh out loud. "I'm ready for it, trust me."

Giving him a dubious side-glance with her round eyes, she mumbled, "We'll see about that."

She returned her attention to her laptop and for a moment, he admired the way her slender hands brushed across the keyboard. There was something so captivating about her that Hunter found it hard to turn away. He couldn't understand what was happening to him, but he knew the signs well enough to recognize that Cary Anderson was working her way beneath his skin. She was getting inside, and dangerously close to his heart. Part of him wanted to push her away, but another part yearned to hold her close. And that long forgotten glimpse into the shadows of his soul was beginning to trouble him. He needed to rein in his feelings, be the tough guy women wanted; otherwise he was afraid he would only end up getting hurt when she eventually walked away.

* * *

Hunter was checking his watch as he waited in his car for Cary to emerge from her triangular apartment building. A close walk from the Donovan Books offices in the Fairlie-Poplar district of downtown, the historic apartment building was known for catering to artists, musicians, and the generally creative. When he saw her at the door of the car, wearing a black leather skirt and billowing black blouse, he could not believe she was the same woman he had seen leaving the office only two hours before. About her neck was a silver chain-link necklace, her eyes were surrounded by deep gray eye shadow, and her full lips were glistening with bright red lipstick.

"Ah, you look very...nice," he said as she took her seat.

"Nice? The place we're going isn't the sort for nice." She inspected his casual blue dress shirt and black slacks. "You, on the other hand, will stand out like a sore thumb."

"We're going to check it out for a photo shoot, not socialize," he disputed while shifting the car out of neutral.

"This might be a chance to introduce you to the real world of bondage. Hitting the club scene and seeing how couples hookup might be good for you."

"I think I had enough of the bondage scene the other night with you." He steered the car into the busy traffic on Peachtree Street. "My arms are still sore, by the way. Whatever you have been picking up in those bondage classes seems to be working for you."

"I thought we were putting the other night behind us."

"We are," he agreed. "I'm just not interested in getting any more glimpses into what you do with your off time." He shifted the car into second and hit the gas as he tried to pass an aggravatingly slow moving black Lincoln.

"What makes you think that is something I do on my off time? Maybe I thought it was something you might enjoy, seeing how uptight you were about the two of us being together."

"I wasn't uptight." He skillfully swerved around the Lincoln. "I didn't think it was a good idea for us to—"

"Are you saying you didn't enjoy the other night?" she edged in.

"No." He slammed the stick shift into third.

"You sure gave me the impression that you liked it."

"It's just not what I intended. I'm not into being tied up, Cary, and…forget about it. We said it was behind us and it is."

"What did you intend?" she pestered.

"Nothing." He jammed the accelerator down, flying past more slow moving traffic.

"Did you want to be in charge? Seduce me and not have it the other way around?"

"I did not want to seduce you, but perhaps...yes, I would have liked to call the shots instead of you...." He stopped, uncomfortable with going on. "Let's drop the subject."

She unfolded her arms and sat back in her leather seat. "Fine, if you feel intimidated."

"I don't feel intimidated." He slowed down for a red light. When he pulled behind a car, he turned to Cary. "Why are you so different from other women? Most are happy to let the man decide the pace of a relationship, but you go barreling forward. Do you know how that makes a man feel?"

"Intimidated?" she said, grinning.

"No. Weak." He saw the light change to green and he directed his eyes to the road. "Men think they are weak when a woman takes control in bed. Every now and then, sure, we all love it. But in the beginning, when two people are starting out, it's not something a guy expects."

"But you did like it, didn't you?"

He shoved the stick shift into first and stomped on the clutch. "Sure, Cary. I liked it."

She leaned in closer to him. "Then why didn't you say that?"

"Because it can't happen again. You work for me," he grumbled.

"So what if I'm your employee. That doesn't mean we can't sleep together."

"That's exactly what it means," he argued in a disgruntled tone.

"What if I quit?"

"What's more important, screwing me or building something together?" He put the car into second. "Besides, you don't want to get involved with me. I'm not into relationships. Eventually, we would break up and it would be hard as hell for both of us at work. This way is better. We had our one night of fun, and now we can get down to business."

She sat back in her seat, furrowing her brow. "So you don't want to try again?"

Hunter kept his eyes on the road. Of course he wanted to try again. Ever since their night together, he had been able to think of little else. But he was also practical. He needed the new line more than he needed a girlfriend.

"No, I don't want to try again. We're better business partners than lovers, Cary. I'm sure you can see that."

She viewed the street ahead. "No, not really."

Anxious to change the subject, Hunter quickly uttered, "Where is this place?"

"Just keep heading along Peachtree. It's a few miles up, by Georgia Tech."

"What's the name of this club?"

"The Hole. Smut Slut told me about it. It's an urban party club, but a lot of the singles going there are into bondage. They have a special back room for hookups."

An uncomfortable thought crossed his mind. "You ever hookup with anyone there?"

"I just do research, Hunter. I don't go there to meet men."

It did not take long to reach a nondescript, two-story, red-bricked building with a few silver sculptures decorating a dimly lit entrance. Cary pointed Hunter to a parking area in back of the structure, and after pulling into a spot, he surveyed the crowded lot.

"It appears busy tonight," he commented as he rose from the car.

"It's always busy," Cary returned, shutting her door.

"So you come here a lot then."

She came around to his side of the car. "Why do I get the impression you're fishing for something?"

He put his car keys in his trouser pocket while avoiding her maddening eyes. "I'm just trying to understand your fascination, that's all."

"My fascination? What are you talking about?"

He placed his hand in the small of her back and ushered her toward the red-bricked building. "I'm trying to understand why this lifestyle—if we even call it a lifestyle—appeals to you."

"You make me sound like some deviant," she groused, pulling away from him. "I'm not fascinated with this…'lifestyle,' as you put it."

He stopped and dipped his head temptingly close to her face. "You could have fooled me."

She swerved away from him. "So what is wrong with wanting to have a little fun?"

"Nothing," he admitted, following her. "But going to bed with someone shouldn't be about games, it should be about emotions."

That made her spin around on her black heels to face him. "That's rich coming from a man who probably hasn't had an emotional moment with a woman in over a decade. Why is it men expect women to feel something in bed, but the same rule does not apply to men? If anything, you guys pride yourself on not getting emotionally involved with sex."

"For us it isn't an emotional issue. For women it is," he loudly argued.

She took a step closer to him. "Do you really think I needed to feel something for you the other night in order to fuck you?"

Refusing to react to her outburst, he went around her. "Don't try and sound like a man, Cary, it doesn't suit you." He strode along the side of the building to the street entrance.

"Oh, I guess you want me to be all sweet and innocent, is that it? I'm more appealing that way." She hurriedly walked behind him.

"Forget I mentioned it," he called over his shoulder. "Forget that night ever happened, and let's just concentrate on the work."

"You're the one who keeps bringing up that night, not me. You're the one having a hard time forgetting."

"I said let it go, Cary." Annoyed, he rushed to a front entrance that was decorated in gray slate with a silver half-moon hanging above the black glass door. He pushed past a small crowd, and when he pulled the dark door open, Cary came alongside him.

"Forgetting something happened doesn't mean it didn't happen, Hunter."

He held the door open and waved her inside. "Yes, it does."

She gave him one last discontented scowl and then entered the building. As she passed through the door, her small butt wiggled beneath her black leather skirt, and Hunter was reminded of Smut Slut walking down the aisle at the Book Expo in her leather minidress.

Together they would make a hell of a woman, he mused.

The interior of the bar was dark, smelled of smoke, and was already thumping with loud dance music. After passing a bouncer all in black sitting on a wooden stool by the door, Cary and Hunter moved into the main bar area. The centerpiece of the long room was a monolith bar of backlit onyx that subtly changed colors. Like an undecided chameleon, the starry pixilated walls appeared to move and change colors, transforming from ice blue to blood red and then to burnt yellow. Three bartenders were scurrying to attend to the orders of the numerous patrons crowded along the bar, while glass tables with blue neon lights beneath and black couches on either side were situated along the wall across from the bar.

"What we want is upstairs," Cary shouted to be heard above the loud music.

She took his hand and led him through the narrow room to a rear door that was surrounded by an assortment of pink and yellow neon lights shaped like arrows. Walking along, Hunter became preoccupied by the feeling of her hand in his. Stirrings in his belly began to trouble him. Why was the mere touch of her hand making him feel this way?

The rear door led to a straight stairway that climbed to a second story. Red neon arrows of various sizes on the walls directed the way up. Emerging from the stairway, they stepped into a second barroom with shiny metallic piping along the walls and around a huge slate bar. Beyond the bar was a dance floor edged in the same metallic piping. A DJ in a booth to the side was cranking out electro pop tunes meant to entice a flurry of dancing, but none of the patrons were interested. Behind the DJ, Hunter spotted a pair of black curtains billowing below an air-conditioning vent. Above the curtains were the words Dungeon Club done in white neon.

"That's where we want to go," Cary told him, and then tugged at his hand.

When they stopped before the curtains, a thick-armed, baldheaded bouncer in a black T-shirt gave Cary and Hunter a going over with his scary blue eyes.

"Hey, Cary," the bouncer greeted, his deep voice as intimidating as his muscular frame.

"Hey, Sid." She nodded to the curtain. "Good night?"

Sid shrugged. "The usual with a few virgins thrown in."

With a forceful jerk on Hunter's hand, Cary pulled him beneath the black curtains. On the other side, his eyes had to adjust to the dark light, but after a few seconds he was able to make out a square room lit with blue neon lights around the walls and ceilings. The only decoration was a few silver chains on the walls, along with an occasional pair of handcuffs thrown in. Black couches and booths were set about the floor and next to the walls. In the corner was a small bar with a single bartender who was also sporting a silver chain around his neck. In fact, as Hunter began to take in the scant group of people scattered about the room, he noticed most were wearing silver chain-link necklaces. He gestured to the one around Cary's neck.

"What's with the chains?"

Her fingertips caressed the necklace. "For members of the club. Everyone wearing a necklace is a club member. One's without necklaces are called virgins."

"And how do you get to be a club member?"

Her eyes scanned the room. "You need a reference from another member who will vouch that you're a B/D gamer. That you are safe to play with, and aren't into bad pain or severe S&M. The owners here like to keep it clean, no rough stuff."

"And what you did to me the other night wasn't rough?"

She sashayed up to him, grinning. "Not in the least. Rough stuff involves bad pain, the hurtful kind of torture that has got nothing to do with pleasure but has everything to do with destroying an individual's will. True gamers are into the fun, the play, the experimentation used to arouse the senses." She played with the buttons on his shirt. "Were you aroused the other night?"

Ignoring her question, he lowered her hand to her side. "Is this the room where you wanted to shoot the author photo?"

She took a step back from him. "Yeah, I like the ambience."

He arched an eyebrow at her, but refrained from telling her what he really thought. Shifting his focus to the patrons in the room, Hunter was surprised to see that no one was decked out in suggestive leather outfits, black hoods, or wearing spikes through their noses. Most were casually dressed, like him, a few were wearing black leather jackets, skirts, or pants, and the only hint that there was anything related to the bondage scene was their silver chain-link necklaces shimmering in the blue neon lights.

"So how do hookups happen?"

"Well, when you see someone you like, you check for the necklace, talk about what you like, and if they are into the same thing you are, you leave," she illuminated.

"What if they aren't wearing a necklace?"

"People without a necklace can only get in by using a member's name at the entrance. They have to be referred. It's a way the owners guarantee that everyone here has been screened."

Hunter turned his eyes from her to the bar across the room. "Where in here were you thinking of shooting this photo?"

She pointed across the room. "By the bar...or perhaps with her in a booth beneath the blue neon lights. I thought the color contrast would be great considering we used the same colors on the cover."

He pictured Smut Slut striking a provocative pose by the bar. "I like it. What about the owners? Do you think they would consent to allowing us to shoot here?"

"Maybe if we mention the club inside the jacket cover. There's also a scene in the book that takes place in a club like this. I'm sure Smut Slut would be willing to add the club name. She often does that to introduce any of her readers to places they can go for hookups."

"So her books cross over into real life?" He nodded with approval. "That's a good selling point."

"Smut Slut always encourages those who are interested to act out their passions in a safe environment." Cary's eyes did a turn of the room. "She feels some responsibility for making sure her readers stay safe."

"And I thought writing about condoms was enough. Now we have to tell them where to go to meet other like-minded individuals so they don't end up on the evening news. Hell of a genre you two decided to work in."

"Maybe that's why she wants to cross over to romance," Cary debated. "Lately the market has changed, and a lot of people are venturing into this world, unprepared for the outcome."

"Yeah, I can understand that." Hunter became distracted by a pretty blonde in a black dress standing by the bar. She was talking to a dark-haired man wearing a black leather jacket, jeans, and black boots. As the young woman flicked back her silky hair from her shoulders, he hungered to talk to her. She had the long legs and lean figure he liked.

"She's not your type," Cary commented beside him. "Too empty-headed."

"Who?"

"The blonde with the legs. Probably your go to type."

"What are you talking about?"

"You like blondes. You look at them first in a crowd. I figure that's the kind of woman you like to chase. But once you get to know them, or get what you want out of them, you move on."

He looked at her, his mouth ajar. "Where do you get this stuff?"

"I watch you. You may not realize it, but you're pretty predictable when you walk in a room filled with people. You first look at the crowd, then start sizing up the women until you find one you like, and then you stare."

He nervously touched his shirt collar. "What are you, a shrink?"

"No, just observant. I like watching people, figuring out what they are thinking, predicting their behavior. Men are a hell of a lot easier to predict than women."

He shoved his hands in the pockets of his pants. "Funny, I thought it was the other way around."

"Would you like to meet her?"

"Who?" he asked, confused.

"The blonde. Her name is Lenore and she works with a PR firm in town."

He gaped at her for a moment. "No, I don't want to meet her."

"She likes to be submissive. She prefers soft ties, but will do handcuffs and rope as long as it doesn't leave bruises. Lenore is particular about bruises. She can't have any of that because of where she works."

"How do you know all of this?"

"She told me. I met her a while back and we spent one night chatting about preferences."

He ran his hand over his forehead, suddenly breaking out in a cold sweat. "Maybe we should just find the owners and ask if we can do the shoot here."

Cary analyzed his handsome features for a moment. "Why does this stuff make you nervous?"

"Are you always like this with men? If you talk to men like this, they will run for the hills."

"Of course I don't talk to men like this, only you."

"Why do I get the special treatment?"

"You said you wanted to learn about this stuff. This is part of it, talking about preferences. There is nothing wrong with it. In fact, it saves a lot of time in a relationship. You don't have to guess what a person wants in bed, you already know." Her eyes eagerly surveyed the room. "Look, I'll prove my point. The guy alone in the booth at the corner by the bar." She nodded casually to the corner of the room. "I'll go over there and show you what I mean."

He grabbed her arm. "Don't you dare leave me!"

"Why can't I leave you?"

"I don't want anyone in here to think…just stay by my side."

"This really makes you uncomfortable, doesn't it?" Her eyes became like two dark slits. "What are you so afraid of, Hunter?"

"I'm not afraid just…uncomfortable with the people in here." He removed his hand from her arm. "I'm not into being tied up, or tied down and having some stranger…let's just find the manager and get permission to set up the shoot."

"It's already done." She slowly grinned. "I talked to Wes today. He's fine with whatever we want to do as long as the club gets a mention."

Hunter glowered at her, the anger teeming in his green eyes. "You manipulative little…why didn't you tell me that before we came here?"

"Then you wouldn't have wanted to come. Scary how well I know you, isn't it?"

"Scary is not the word that comes to mind." He took her elbow. "Let's get out of here."

She let him pull her back to the black curtains at the entrance. At the metallic and slate bar beyond, Cary leaned in closer to him.

"Why don't we have a drink?"

"No thanks." He kept urging her toward the stairs. "I think we should just get out of here and I will bring you home."

Pouting with disappointment, she did not argue but let him escort her down the stairs and through the main bar on the first floor. Only once they had exited the bar did Hunter let go of her arm. Breathing in the cool night air, the tension in him started to dissipate. It wasn't until he spied his car that Hunter finally relaxed.

"Maybe we could stop somewhere along the way back to my place and have a drink?" Cary suggested as she went around to her car door.

Hunter retrieved his car keys from the pocket of his black pants. "I shudder to think where we will end up next."

"Oh, come on. It wasn't that bad. It's not like you hooked up with anyone in there."

He observed her over the top of the small roadster. "I hooked up with you, didn't I? That's enough for one evening."

"But you've already had me. There is no surprise left for you."

"I beg to differ." He opened his car door. "There is nothing but surprises with you."

She opened her car door. "Fine. Don't let it be said I didn't try and change you. I guess you're just too set in your ways."

He waited behind the wheel as she shut her car door and then fastened her seat belt. "I am not set in my ways. I know what I like, Cary, and whips, chains, and submission isn't part of it." He put the key in the ignition and turned the engine over.

"I was just trying to open you to new experiences."

"I like my old experiences. Less painful."

"And way too vanilla," she countered.

He put the car into gear. "Exactly."

* * *

After a quiet ride back, Hunter eased his car next to the curb in front of her triangular apartment building. When he turned off the engine, he veered his eyes to her. As she freed the seat belt from around her shoulder, he felt a twinge of regret. Perhaps he had been a tad harsh.

"I'm sorry about the way I acted back at the club. I should have been a bit more open to your…alternative lifestyle."

She collected her purse from the car floor. "What makes you think it's my alternative lifestyle? It's my business to stay up-to-date on such things. I can't be a very good editor if I don't know what is happening in the bondage scene."

"I think you know plenty about the bondage scene. Maybe more than you should. After our night together, I learned you—"

"You don't know me, Hunter," she blurted, cutting him off. "We had sex, not a relationship. So don't sit there and pretend you have me figured out."

He sighed and rocked his head back against the seat rest. "Fine. You're right and I'm wrong." He glared at her. "Is that what you needed to hear?" he added.

"You don't have to be such an asshole about it."

"I'm not being an asshole," he refuted, raising his voice. "It's just so hard trying to talk to you. I feel like…forget it."

"There you go again. Just when you start to talk and open up, you shut down."

"No I don't. I open up."

"Like you opened up at the club?" She reached for the car door. "Good night, Hunter."

Feeling exasperated, he slapped his hand on the black leather steering wheel. "Now why do I get the distinct impression you're mad at me?"

She climbed from the car without saying anything. After she slammed her door, his hands gripped the steering wheel. Shaking his head, he opened his door.

"I'm sorry, Cary," he told her as he stood outside of the car. "Yes, I was an ass at the club."

She stopped on the sidewalk just a few feet from the glass entrance to her building. Slowly, she turned to face him.

"Let me make it up to you," he posed, sounding cheerful. "I'll buy you a drink…or better yet, dinner. How does that sound?"

She stood on the sidewalk, cradling her black purse in her hands and shifting her weight back and forth on her black heels as if she were considering his offer.

"I've got some leftover Chinese food in the fridge if you want to come up," she eventually called out.

He saw her standing there, looking like a little girl playing dress up, and knew he could never resist her.

"Let me just park my car and I'll come up."

She smiled. "I'm in 608."

"608. Got it."

He stepped back into his car, feeling happy and at the same time nervous about being alone with her. His mind kept reassuring him that there would be no harm in having a bite to eat with his employee. Besides, the idea of leaving her hurt and angry was more than he could bear.

As she walked inside the glass doors to her building, his stomach jumbled into a thick knot. "I'd better hurry up and find out why she has this effect on me before I lose it completely."

Chapter 11

Cary answered her white front door wearing faded blue jeans and an extra-large, white T-shirt, but had not removed her dark gray eye shadow or deep red lipstick. Hunter found the contrast between her innocent attire and seductive makeup alluring as hell.

"You changed," he commented, fighting to keep the apprehension from his voice.

"Just getting comfortable," she assured him.

The knot in his stomach twisted even tighter.

"Come on in," she drawled. "I hope you don't mind cats."

"Why, do you have one?" As soon as he spoke the words, he felt something wind around his right ankle.

Cary pointed to the fluffy orange and white cat at Hunter's feet. "That is Sex Kitten."

"Sex Kitten? You're kidding?"

"Nope." She shook her head. "It suits him. He's the biggest flirt in the building."

It was a tastefully decorated apartment with shiny oak hardwood floors, muted tones of beige, copper, and sienna painted on the walls, high ceilings, and tall windows that overlooked the surrounding downtown buildings. The furniture was a hodgepodge of modern, sleek leather and chrome chairs, a pine coffee table, and an oversized, plush white sofa stuffed with a colorful assortment of throw pillows. The living area was triangular in shape with a small kitchen in an adjoining alcove, and dining area just beyond the kitchen. Posters of famous French Quarter attractions, such as Café Du Monde and Jackson Square adorned the walls.

"You like to keep pictures of New Orleans close by?"

"Always." She shut the front door. "It keeps me sane."

"How many bedrooms do you have?" he asked, admiring a poster of the entrance to The Court of Two Sisters Restaurant.

"Two," she replied, waving to an archway past the kitchen. "I use one as an office."

He walked over to a window that faced the thirty-three foot neon Coca Cola sign on top of the Olympia building near Woodruff Park. "Great view."

She came up beside him. "Yeah, nothing like gazing out your window and seeing a great big advertisement for a soft drink. Wait until the lights go on. My living room glows red."

"If you hate it that much, you could move."

"Believe it or not, I've gotten used to it. It's kind of comforting in a way. Always there flashing its bright red neon display. Anyway, downtown is convenient for me. Close to my job."

"I hear your boss is a real jerk though."

"He's not that bad once you get to know him." She started for the kitchen. "I hope you don't mind wine. It's all I have."

"Wine is great." He grinned as Sex Kitten trotted into the kitchen alongside him.

"I never pictured you being into wine." She directed her gaze to the cat at her feet. "Go sit on the couch."

"Actually I used to drink it all the time when I was writing." Hunter stared in amazement as the big white and orange cat ran back into the living room and jumped on the white sofa. "Does he always listen like that?"

"Yeah, I know it's weird. Ever since I brought him home, he seems to understand everything I say." She went to a white refrigerator. "I thought you only drank vodka," she added.

"I didn't get into drinking chilled vodka until after I took over the company. I never touched hard liquor before then."

She pulled out a few white cartons from the refrigerator. "That's not good. Makes it sound like you hate what you do."

"Not hate." He came up to her and took the cartons from her hands. "Just not real crazy about it." He carried the cartons to the table.

Cary opened a polished oak cabinet and retrieved two white dinner plates, then she gathered forks and spoons from a drawer. "So how long do you plan on doing this job you're 'not real crazy about'?"

"I don't know. Might have to stick with it for a while." He rested his hand on the arched back of a wooden chair against the table. "I don't have anything else to fall back on."

After putting the plates and utensils on the table, she raised her eyes to him. "You still have your writing." She went to the refrigerator and removed a bottle of wine. After stopping by a drawer to get a wine opener, she came back to the table. "I read your manuscript, Hunter. You have a great shot at making it as a writer." Handing the wine bottle and opener to him, she returned to the kitchen.

"But that's not a career, Cary. Not a career I can eat with anyway." He peeled the foil back from the wine bottle and placed the opener in the cork. "I have to be practical."

She collected two wine glasses from a cabinet above the sink. "Practical?" She shook her head. "Now you sound like your father. Is that why he insisted you take over the business? You had to be practical and go to work at the publishing house."

He popped the cork from the bottle. "No, my bank account made me practical. I got tired of asking my father for money, squeaking by on my measly allowance, and living in general squalor so I could fulfill some silly dream of being a writer. After my mother died…I decided enough was enough."

"So now you have a lucrative job, but are you happy, Hunter?"

"I'm happy," he assured her, filling a wine glass on the table. "I'll be even happier when we launch this book. Having Smut Slut as my debut author for the Hot Nights line was a stroke of luck." He handed her the glass of wine.

"She's pretty excited about it, too." She took a sip of the wine.

He filled the other glass. "With her on board, things might finally start picking up at Donovan Books." Putting the bottle down, he pulled out a chair.

"Has business been that bad?" Cary probed, taking a seat next to him.

He inspected the contents of one of the cartons. "Not bad. Just difficult. We lost our premier author last year."

"Monique Delome, yeah I know. What exactly happened with her and your brother? He was pretty tight-lipped about it at dinner the other night."

While spooning shrimp fried rice onto his plate, he shrugged his wide shoulders. "Monique and my brother had worked together for years, Chris was always interested in her, but she put him off. Then she got involved with some old flame, an oil guy from Dallas. The affair turned out badly and Monique leaned on Chris for support. I didn't find out they were engaged until a month after it happened." He plopped the carton beside her. "A month after that I found out she was pregnant."

Cary almost dropped her spoon. "Pregnant?"

Hunter opened another white carton and peeked inside. "It wasn't Chris's baby. The oil guy was the father. Tyler Moore was his name. Anyway, Tyler found out she was pregnant, won her back, and then she fired Chris as her manager. In the process, she gave her last release, *A Chance with You*, to another publisher. I would have killed to get my hands on that book, but my idiot brother told Monique it was too risqué for Donovan Books."

Cary selected a cold egg roll from another carton. "Was that when you decided to branch out into erotica?"

He nodded as he loaded some chicken and noodles on his plate. "That was when I knew we had to change. Losing Monique Delome hurt, and since then other authors have been pulling away." He took a bite of noodles. "Hey, I get it. Authors need to grow, but my father is old-fashioned, so is my brother."

Cary snatched up her fork. "Your brother is also clueless."

Picking up his wine glass, he snickered. "Clueless? How?"

"He thinks he knows writers, says he can anticipate their needs. He even claimed he was the best manager there is, but I didn't buy it. A good manager would know he could never anticipate any writer's needs. Needs change with every book." She deposited a small serving of chicken and noodles on her plate. "Sometimes you need someone to listen to your ideas as you write; sometimes you just need peace to write. Every book requires something different from a writer."

He sat back in his chair, holding his wine glass and studying her. "Now that sounds like something a writer would say."

She fidgeted in her chair, shaking her head. "I've heard my writers tell me that, that's all." She daintily tried to push a forkful of noodles into her mouth without spilling a drop.

"I think you've been keeping a very big secret from me, Cary." He put his wine glass down and leaned over to her. "I think there is something you want to tell me but are too afraid."

She munched on her noodles, her eyes nervously darting about the kitchen.

"You want to be a writer, don't you?" Hunter softly asked. "You edit books, hang out with writers and took this job with my publishing house because you secretly want to write. That's why you go to those bondage clubs and spend time in those weird bars. You're doing your research in hopes of penning your novel one day."

Cary almost choked on her noodles, then she burst out in a fit of laughter. "You don't know how wrong you are about me, Hunter." She took a hurried sip of wine. "Cary Anderson is not a writer."

"No, I'm pretty sure I'm right about you." He pointed his fork at her. "And it's all right to want to be a writer, Cary. There's nothing wrong with it."

"If there is nothing wrong with it, why aren't you trying again with your book?"

He gathered up some noodles on his fork. "I had my shot, but you could still take yours."

Waiting as he chewed on a mouthful of noodles, Cary cradled her wine glass in her hands. "How 'bout I make a deal with you?"

He stopped chewing, leery of her suggestion. "A deal?"

She exuberantly thumped her glass down on the table. "I will take a shot at writing a book, if you finish the book you started."

He furrowed his brow at her. "Why would I do that?"

"Why not? We could work together, compare notes, and urge each other on. When you get frustrated you could bounce ideas off me, and I can do the same with you when I get stumped. We'll help each other."

He put his fork down and contemplated her eyes, attempting to read her thoughts. "Why are you so determined to see me pick up that book again?"

Appearing as if she were suddenly reinvigorated, she snapped up her fork. "I don't know. Maybe I want to see how your book ends. I've always been a sucker for endings, good, bad, boring; I love to see everything brought to a conclusion. I guess it's the editor in me. I can't move on to another book until I know how the last one ended. And I want to see you finish your book, Hunter. I think you want to see it finished, too."

"I'll think about it," he sighed. "But if I did agree to such a scheme, it could not interfere with work. We have to stay on track with *The Bondage Club* release."

"Absolutely. We can start tonight, after we eat." She heaved a hunk of noodles onto her fork. "I have this idea for a book, but I need help getting started."

He enjoyed her enthusiasm. "All right. I guess we can brainstorm for a little while."

"Great." She shoved the noodles into her mouth.

Her childlike exuberance was infectious and Hunter rolled a thick wad of noodles on his fork and then crammed it into his mouth, mimicking her. They laughed together as the Coca Cola sign began to flash its bright lights into her living room, bathing them in a warm red glow.

* * *

They were sitting in her office, next to her white Ikea desk with an add-on unit of shelves and a matching white printer stand, each with yellow legal pads and pens in their hands. The half-full bottle of zinfandel and two almost empty wine glasses sat on a corner of the desk just down from her closed black laptop, while Sex Kitten was curled up next to the computer. Scattered on the walls were peg boards, a large calendar, and a framed poster of St. Louis Cathedral in the moonlight. A long window next to the desk was allowing the amber glow of the street lights into the room, while the single black desk lamp added a stringent hue.

"You have an outline for the middle and an end. They fall in love, get torn apart, and then find their love again," Hunter began as he sat back in the oak chair he had dragged in from the dining room. "But you need a sharp beginning. Something to draw the reader in."

"I know." Cary sank in her black desk chair. "That's my problem. I can't figure out how to start it."

Hunter glanced down at his legal pad, reviewing his notes. "Perhaps start with the character of Sylvia. Offer the reader a glimpse of her life before you bring James into the story. That way they can see how much meeting him will change her life. Make it from her viewpoint."

"Yeah." Her eyes danced in the light from the desk lamp. "That's it. I can have her come home from work and show the drudgery of her existence as a librarian. It will add to the excitement when James runs into her on the street. Then as the relationship builds, I can show how his love changes her life and opens her eyes to the world around her."

"From what you describe, it sounds like a romance. But you still need something that will make it memorable. You know, beyond the boy meets girl scenario."

"Yeah, you're right" she agreed. "I guess I'm still putting it together in my head."

"You just need to hone the characters down. When they become real to you, the story will take shape." He tossed his pad on the desk. "From the way you describe her, I can see bits of the shy and reserved Sylvia in you."

She put her pad and pen down. "What makes you think this is autobiographical?"

Hunter picked up his wine glass and the bottle. "Every writer puts part of their life into their stories. Our experiences shape what and how we write." He poured some wine into his glass. "So who was James? Who was the guy who turned you from a recluse and into a woman of the world?"

She lifted her glass and held it up to him. After he finished pouring his wine, he tipped the bottle over the rim of her glass. "There was never a James," she divulged.

He topped off her glass, frowning slightly. "No one ever came close? Not even your fiancé?"

"No, Winter and me…well, we started out all right, but he eventually walked away. With other guys I was never…very successful. I guess James is the guy I would like to meet. Someone who can rescue me from this life."

"What's wrong with your life? You've got a great career, are well-known by some famous authors, are highly respected, and you just started a new job with a great company."

"But...." She peered into her wine. "I'm also thirty-one, never been married, and according to my mother that makes me something of a spinster. And I've even been considering getting another cat, which, as you know, is the death knell for any spinster."

He cast his eyes to Sex Kitten. "I don't think he wants a playmate. He strikes me as a lone wolf."

Scratching behind the cat's right ear, she said, "Maybe we're both like that."

"I don't buy that." He paused for a moment and rolled his glass in his hands, debating if he should say what was on his mind. "Maybe if you weren't so...pushy."

"Pushy?" She thwacked her wineglass down on the desk. "Do you think I'm pushy?"

"Yes," he calmly told her. "You should never tell a guy about your interest in bondage, at least not until after quite a few dates, maybe even later than that. It might scare some guys away."

"It didn't scare you away."

"But I'm not dating you, Cary."

She took in a breath, allowing a long silence to linger between them. "Would you ever date someone like me?" she eventually asked with an alluring smile.

He put his wine down, fighting like hell to not let that smile get to him. "If you weren't my employee, then...sure, I would ask you out on a date." He abruptly rose from his chair, feeling uncomfortable. "It's getting late. I should go."

"Sure. I'll walk you out."

When Cary stood up, she teetered a little to the side. Hunter caught her before she stumbled into her desk.

"Are you okay?"

She rested her hands against his chest. "I think I had too much wine."

The smell of her flowery perfume and the softness of her skin aroused his desire. Without thinking, Hunter wrapped his other arm about her. As her body pressed into him, he became hypnotized by her red lips and before he could stop he was lowering his mouth to hers.

The kiss was spontaneous, but as the warmth of her lips caressed his, Hunter realized that this was exactly what he had been craving from her all night. He had been yearning to hold her close and taste her hypnotic smile. When she kissed him back, his grip about her waist tightened, crushing her to him. He traced his lips along her cheek and down her neck to the tender spot at the nape. His teeth scraped her skin, and when he bit into her flesh, she rocked her head back and moaned.

"I know we shouldn't," he murmured against her throat. "But what if we—"

"Moved this to my bedroom?"

Hunter eased back from her, feeling his resolve weakening. "We have to be smart about this."

She clasped his hand and pulled him toward her office door. "Admit it, Hunter, it's what we both want." She stopped at the doorway and kissed him. "Am I right?"

He shook his head, hating his inability to push her away. "Where's your bedroom?"

She nodded to a door just down the short hallway from her office. When she turned back to him, he picked her up in his arms and tossed her over his left shoulder. He was laughing as he carried her down the hallway, and when Hunter came to her bedroom door he kicked it open.

Lit by the streetlights, the bedroom was painted in alternating shades of pale blue with white trim. A blue bedspread was neatly made on a white canopy, queen-sized bed in the center of the room. A wide square, blue and white throw rug lay beneath the bed, blue curtains covered the two tall white windows on the far wall, and a white chest of drawers with a white mounted mirror on top hugged the opposite wall.

"This is not what I expected," Hunter declared, depositing her on the bed.

She reclined back on the blue cover, and turned on a brass lamp sitting on a white night table. "What did you expect?"

He stood at the foot of the bed and kicked off his black loafers. "Something less…girly." He curiously fingered the blue drapery hanging from the canopy beside him.

She sat up. "But I am a girl, you know?"

He hurriedly undid the buttons on his shirt. "Yeah, I noticed." He leapt onto the bed and encircled her in his arms.

Cary wrestled the shirt over his shoulders and threw it to the floor. Hunter finished pulling her T-shirt over her head, while she unzipped his fly. She was tugging his boxers and black pants down his hips while he fought to undo the last clasp on her bra. Giggling, she finally got him out of his pants as he dropped her bra over the side of the bed. When his hands went to the zipper on her jeans, Cary rolled over, and opened a drawer in her night table.

"What are you doing?" he questioned, lowering her jeans to her ankles.

"Protection," she answered.

He finished getting her black silk panties from around her ankles. "For a girl who claims to not be too successful with men, you sure have a ready supply of condoms."

She lay on her back, naked beneath him. "Is that a bad thing?"

He kissed her lips. "No, it just makes me wonder." He wrapped her legs about his hips.

"I'm not easy, Hunter."

"Neither of us are exactly easy, Cary."

"You're right," she whispered, arching her body into his.

He fondled her folds and when his fingers slid inside her wet flesh, Cary groaned. His need for her took over as her body responded to his touch. Unable to wait any longer, Hunter grabbed her butt, elevating her hips.

"Wait." She placed her hand on his chest.

He searched her eyes. "What is it?"

She sat up and gently eased him over on his back. "Not that way. I like to be on top." Kissing the scar on his left upper chest she snaked her hands up his arms, raising them above his head. "Are you ever going to tell me how you got that scar?"

"Not right this minute."

"What if I make you talk?" She tempted his neck with her teeth.

He went to put his arms about her, but she held them above his head. "What did you have in mind?"

Hunter felt something cold clamp over both of his wrists. "That's better," she mumbled into his ear. "Now you're my captive."

Hunter opened his eyes and saw a pair of silver handcuffs secured to the corner post above his head. He frantically pulled on the handcuffs while Cary straddled his hips. "For crying out loud, Cary, not again."

"You'll like it this way." She nibbled his ear.

"Can't we try it the normal way?" he beseeched in a raised voice.

She placed her hand over his mouth. "No talking." She kissed his chest, bit his right nipple, and then worked her lips down his stomach to his erection.

When her mouth closed over him, Hunter gasped. Her lips worked up and down his shaft, tantalizing him, encouraging him, and building tension in every muscle of his body. Hunter dreaded what was coming, but as his climax charged upward, he prayed that she did not intend to tease him like before.

And when that white heat took over his senses, his back arched and his hands tugged against the handcuffs. His orgasm was swift and relentless, and he moaned as his body shook. Breathing hard and trying to relax against the bed, he felt her shimmy up his body and settle on top of his hips.

"Okay, undo the handcuffs, Cary."

She kissed his neck. "Not yet. I'm not done."

"Come on, this isn't comfortable."

Her fingernail scratched down his chest to his groin. The throbbing in his body had not even ebbed when she began stimulating him. Hunter sucked in a breath when her fingers gently teased him, creating that welcomed tingle. He could not believe that he could feel any excitement so soon after coming, but he did. Her hand enticed him, and soon he was growing hard again.

Before he knew what was happening, she swiftly maneuvered a condom over him, and straddled his hips. "Now it's my turn," she whispered to him.

"I swear I've never known a woman like you. But if you don't take off these handcuffs soon, I'm never going to regain sensation in my hands again."

She kissed his lips as she lowered her hips on to him. "I don't need your hands, just this." Taking him all the way into her, he sighed as her flesh closed around him.

She rode him hard, compounding the pain in his arms. Cary was writhing above him, slamming her hips against him, causing Hunter to wince as his shoulders stretched out further. But soon his discomfort was erased by the fire growing in his loins. He wanted to hold her, urge her hips to move faster, but he was at her mercy. He found the sensation compelling and yet frustrating as hell. He was plotting his revenge when his second climax surged forward. His body tensed and he heard Cary call his name as her body trembled. When he finally let go, he swore it was better than before.

Catching his breath, Hunter opened his eyes and saw her curled up on his chest, breathing hard. He went to hold her and then the uncomfortable burning in his arms returned.

"Cary, undo my hands, please."

She sat up. "What if I want to go again?"

"Then I will get on top, or from behind or any way you want, just get me out of these damn things."

Grudgingly, she undid the handcuffs, and when his arms fell from the post, shooting pains burned all the way from his left shoulder to his hand.

"Shit!" he yelled.

"What?" She hovered over him, frowning.

"My arm." Tears began welling up in his eyes. "Christ, it's on fire. My left shoulder feels like it has been ripped from the socket."

She sat up next to him and gently helped lift his arm over his chest. He grimaced and gritted his teeth as Cary moved him to an upright position in the bed.

"Maybe I should take you to the ER."

"And tell them what? You practically raped me?"

She sat back on her heels. "I didn't rape you."

"That's a matter of opinion."

"I thought you enjoyed it," she returned, almost shouting.

"Every time I end up in bed with you I'm either tied up or in handcuffs. What is it with you?" He was quickly silenced by the pain tearing through his shoulder. "Christ this hurts."

Cary jumped from the bed. "Come on, let's get you dressed. I'm taking you to a place I know just up the road from here." She collected her jeans and panties from the floor.

Holding his left arm against his chest, he sat on the side of the canopy bed. "What place?"

"An urgent care clinic." She hiked her jeans up her hips. "I went there last year when I sliced my finger and needed stiches. They can help you."

"Forget it. It's probably just a cramp."

She poked her finger into his left shoulder, making Hunter curse out loud. "There see, it's not a cramp. I'm a woman, I know cramps and that's not a cramp."

"It's in my arm, not my…." His eyes ran down her semi-naked body. "Uterus."

"Stop arguing with me." She yanked up her zipper and began to look around for her T-shirt. "You need to go and make sure you didn't dislocate it."

"I would know if I dislocated my shoulder, Cary."

She grabbed for her bra and T-shirt. "Are you a doctor?"

"What kind of stupid question is that?"

She finished putting her bra in place. "Then we're going to take you to the doctor." Yanking her T-shirt over her head, she added, "The least a doctor can do is get you some pain medication in case you sprained it or something."

"Can you sprain a shoulder?" He stood from the bed.

"How should I know?" She retrieved his boxers and jeans from the floor. "Use your good arm to lean on me and I'll help you dress."

"This so humiliating," he huffed as she lifted his black pants and boxers up his legs.

"Stop acting like a baby." After zipping up his trousers, she eased his shirt around his good shoulder, and draped the empty sleeve over his left shoulder.

"I can't drive like this," Hunter admitted, adjusting his shirt.

"I'll drive your car," she assured him, while he stepped into his black loafers.

By the time they made it to Hunter's car, parked on the street down from her building, the pain in his shoulder was a little better, but he was still unable to use his arm. Concern began to cloud his judgment as a plethora of worst case scenarios crossed his mind. He worried about how he would get to and from work, how he would manage his business, even the mundane tasks of everyday activities became a vexing problem if he could not use his left arm. When the rear lights flashed on his car as Cary hit the remote entrance key, an unexpected consideration overtook him. What if he could not type, but more to the point, what if he could not write?

"You all right, Hunter?" Cary inquired as she stood beside the open passenger side door.

He came back from his imaginings. "Yeah, look it's feeling better."

She pointed to the car. "Get in. If it's nothing, then they will tell us that instead of us worrying if it is something. 'It's better if you know the name of your demon,' my father used to always say."

Shaking his head, Hunter eased into the passenger seat. "I don't think that's what I needed to hear right now, Cary."

Speeding along Peachtree Street, Hunter was amazed at how well Cary handled his car. She pushed the little roadster through some moderate traffic and was able to gear down at red lights and shift from neutral to first without any problems. Hunter hated to admit that when he had first bought the sporty car, he had spent several days trying to get the feel of the stick shift.

"Where did you learn to drive a stick?"

She maneuvered the car around a van. "I had three older brothers. They taught me everything. How to throw a football, pitch a curveball, hot wire a car, drive, fight…drink." She smiled as memories warmed her delicate face. "They took care of me, but my brothers were the main reason I wanted to go out of state for school. I needed to get away."

"Still, it must have been hard to leave your family."

"It was at first, but then when I finished school and started making my way in Atlanta, I was glad I left. I needed to find out who I was and what I wanted."

"And what is it you want, Cary?"

She shifted her attention to an orange building just up the street. "Here's the emergency clinic."

Tucked between two higher buildings, the boutique-looking exterior resembled a retail business more than a medical clinic. The only thing that gave Hunter any reassurance was the glowing red cross placed above the glass front doors.

After parking outside the entrance, Cary went around to the passenger door and helped him from the low car. "I'm not helpless," he barked as she tried to lift him to his feet.

"You don't have to get snippy. I'm trying to help you."

"Handcuffing me to your bed was helping me?"

She fixed his shirt over his left shoulder. "I thought the surprise would help loosen you up."

"Just tell them I hurt my shoulder moving furniture or something heavy." He rolled his green eyes as she held the glass front door to the urgent care clinic open for him. "They don't need to know the truth."

"Fine," she agreed, following him in the door. "I'll tell them it was a huge dresser. Way bigger than you. Will that make you feel like a real man?"

"Maybe you'd better let me do the talking."

* * *

Thirty minutes later, after filling out pages of paperwork, answering a slew of medical questions, and giving them his insurance card, Hunter was seated on an exam table in a cubby hole-sized room, waiting to be seen by the doctor.

"By the time I actually see a doctor, my shoulder will be better," he complained to Cary, who was sitting in a chair across from the exam table.

"How's the shoulder feeling?"

He tried to move his left arm and winced. "Not as bad as before, but still hurts like hell to move."

"I'm sorry." She stood from the chair and came up to him. "I shouldn't have done that to you. I broke the first rule in all bondage clubs and that is to make sure all activity between two partners is consensual."

"Bondage clubs?" He paused and stared at her in disbelief. "How many of these things do you belong to?"

"I don't know. It's hard to keep track." She paused and reflected for a moment. "There are a few straight clubs, some gay clubs, sugar daddy clubs, under twenty-one, over fifty, S&M clubs, fetish clubs...you've got to cover a lot of clubs when you work in this genre."

He sank into the exam table and the paper sheet covering crinkled beneath his weight. "And what club taught you to pull that stunt in the bedroom?"

She wrung her hands together. "I never...meant for us to end up here."

"I find that hard to believe." He rubbed his shoulder. "I could have sworn you liked tying me up."

"I thought a man like you would want an experienced woman in bed. Doesn't that turn you on?" she questioned, sounding like a little girl.

"Taking someone to bed isn't a competition, Cary. It's not about being experienced or experimentation. It's about feeling good."

"And what about emotion? Shouldn't you feel something for someone you want to be with?"

"Mr. Donovan?" a voice inquired from the doorway.

Hunter turned and took in the radiant round face and lovely blue eyes of a young blonde woman. In her hands was a clipboard, and in the pocket of her long white coat a black stethoscope poked out.

"Yes, I'm Hunter Donovan, are there more papers I have to fill out?" he demanded, assuming she was part of the staff.

She flashed him a breathtaking smile. "No, no more papers. I'm Dr. Kendrick." She glanced at her clipboard.

Hunter felt his embarrassment complete. Not only was his doctor female and blonde, she was also reasonably younger than him.

"Are you his wife?" Dr. Kendrick asked Cary.

"No, ah...." She looked over to Hunter. "His employee. He was helping me move some furniture in my apartment and he hurt his left shoulder."

"Your left shoulder? Let's see what we've got." Dr. Kendrick put the clipboard down on the end of the exam table and directed her eyes to his naked left shoulder. She pushed his shirt aside and inspected the scar on his left, upper chest.

"Is this a surgical scar? Clavicle injury?"

"Yes. It happened ten years ago," he told her.

"Bar fight?" Dr. Kendrick joked with a smile and placed her cool hands on his injured shoulder.

"Ah, no. It was a car accident." He winced as her fingers poked and prodded. "I was ejected before the car went into a ravine. I broke my collarbone in three places when I hit the railing."

Hunter noticed the startled look on Cary's face, but the doctor's continued probing of his shoulder made him glance away.

"How long ago did you hurt your shoulder?" Dr. Kendrick queried.

"An hour, maybe," Cary confirmed, hovering about the exam table.

Dr. Kendrick took his left hand in hers and gently raised his arm. Hunter damn near screamed out with the pain. "You think you could knock me out before you do that?" he said between his gritted teeth.

"What kind of furniture were you moving, Mr. Donovan?"

Hunter froze. "A bed," he eventually told the doctor, figuring it was as close to the truth as he wanted to get.

"A bed?" Dr. Kendrick returned to her clipboard. "Did your arm get caught or yanked in any way when you were moving this bed?"

"Ah, I guess," he answered. "I wasn't really paying attention."

Dr. Kendrick removed a black pen from her top coat pocket. "Mr. Donovan, were you tied to this bed when it was being moved?"

He shook his head. "I don't understand."

Dr. Kendrick smiled for him. "Your shoulder injury is nothing more than a bad muscle spasm. We've been seeing a lot of this lately."

"You have?" Cary questioned.

Dr. Kendrick jotted something down on the clipboard. "We call it FSOGS."

Hunter's throat tightened with dread. "Which means what?"

"*Fifty Shades of Gray* Syndrome. We get about a dozen cases a week." Dr. Kendrick held her clipboard against her chest. "Just ice your shoulder for the next twenty-four hours. Take Advil for the pain and by tomorrow it should loosen up. You'll be sore for a day or two, but that's it. If you're still having problems after that, come back here and we will do some x-rays." She was about to turn for the door when she stopped. "I might suggest laying off the handcuffs for a while."

Hunter shook his head, chuckling. "How did you know it was handcuffs?"

"The pattern of bruising popping up about your wrists; it's a dead giveaway." She turned to Cary. "Just keep an eye on him and make sure he doesn't overexert himself any more this evening."

Cary blushed and lowered her eyes to the floor.

"Thank you, Dr. Kendrick," Hunter said as the physician moved toward the exam room door. "I appreciate your…advice."

"You two have a good evening," Dr. Kendrick offered with a grin, and then exited the room.

After the door to the exam room had closed, Hunter turned to Cary. "I guess this is one of those little lessons they left out of your bondage club class, eh?" He climbed off the exam table. "I don't know what was more humiliating, you handcuffing me to that bed, or the doctor's face when she figured out what was going on." He struggled to fix his shirt over his injured shoulder.

"I already said I was sorry. What else do you want, Hunter? My resignation?"

"That's not what I'm saying. I just get the impression you are trying to be something you're not with me. The handcuffs, the bondage clubs, all of it." He winced and held his shoulder. "Then there are times I swear I see the real you. Like in the car on the way over here; you weren't trying to be someone else. You were...you."

She hesitated as her eyes weighed his. "The car accident you spoke of, was that when your mother died?"

He took a moment to adjust his shirt, before he spoke. "We were coming from the office one night, heading back to my parent's home in Decatur. She hated driving alone at night and I had gone along because I knew what would happen when...." His eyes darted to Cary. "She caught my dad with his secretary that night...me and Chris always knew about Dad's affairs, but Mom...well, she was so upset she lost control of the car in a sharp turn. I was tossed out before the car went over the railing."

"Why didn't you say anything before?"

"It's just another dirty Donovan secret. No one wants to hear about it."

"I want to hear about it, Hunter."

He was stumped for a comeback. He knew he should say something to break the deafening silence in the exam room, but the ache in his shoulder, and the innocent glint in her eyes was distracting the hell out of him.

"Let's get out of here. You can drop me at my place, then take my car home and pick me up in the morning," was all he could think to say.

"No," Cary argued. "The doctor said to keep an eye on you. You're coming home with me. We'll ice your shoulder, and you can sleep in my bed. I'll take the couch."

"Not a good idea. I'll be fine at home."

She stood before him, defiant. "You'll go home, probably open a bottle of vodka, and pass out on your couch. In the morning, you'll be worse off than you are now. You're coming home with me." She gave him a tolerant smile. "It's the least I can do for humiliating you."

His determination to shut her out faltered. "You didn't humiliate me, at least not before coming here."

Her smile deepened, highlighting the curve of her pink cheeks. "So you did enjoy it, maybe a little bit?"

He turned for the exam room door. "I think you and I should stick to working together and nothing else. As a couple, we're a danger to society."

Hunter hurried into the stark white hallway beyond the exam room, anxious to get out of the emergency clinic. Even though he was apprehensive about spending any more time with Cary, he did have to admit he wasn't ready to go home and face his empty condo. Despite their disastrous attempt at being a couple, he still enjoyed her company and wanted to be able to spend a few hours together without the added pressure of sex. Never before had he wanted to spend time with anyone, even his family. People usually bored him with their predictability and self-centered conversation, but Cary was different. His opinions and ideas mattered to her. She encouraged him and that was what touched Hunter most of all. Everyone yearned to be heard; it was just a shock to the system, in a world filled with talkers, to find someone willing to listen.

Chapter 12

The sun was shining through the blue curtains on the side of the white canopy bed when Hunter opened his eyes. Staring up at the sheer blue drape, he had to blink his eyes a few times before he could comprehend what he was seeing. When he moved to sit up, the shooting pain in his left shoulder stopped him. After rolling to his right side, he was able to push himself to a sitting position and take in the blue bedroom.

In the daylight, the room was surprisingly unlike the Cary he knew. Porcelain knickknacks of ballerinas were spread out along the wide dresser, neatly bowed white ribbons held back the thick curtains, and about the bed were several white heart-shaped throw pillows. He picked up one of the pillows and turned it over in his hands. This was something he expected to find in the bedroom of a devoted romantic, not a bondage enthusiast.

A gentle rap at the white bedroom door made him glance down at his black trousers. Thankful that he was still partially dressed, he searched the room for his shirt. "Come in."

Cary glided into the room, wrapped in a thick blue robe and with a white mug in her right hand. At her feet was the orange and white cat he had met the previous night. When

Sex Kitten's green eyes spotted him on the bed, the creature went running across the room and leapt onto the blue bedspread. The cat came up to him purring, and Hunter scratched behind its fluffy orange ears.

"I brought you some coffee," Cary told him as she came up to the bed. "How's the shoulder?"

"Stiff," he confided while petting the cat. "But I think the ice helped last night."

She handed him the mug. "If you're hungry, I've got some eggs and toast waiting in the kitchen."

He took the mug and sipped the black coffee. "Actually, I'm starved." He smiled up at her and lifted the mug. "Thanks for this, and thank you for last night. You really didn't have to bring me back here and take care of me."

"Well, I felt responsible, and I couldn't have you go home and not be able to do anything."

He rested the mug on his thigh. "But I feel guilty for kicking you out of your bed."

"Sex Kitten and I were fine on the couch."

He glimpsed his watch on the night table, and after putting his coffee mug down beside it, he gingerly slipped the watch on his left wrist and checked the time. "I need to get home and change before we head into the office."

"Perhaps you should call in sick today," she suggested.

He slowly stood from the bed. "I haven't called in sick in ten years, I'm not about to start today. And we have a lot to do for the launch."

"Yeah, I know." A small frown marred her lips. "Why don't you get something to eat while I change, and then I'll drive you to your condo."

Hunter's certainty about keeping the woman at a distance languished in the pit of his stomach. For some reason, Cary's happiness was becoming very important to him.

"I want to thank you again for everything you did last night." He took a breath, trying to think of something to add, but the right words escaped him.

She walked to the bathroom door in the corner of the room. "I handcuffed you to the bed, so I sort of owed you."

"Cary, despite what happened, I would like to get to know you. I think we work well together and I like being around you...as a friend."

She placed her hand on the bathroom doorknob, but did not gaze back at him. "As a friend; sure, Hunter." Her voice sounded flat and bereft of its usual life. "I understand." She stepped into the bathroom and quietly shut the door.

As Hunter walked out of the bedroom, a stitch of regret caught his insides. He had wanted to reassure her, but he sensed all his words had done was add to the tension between them. He needed to find a way to keep her whimsical smile and soft brown eyes from affecting him. But he wasn't sure exactly how to go about it. After all, it was easy enough to shut out people who made him uncomfortable, but how did he rid himself of someone who had finally made him feel content?

* * *

The next day Hunter kept his distance from Cary. Avoiding his office, he spent the morning with his accountants, going over a budget for the new erotica line. Then, he went to visit with Jesse Hart, his IT guy, wanting to update the website.

When Hunter exited the elevator on the basement floor he entered a hallway filled with metal shelves lined with laptop computers, hard drives, monitors, telephones, printers, fax machines, and a whole host of other IT paraphernalia. Making his way toward Jesse's office, he wondered how the man kept his sanity working in the cool, windowless basement all day.

"Jesse? You in here?" he called when he came to an open area at the end of the hallway.

"Hey, Hunter," a baritone voice returned from the corner.

Leaning over a worktable with several laptop computers spread out before him was a dark-haired man. When he stood from the table, his massive shoulders and thick arms towered over Hunter. At six-foot-five, Jesse Hart was a tree trunk of a man, with bulging muscles poking out around his short-sleeved shirt, a square face, and deep brown eyes. His coffee-colored skin glistened beneath the harsh fluorescent lights, and when he smiled at his boss, his bright white teeth shined.

"What you doing down here?" Jesse asked. "You hate the basement."

Hunter nodded, glancing around the dimly lit workroom. "Yeah, but I have to go over a new website design with you and I figured this was better a place than doing it in my office."

Jesse's deep chortle bounced about the compact basement. "Oh, I get it." He shook his head and waved Hunter to his desk. "The new girl driving you nuts, huh?"

Hunter walked over to a long wooden desk with two desktop computers on top of it. "Not exactly." He briefly massaged his left shoulder.

"Not exactly?" Jesse chuckled once more. "If I had to be in the same room with her every day, it would drive me crazy. She's cute as hell, and those eyes...." He let loose a low whistle. "Better you than me."

Hunter pulled out a wooden chair next to the desk. "So you think she's cute?"

Jesse's brown eyes were all over Hunter. "And obviously so do you…that's why you're here, right? There are only two reasons why a man avoids a woman: he's either fed up with her and wants to bolt, or he can't get enough of her and he's scared to death."

Hunter snorted with incredulity. "I am not scared of her."

Jesse knitted his black eyebrows. "Uh, huh. Scuttlebutt is your brother tried to take her out and you two fought over her. Which personally pleased the piss out of me, since I think your brother is a piece of shit."

Hunter flopped back in his chair, his features furrowed in amazement. "How in the hell did you hear about our fight?"

"Man, how many times do I have to tell you, ain't nothing secret in an office. Your girl told those two blabbermouths in accounting about your fight with Chris at some art gallery. Everyone was already talking about your face, so Cary filled in the details. I'm sure the FBI already knows the rest by now." Shaking his head, he took his chair at his desk. "You know how women talk."

"What else have you heard?"

Jesse arched one eyebrow at him. "Why, you want me to ask around?"

Hunter anxiously rubbed his left shoulder again. "No, forget it." He motioned to the desk. "Pull up the website and let me show you what changes I want to make."

"This is about the new line?"

Hunter gave him a wary side-glance. "Cary told you about it?"

"Didn't have to." Jesse shrugged his impressive shoulders. "I made that new book cover for her. It wasn't what we usually put out, and I got the impression that wasn't going to be the only one."

"What does the final cover look like? I never saw it."

Jesse punched up the desktop on the right and then turned the monitor to Hunter. "Here it is. Pretty racy, huh?"

On the computer screen was a blindfolded woman on a bed, wearing only black lace panties and a bra, with her hands tied behind her back with rope. A faceless man was leaning over her shoulder and had his muscular arm wrapped about her slender waist. The title was done in blood red across the top of the picture.

"Your father's going to shit on himself when he sees it," Jesse declared.

Faced with such a provocative cover, Hunter suddenly realized keeping *The Bondage Club* a secret from his father was going to be a lot harder than he had originally anticipated. "Let's not spread this around too much, all right?" he proposed to Jesse. "I've got to keep my old man in the dark for as long as possible."

"Smart move." Jesse nodded his approval. "If he finds out before the launch, he and that idiot brother of yours will probably try to shut it down."

Hunter chuckled at the big man's disclosure. "I should have known nothing would get by you, Jesse."

"Only you would say that, Hunter. Everyone else thinks that just 'cause I lift weights that I'm not smart enough to know everything that goes on around here."

Hunter took in Jesse's herculean profile. "Still don't know why you took the job with me. With your credentials you could work for any top five hundred company."

Jesse squinched up his face with a sour grin. "You know I hate busy offices with a lot of nosy people. With your company, I get to take off early every afternoon to hit the gym. No other boss would give me that kind of flexibility. And I like the creative side here. Not only do I get to do all your IT, I get to make book covers, and run your website, too. Not a lot of jobs give you that kind of variety."

The Bondage Club

Hunter had always considered Jesse one of his best employees, and over the years he had come to value the large man's advice. "Well, I'm lucky to have you."

"You're lucky to have Cary, too. Sweet girl." Jesse's eyes swept over Hunter's face. "Are you going to ask her out?"

"Hell, no," Hunter loudly proclaimed. "She's an employee."

"Then you won't mind if I take a stab at it?"

Hunter nervously cleared his throat. "I don't think she would be interested. She's, ah...mentioned a boyfriend."

Jesse slapped his back, sending Hunter forward in his chair. "You're a crappy liar, Hunter. You know, it's all right if you like her."

Hunter shook his head. "I can't like her."

"Yes, you can. You've got what...fifteen employees here. It's not like you would be creating some big scandal if you took the woman out. Other bosses have dated their employees and it never ended up in court. Ask her out, see where it goes. If things turn to shit, then you can be friends, but you'll never know until you give it a try."

Hunter directed his attention to the computer screen with the book cover still glaring back at him. He thought of his two previous encounters with Cary, and wondered if he could survive a third. But as he recalled moments of their time together, he began to forget the awkward feelings she had aroused in him and lingered over the intense desire she had awakened. With many women his desire had been short-lived and satisfied almost as soon as he was reaching for his clothes, but with Cary his hunger only intensified with each encounter.

Pulling his mind back to the job at hand, Hunter concentrated on the computer monitor. "Why don't you pull up that website and let's see what we can do to give it a little more sizzle…like that cover."

Jesse's hearty laugh echoed about the cold basement. "Sizzle? Now you're talkin'!"

* * *

After ordering in lunch and spending most of the afternoon in the basement, Hunter finally made his way back to his office. But as he stepped into the open door, he discovered his brother hovering about Cary's desk, and drooling like a jewel thief over a rare diamond.

"Hello, asshole," Hunter said as he walked to his desk. "What are you doing here? Didn't think you would have the balls to show your face at least until Thanksgiving."

"Lovely to see you, too, little brother." Chris swerved around to Hunter. "But I didn't come here to talk to you. I came to speak with Cary."

Hunter leafed through a few yellow message notes left on his desk. "What? Came to ask forgiveness for making an ass of yourself the other night?"

Cary stood from behind her desk. "Boys, why don't you two play nice for a change?"

Chris held up his hand, wanting to allay her concern. "No, it's all right. I'm used to dealing with my brother's temper tantrums."

Hunter dropped the messages on his desk. "Temper tantrums? Who's the spoiled brat who had a fit at Mom's funeral when he was left off the program?" Hunter sat down in his chair. "The middle of our mother's funeral service and all he can think of is that his name isn't mentioned on some stinking piece of paper."

Chris turned his cold blue eyes back to Cary. "We can't talk here. Why don't we go down the street for that drink?"

"She's got work to do, Chris," Hunter growled.

"Actually, I'm all caught up on everything," she professed to Hunter. "I can afford to leave a few minutes early for—"

"What about our dinner plans?" Hunter edged in.

Cary stared at him. "What dinner plans?"

"We're supposed to meet that new author tonight. The one I'm considering for the romance line."

"We are?" Her eyebrows went up.

"New author?" Chris perked up. "Anyone I can handle?"

"No." Hunter's eyes never left Cary. "This is an author Cary knows who has written a stunning book about man and a woman trying to find balance between their working life together and their secret affair. I haven't read the ending yet, but I'm real damned interested in finding out what happens."

"That sounds pretty lame," Chris snorted. "Is it sellable?"

A crafty smile eased its way across Cary's heart-shaped mouth. "I guess I did forget about our dinner plans." She turned to Chris. "Sorry, it looks like I won't be able to join you for that drink, after all."

"What about tomorrow night?" Chris persisted.

"She's busy then too, dickhead," Hunter declared in a thunderous tone.

Cary frowned at Hunter and then slipped around her desk to Chris. "Why don't I call you when I'm free?" She took his arm while smiling sweetly. "Things are just getting so busy around here and we have a lot of late meetings planned for this week."

Chris allowed her to walk him to the office door. "Don't let my brother work you too hard. The bitter recluse has no life, but don't let him do the same thing to you."

"I heard that," Hunter shouted.

Cary's light giggle sounded so fake that Hunter could not help but flash a smug grin as she escorted Chris into the hall.

After she had shut the office door behind them, Hunter sat in his chair and waited for her return.

Several minutes passed before Cary re-entered the office. As she stood just inside the doorway, she folded her arms over her chest and glared at Hunter.

"Was that bullshit about dinner or were you being serious?"

He flipped up his laptop. "Do you think I'm honestly going to stand by and let my depraved brother ask you out?"

"This has got nothing to do with Chris." She hurried to his desk. "Were you asking me out on a date?"

He pretended to be distracted by his e-mails. "I was asking you to dinner. Do you have a problem with that?"

She leaned over his laptop, demanding his attention. "No, but I thought you wanted to be friends. You acted pretty adamant about it up until a few minutes ago."

Hunter pushed back in his chair, skeptically eyeing her frown. "Well, maybe I want to try something else. Get to know you away from the bondage clubs and without the handcuffs."

She stood from his desk, and her frown quickly dissolved into beaming smile. "How about you pick me up at seven?"

He took a moment before he spoke, trying not to return her infectious smile. "Why don't you let me choose a time?"

"Oh, yeah right." She cleared her throat, attempting to be serious. "What time do you want to pick me up?"

The wide grin that spread across Hunter's lips accentuated the irresistible dimples in his cheeks. "Seven o'clock."

"That sounds great." Seeming unsure of what to do next, she scurried back to her desk. "And I wanted to let you know I set up the photo shoot for the twentieth of this month," Cary stated in a businesslike manner. "I've got a photographer

Jesse Hart knows and we secured the club room in The Hole for two hours. I've already contacted Smut Slut about the date and time."

He nodded his head, impressed with her progress. "You were busy while I was out."

"You did seem to be out of the office most of the day. I was beginning to wonder if there was something wrong." She sat behind her desk. "By the way, how's the shoulder?"

"Still sore." He directed his eyes to his laptop. "I was downstairs working on a new website with Jesse. I want to get something going for the launch." He paused as he typed something on his keyboard. "I saw the new cover, by the way. Very...enticing."

"Does that mean you approve?"

He never raised his eyes from his computer. "Where are you on editing? We need to get that done."

"I'm going to start reviewing the manuscript later this week."

He frowned at her. "What about sooner, like today?"

"I can't today. I have to go home and get ready for a date."

"Maybe we could make it a working date."

She shook her head, appearing obstinate. "No, no work tonight. I think we need to try and make this a real date."

"A real date?" Hunter refrained from chuckling. "I think it's a little late for that...considering."

She rested her elbows on her desk, pensively gazing over at him. "Just because we've gone to bed together doesn't mean we can't have a date. A date isn't about sex or the eventuality of it; it's more about getting to know each other and sharing your stories with someone. Sort of like sex for the mind."

"You have sex on the mind, if you ask me," he teased.

"What makes you think that women don't think about sex just as much as men?"

"Aw come on, Cary." This time he did not hold back and let loose a loud chortle. "If women thought about sex just as much as men, there would be a lot more of them having it."

"You don't get it, do you? Sex for women has always been determined by the society they live in. Get too aggressive and you're a whore; too afraid of sex and you're frigid. I don't see men getting those kinds of labels." She shifted her eyes to her laptop. "That's what I like about all those clubs I go to. There are no labels. Sex is sex."

"Can you imagine what the world would be like if all women were like the ones in your clubs?"

"Yes, I can." Her features were hard and steadfast. "It would be equal."

He went back to his computer. "You'd better not talk like that in front of my father or brother; they'll want me to fire you."

"They've just never met anyone like me before. There are a lot more women like me than you think."

"One of you is about all I can handle right now," he muttered under his breath.

Cary glared at him. "What was that?"

Hunter just shook his head, smiling innocently. "Nothing, dear."

"Now you develop a sense of humor." She rolled her eyes. "Great."

Chapter 13

Standing before his closet, Hunter could not make up his mind about what to wear for his date with Cary. It had been a long time since he had been confounded by something as simple as choosing an outfit. In the past when he had taken women out, he had been more concerned about taking his clothes off, and not so much about how he looked in them. His confidence with women had never been a problem before now, but with Cary he felt inexperienced, confused, and completely insecure.

"Someone please shoot me."

Giving up, he chose his usual pair of khakis, a pale blue dress shirt, and then eased on his favorite brown loafers. Checking his image once more in the bathroom mirror, he waved his hand at his reflection and turned away. It was good enough.

In the car on the way to her apartment, he analyzed his feelings for Cary. Every time they had been together ended in disaster, but despite the dire warnings of his head, Hunter's heart was warming up to her. He was not sure if it was her vulnerable looks, determined attitude, or just the way she lit up a room, but something about Cary was definitely unique. Unlike the other women he had bedded and abandoned, Cary had somehow endeared herself to him. At this point in his life, he wasn't sure if that was a blessing or a curse, but since meeting the assertive editor, Hunter had become painfully aware of how lonely he was. It was as if her existence shone a harsh light on the reality of his emptiness.

Standing in front of her door, he held up his hand to knock and then hesitated. Was he doing the right thing? He could dismiss their previous intimate encounters as lapses in judgment, but tonight was going to cast them headlong into that dreaded tangled web called a relationship.

Brushing off his rising panic, he knocked on the door. "It's just a date, idiot," he chided. "Not a lifetime conjoined at the hip."

When the door opened, the first thing he noticed was the bright yellow dress hugging her curves, and then his eyes rose to her devastating smile.

"I'm ready," she asserted. "I just hope you are."

Shaking his head, he entered her apartment. "Keep talking like that and I may have to make a run for it."

After patting Sex Kitten on the head, and escorting her back to his car, Hunter settled behind the wheel.

"So where are we going?" she asked, securing her seatbelt over her shoulder.

"I have a special G-rated evening planned. There are going to be no bondage clubs, ultra-hip urban crowds, or any shiny metallic devices to tie me to any more bedposts."

She scrunched her eyes together. "Where exactly are we going?"

He put the car into gear. "Just think...Disney World."

* * *

After a short drive to the Lucky Marietta District, Hunter pulled his car into a parking lot next to a stone and red-bricked building that sat adjacent to the grounds of the

Centennial Olympic Park. Cary eyed the Hilton Garden Inn across the street, and then the cozy shops on the first floor of the structure next to them.

"What are we doing here?"

He opened his car door. "Our evening starts with a quick dinner."

Cary was about to open her car door, when Hunter stopped her. "Wait, I'll get it." He jumped from his car seat and went around to her side. After opening her door, he held out his hand. "If this is a date, I should at least try to act like a gentleman."

Cary took his hand and climbed from the roadster. "You a gentleman? That would be a nice change of pace."

"Believe it or not, my mother raised Chris and me to be gentlemen. She would always be scolding us about how to act, what to say to a lady, our manners...you know, the usual."

"Where were all these good manners hiding before tonight?"

He led her across the parking lot. "Since this is a date, I figured I should be on my best behavior to impress you. Isn't that what I'm supposed to say?"

She gazed down at their intertwined hands. "Just feels a little weird, you trying to impress me. I think I prefer it when you are just being your ornery self."

"You think I'm ornery?"

Glancing up at the ten-story building ahead, she grudgingly conceded, "Well, you're not always pleasant."

"I promise to make a concerted effort to be different tonight."

She dissected him with her suspicious eyes. "Why tonight?"

"Come on." He started toward the building. "I'm starving."

When they climbed the white stone steps to one of the first floor shops set behind a stone archway, Cary examined the sign hanging from above.

"Frazier's Ice Cream & Coffee Bar?" She turned to Hunter. "I thought you said we were going to dinner."

He opened the glass front door for her. "We are. My mother always said the best dinner is just dessert."

A smattering of white iron tables and matching chairs filled a red-tiled room, with posters of coffee houses in Europe hanging on the walls. A long deli counter displaying a variety of pastries, along with a frozen yogurt and ice cream section, stood beneath a wide blackboard mounted above advertising all the specials being served. The aroma of fresh baked bread and coffee hung in the air, making Hunter's stomach growl.

"Do you come here a lot?" Cary browsed a row of decadent chocolate cookies beneath the glass counter.

"When I'm hankering for some time away, yeah, I like to come here." He took a turn of the room watching a few couples gathered about the tables, while a handful of children enthusiastically licked their ice cream cones. "It grounds me."

"Grounds you? How?"

"It shows me how the world really is. Parents, kids, families, things I don't get to see too much every day. I don't know a lot of people like this." He turned to a family of four sitting at a table together.

"What about your family? You must have cousins and distant relatives."

"My mother's family lived in California, and we were never close." His eyes gleaned the chalkboard above. "My father never really had much family. His parents died when he was young and his only brother, Uncle Marty, died when I was a kid. So it was always just the four of us."

"There are advantages to what you have, Hunter. I have six nieces and nephews, and every Christmas I go broke buying presents; and then there are all the birthdays I have to remember, lectures I get from my mother when I don't go home for the holidays, phone calls about assorted family dramas...consider yourself lucky you don't have to deal with all of that."

A young girl with ash-blonde hair working behind the counter smiled at them. "What can I get you folks?"

Hunter turned to Cary. "Do you trust me?"

"Yeah, I trust you."

Hunter faced the young girl and held up two fingers. "Two hot fudge sundaes."

"Two hot fudge sundaes, got it," the young blonde replied, and then turned toward the ice cream section of the counter.

"You like to live dangerously," Cary imparted with teasing grin.

"I think you already know the answer to that." Hunter paused as the young woman behind the counter piled scoops of ice cream into two long glass dishes. "That guy, Winter, you mentioned...do you mind if I ask what happened?"

She shrugged her shoulders, sighing lightly. "With Winter St. Cyr things got...complicated."

Hunter eased his hip against the counter. "Was he the first guy you ever loved?"

"Loved? I'm not sure I ever loved Winter. We were good friends, had a lot of the same interests, but I wasn't absolutely shattered when he told me he had found someone else." She folded her arms over the front of her yellow dress. "I was relieved."

Hunter's eyebrows went up. "What woman doesn't want to marry a doctor?"

"The kind of woman who wants to live her life before being tied down by his. My mother kept reminding me that when I married a doctor I had a duty to act a certain way, look a certain way, and I would have to consider his needs before mine."

"And is that why you didn't want to marry him?"

Cary waited as the attendant brought two glass dishes filled with vanilla ice cream, fudge, and topped with whipped cream and cherries to the counter.

"Can I get you anything else?" the young woman inquired.

Hunter reached for his wallet in his back pocket. "You want anything else?" he asked Cary.

She shook her head. "No, that should put me into sugar coma for a while."

He handed the young woman a twenty dollar bill.

Taking their ice cream sundaes to a nearby table, they had a seat and as Cary pulled her pink plastic spoon from the center of her sundae, Hunter decided to pursue the topic of her ex. "So why didn't you want to marry the Winter guy?"

She carefully dug her spoon in the center of her sundae, making sure to get a hefty amount of whipped cream. "The moment he asked me to marry him, I saw my whole life flash before me, and I wanted more."

"Had you started editing then?"

She nodded and swallowed the ice cream. "I was just getting a name for myself, but Winter didn't want me to continue with my erotica authors. He was too embarrassed to tell anyone what I did."

Hunter dragged his pink plastic spoon over the edge of his sundae, scooping up a mound of hot fudge and vanilla ice cream. "Sounds like a jerk to me. What kind of name is Winter?"

Cary strategically filled her spoon again. "A family name. He came from an old Southern family in Alabama where tradition was very important. That had a lot to do with why it never worked out. I'm not a very traditional woman"

"Yeah, I noticed. Be thankful my brother didn't."

"Chris did remind me of Winter in a way." She twirled her spoon in her whipped cream. "They were both egotistical and insincere."

"How do you know I'm not the same way?"

She glanced up from her sundae. "The other night when you sat down and went over my story line for my book, never once did you ask me about your book. You were focused on what I needed, and you've been willing to let me be who I am. A lot of men aren't that…selfless."

"I'm not selfless, Cary. I promise you there are parts of me that are just like all the other men out there."

"Perhaps." She held another spoonful of vanilla ice cream and hot fudge in front of her lips. "You ever almost settle down with someone?"

"After Kathleen, I gave up thinking about settling down. For the last few years I've…well, I haven't lived like a saint."

A happy burst of laughter came from two children at a table a few feet away. As Cary took in the children's exuberance, Hunter admired the curves of her profile. When she turned back and caught him staring, Hunter blushed. Smiling sheepishly, she returned to her sundae.

"You don't have to eat all of that." He gestured to her sundae. "I know a great little sushi place up the road if you want some real food."

"No, this is perfect. Your mother was right about the best dinner being just dessert." She raised a large spoonful of the melting ice cream to her mouth. "What was she like, your mother?"

Hunter put his spoon down and reached for the paper napkin next to his glass bowl. "A lot of fun. My mother made everything fun. We always had birthday parties, holidays, lazy weekends, and all of it was fun." He wiped his hands on his napkin. "She had this great laugh. Mom was a real small woman, but she had this big, bellowing laugh. When I was a kid, I loved listening to her laugh. Unfortunately, as I got older, I heard that laugh less and less."

"Why was that?"

"My old man. I think the years of his screwing around ate away at my mother. The last time, when she caught him at the office, I never saw her so torn up."

"That must have been hard on you and Chris growing up."

"Nothing is hard on Chris. He's just as cold as Jim Donovan."

"And are you like your mother?"

Hunter dropped his napkin on the table, considering the question. "Yeah, I guess I am."

She dug her spoon into her sundae. "So what else do you have planned?"

"You'll have to wait and see."

* * *

After finishing their sundaes, Hunter escorted Cary back to his roadster. Leaving the parking lot, he made a right on Baker Street and then drove the short distance to the largest aquarium in the world, the Georgia Aquarium. When he entered the parking garage, Cary peered over at him, a huge grin on her face.

"You're taking me to the aquarium?"

He took a parking ticket from the toll gate. "Actually, it's a special event; Donovan Books is one of the sponsors. I donate books every year to the libraries across the city, and this is their annual fundraiser."

"But we're not dressed up," Cary objected, glancing over her simple cotton dress.

"It's a family benefit. There will be children here, so it's casual."

"You know I've lived in Atlanta for years, but I've never been here," Cary confessed.

Hunter stuck the ticket under his visor. "Then you're in for a treat."

After passing through the blue-metal and glass exterior that was meant to represent the giant arc of a wave, they checked in at a registration table just inside the main entrance. As Cary explored the ceiling painted with manta rays floating through a blue ocean, Hunter gave an older man at the table his name and then collected two name tags with Donavon Books printed on them.

"I didn't realize you worked with any of the local charities," Cary reflected as she removed the adhesive back from her name tag.

"If you run any business in this town, it's a great way to get connected. I donate all the books I can't move to libraries, hospitals, and nursing homes." He patted his name tag over the right side of his shirt. "I like knowing our books get read by those who might not have access to them."

"That is a side of you I never expected, the altruist."

He clasped her hand. "I'm a businessman, Cary, and far from altruistic."

Stepping into a dark entrance with tanks on either side filled with shimmering silver fish, Cary squeezed his hand.

"That's not what I see, Hunter. I hope one day you figure out that you're more of a writer than a businessman."

A jazz band playing a lively melody greeted them as they stepped in the blue neon lights of the atrium. All around guests were milling about in an array of fashions from casual to dressy, while children screamed and chased each other about the entrance to the different exhibits.

Cary glimpsed the long blue-lighted sculptures of waves above adding to the soothing ambience of the grand atrium. Ahead in a seated dining area, people were hovering around several white-linen buffet tables offering a myriad of dishes. Black-tie waitstaff scurried back and forth serving drinks, while other guests walked in and out of the open exhibits surrounding them.

"What do you want to do first?" Hunter eyed the different exhibit marquees. "We can see the dolphins, cold water aquarium, or—"

"Where are the otters?" Cary cut in.

Hunter surveyed the atrium. "Let's start in the River Scout exhibit. They're probably in there." He guided her toward the brightly lit entrance to the exhibit.

As they passed beneath Spanish moss strewn archways built to resemble thick trunks of cypress trees, a swarm of children eagerly ran past them. Checking the aquariums built into walls that were sculpted to look like trees, Cary and Hunter marveled at the many different types of fish found in the rivers of South America, Africa, Asia, and even Georgia. When they found an old cypress log with the words River Otters and an arrow carved into it, Cary tugged on his hand.

"Come on," she excitedly chirped.

Set behind wide Plexiglas, the brown otters were slinking their way in and out of an octagonal pool, allowing visitors to watch in amazement as the animals skirted below the waterline, appearing more like fish than mammals. A rock-like surface climbed up the far wall, and a slide made to appear like natural rock came down from the top of the wall and into the water.

"So you like otters," Hunter remarked while the fascinating creatures dipped and played below the water's surface.

"Yeah, I love them. They are always so cool to watch."

"I'm surprised you didn't want to see the alligators. You know all those rough hides and such. Thought that might be more your style."

As Cary went to elbow him, a little boy, no more than three, squeezed between them. The dark-haired urchin pushed against Hunter's trouser leg, shoving him aside.

"Hey," Hunter called as he moved away from Cary.

The small human ran behind them to a couple standing a few feet away.

"Sorry about that," a tall man apologized, picking up the boy.

For a moment, Hunter was amazed at how closely the child resembled the man. But when Cary turned beside him, he swore he heard a surprised gasp escape her lips.

"Cary, is that you?" a throaty voice questioned.

"Son of a...." Cary's voice faded when the man put the child down and came forward.

He had thick shoulders, jet-black hair, and a narrow face that gave him a sinister appearance. His dark eyes were the most disturbing feature on his pale countenance. Hidden behind a pair of silver wire-rimmed glasses, they made Hunter feel as if the man was not at all trustworthy. His wide brow, slender chin, and sunken cheekbones only added to his intimidating presence. Wearing a tailored gray suit, he appeared completely out of place next to the playful otters.

Beside him was a petite blonde with wispy arms and perfect features, and as she drew near, Hunter almost felt sorry for the tiny woman, being paired with such a menacing-looking individual.

"How have you been?" the handsome man inquired.

"Winter, what a surprise," Cary said in a uncharacteristically monotone voice.

Hunter studied Winter with a newfound sense of dislike. *He even looks like winter*, he thought. *Cold, distant, and utterly lifeless.*

"I was just telling Melissa that I thought that was you." Winter kissed her cheek and motioned to the pale, mousy blonde holding the small boy's hand. "Melissa St. Cyr, my wife, this is Cary Anderson."

Melissa uttered a faint "hello" as the child stood before her, grasping at the skirts of her green dress.

"You still working on all those naughty books of yours?" Winter's amused chuckle immediately grated on Hunter's nerves.

Cary waved to Hunter. "Ah, Hunter Donavon, this is Winter St. Cyr. Hunter owns Donovan Books."

Hunter and Winter briefly shook hands, while Hunter appraised the man's firm handshake. "Is he yours?" Hunter pointed to the small boy.

"Yes," Winter beamed. "Winter St. Cyr the fourth."

Hunter smirked. "The fourth?"

"Winter was the third," Cary informed him.

"It's a family tradition," Winter explained. "Every first born son is named Winter."

"What happens when you get to double digits?" Hunter joked.

But Winter didn't seem too pleased with the jest. "So, ah, Cary," he went on, ignoring Hunter. "What are you doing these days?"

"Oh, I'm still working on those naughty books as you put it, Winter."

"I had hoped you would have become more respectable in your old age. You always had so much potential."

Hunter's anger stirred. "Actually, Winter, Cary is one of the most renowned editors in erotica. Everyone wants her services."

Winter pursed his lips together. "Editor? I thought you were—"

"What are you doing here, Winter?" Cary interjected. "I seem to remember you never had time for anything other than work."

Winter fidgeted with his black tie. "Melissa works for the Atlanta Library System, so we had to come. Luckily, I was off from the hospital tonight and could join her and little Winter."

Cary turned to Melissa. "I thought you worked with Winter at the hospital."

Winter cleared his throat. "No, you're thinking of Bethany, my first wife, the one I met…that marriage didn't last very long. I met Melissa after my divorce and we just hit it off."

Hunter observed the diminutive woman who never said a word and only had eyes for her husband. "Yes, I can see that," he softly murmured.

"You know, Melissa has always been interested in writing, Cary. I told her all about you and your books. You two should get together. I'm sure she would love to hear about what it takes to get ahead in the literary world."

Cary quickly took Hunter's hand. "We really should get to those dolphins, Hunter." She glanced back at Winter. "Good to see you again." She nodded to his wife. "Melissa, great to meet you."

Melissa merely smiled as the young boy in front of her suddenly dashed off to a corner of the otter room where two other children were pulling on an interactive children's exhibit demonstrating the strength in an otter's hand.

"Oh, lord." Winter was about to start after the boy when he halted. "Good to see you…both," he stated and then ran after his son.

Hunter spotted Melissa, who still was standing before them, not uttering a word. Cary then quickly jerked Hunter toward the exit.

"That was Winter?" he pressed, once they were safely out of the room. "How on earth could you have ever considered marrying him?"

Cary wiped her hand over her brow while letting out a ragged sigh. "Temporary insanity." She led him toward the exit of the River Scout exhibit. When they were out in the atrium, Hunter gave her a worried going over with his green eyes.

"You okay?"

She let go of his hand and walked over to a metal railing at the edge of the platform next to the stairs leading to the atrium floor. "I can't believe I ran into him of all people." She spun around to Hunter. "His second wife? Can you believe that? And they have a kid? He has to be what two, maybe three?"

"I guess." Hunter shrugged. "But they all look the same age to me."

"Winter and I broke up four years ago. Since then he has had two wives and a kid?" She ran her hands up and down her bare arms. "Christ, that could have been me."

He came up to her and placed his hands on her arms, rubbing them. "But it's not."

"Thank God. I saw that poor woman he married and I actually felt sorry for her. She looked just how I felt with him; oppressed and stifled."

Hunter noted the anxiety in her brown eyes. "I got the impression he was surprised you were an editor. Why is that?"

She waved her hand to the exhibit entrance behind them. "You saw the kind of man he is. Do you think he could honestly tell if a woman was a writer or editor? As far as Winter was concerned, it was all just busywork."

Hunter slipped his arm over her shoulders. "Yeah, I got that." He perused the atrium, filling with patrons spilling out from the other exhibits. "Where to now?"

She rested her head against his chest. "If you don't mind, I would really just like to get out of here. Go somewhere quiet for a drink."

"Great idea. Any suggestions?"

She curled into him. "I put a bottle of vodka in the fridge before I left; interested?"

"That's the best idea I've heard all night."

Alexandrea Weis

Chapter 14

When Cary pushed the white door to her apartment open, a pair of vivid green eyes was staring at the two of them from the hardwood floor. With an insistent "meow," the orange and white cat came up to Cary as they walked inside.

"I wasn't gone that long, Sex Kitten." She gave the cat a quick stroke.

Hunter pointed to the cat. "How long have you two been an item?"

Cary placed her yellow purse on the sofa by the door. "Four years. I found him on the street outside when he was a kitten. I had just broken up with Winter and was pretty down on life, and then he came along and perked me up. I always figured it was meant to be."

"Still can't believe you ended up with a guy like that." Hunter shut her apartment door and turned the deadbolt.

"I think I was still suffering from all the years of listening to my mother tell me that I needed a man to be complete." She walked toward the kitchen.

"Yeah, my mother used to tell me I needed a good woman to feel complete."

Cary went to the refrigerator. "I think you need a fulfilling career to feel complete; you need another person to make you feel...real."

He came up to her side. "Real? What do you mean?"

She pulled the bottle of vodka from a shelf in the refrigerator. "You and I work in a world of fantasy. Happily ever afters are the norm, but that's not how life works. You need the bad to appreciate the good, the ugly to learn what is beautiful, and periods of hopelessness to teach you to always be hopeful. Without experiencing such opposites, we never learn how to be grounded in the middle. Having a relationship with another person takes you to those extremes, and also teaches you to realize that it's not always about being happy, it's about appreciating life...all of it."

He folded his arms over his chest, considering her words. "You should put that to paper. Make that the cornerstone of your story. Two people who go through the extremes of emotions between them, but learn how to appreciate the middle ground they find."

She paused, putting the bottle on the white Formica countertop as she thought for a moment. "That sounds like a really good idea. Thanks for that."

"Anytime." He took in the curve of her hips as she stretched for the oak cabinet above and selected two old-fashioned glasses. "I still find it hard to imagine that after all the years of dealing with writers that you never wanted to become one."

She turned, placing the two glasses on the counter next to the bottle. "I told you I was never brave enough to put my name to paper."

"Funny, I don't see that." He came up behind her. "You're not afraid of anything. There is something else to this."

She picked up the vodka bottle and twisted the top. "If I become a writer, Hunter, my editing clients will drop me. I'll become the competition. Anyway, if I write a book, it may still never get published." She poured out some vodka into the first glass.

"If you write it, I'll publish it." He took the bottle from her hand.

"What if it's horrible?"

"It won't be." He placed the bottle on the counter. "We will work on it and work on it until it's perfect." Hunter put his arms about her.

"I thought you wanted a drink."

He lowered his mouth to hers. "Not at this particular moment."

Hunter became undone when he kissed her. Her tongue enticed him, making him tighten his grip and lift her from the floor. There was no doubt in his mind this time. He wanted her. He wanted to feel her naked body next to him, kiss her tender skin, and lose himself in the pleasure of her.

Hunter was carrying her down the short hallway to her bedroom while Cary tore at the buttons on his shirt. When he reached the open bedroom door, he stopped. Putting her feet on the floor, he flipped the switch on the wall, bathing the room in the warm light from the ceiling fan above.

"What is it?" she asked, alarmed.

He stepped into the room, checking the bed. "Just making sure there are no hidden handcuffs, or leather straps." He pulled open the drawer on the nightstand and eyed the box of condoms. Removing one of the foil-wrapped condoms, he flung it on the bed.

She strutted into the room. "I keep that stuff in my closet. You want me to get something?"

"Hell no." Hunter sat down on the bed. "For once, I want it to be just you and me. No gimmicks, no games, and no paraphernalia."

She nestled in next to him. "What difference will that make?"

He pushed her down on the blue bedspread. "It makes a great deal of difference to me."

"Why? It's just sex, Hunter."

"No, it's not, Cary." Kissing her again he slowly undid the buttons down the front of her yellow dress. "I want to know who you are. To be with you and not some woman you're pretending to be." He opened the dress and caressed her skin.

"I'm not pretending," she adamantly denied, sitting up.

"Yes, you are. You're a walking contradiction. You wear these flowing, feminine dresses, have white ribbons tying back your curtains, and even have a cat."

"A cat named Sex Kitten," she defended.

He eased one shoulder free of her dress. "But then you like to tie me up, go to bondage clubs, and act as if sex is no big deal." He nuzzled her ear. "But it is a big deal. It shows me the real you."

"The real me?" A reflective sigh escaped her lips as her shoulders drooped. "I very much doubt if you would like that Cary Anderson."

"But I want the chance to know her." He eased the dress over her other shoulder, slid it down her hips, and then tossed it to the floor. "Let's do this my way for once. We might like it."

Her hands went to his wide chest and finished undoing the buttons on his shirt. "I'm game." After helping to gently remove the shirt from around his sore shoulder, she traced the outline of ripped muscles in his abdomen with her fingertips. "But what if we don't like it your way?"

Hooking his finger beneath her black bra strap, he slowly lowered it down her arm. "Give me tonight."

Hunter slipped the other bra strap down and then freed it from her body. Easing her on the bed he kissed her right nipple, and as his teeth grazed her flesh, Cary shuddered beneath him. His hands began their eager quest of her soft skin, and when he came to the elastic waistband of her black silk panties, he hesitated.

Kissing her again, he slipped his fingers inside her underwear and pushed the silky fabric down her hips. Hunter's mouth traveled the hills and valleys of her chest, lingering over her nipples and kissing the recesses of her stomach. She wrapped her legs about his waist, encouraging him, but Hunter pushed her legs back on the bed. Cary's movements became like a woman on fire. She dug her short nails into his flesh, kneaded the muscles in his firm butt, and when her hands found the fly on his pants, he stopped her.

"Tonight, you're my captive." He removed her hands from his trousers and stood from the bed. "Get on your knees."

Cary sat up, her eyes wide with trepidation. "What?"

Flipping her over, he curled his arm underneath her stomach and brought her to the edge of the bed. He positioned his hips behind her while rubbing his hand over her smooth, round ass. His fingers found their way to her delicate folds, teasing her wet flesh. Slipping two fingers inside, he pressed his thumb into her nub and rhythmically moved in and out of her. Cary moaned as her body rocked back and forth against his hand. And just when he felt her muscles tense, he removed his fingers.

"No," she cried out.

Hunter kissed her back while his fingers lightly skimmed the outline of her folds. "It's my turn to see how hot I can get you."

She was about to face him when he shoved his fingers deep inside her, forcing them as far as they could go. Slowly thrusting in and out, he brought her closer to climax once more. Just when her breath was coming in short needful gasps, he stopped and Cary whimpered with frustration. But he ignored her, and then started his teasing all over again.

Cary was bathed in a light film of sweat and panting as he brought her to the brink yet again, but when he stopped this time, he roughly turned her over. He hurriedly spread her legs apart and kneeled at the side of the bed. Covering her folds with his mouth, she groaned when his tongue flicked over her very sensitive nub. He was merciless in his assault, sucking, nipping, and licking until he felt her body buck. But when she screamed at the height of her release, Hunter did not stop; he kept on tempting her with his mouth until he made her come again and again.

When he finally stood from the floor and angled over her body, kissing her stomach and chest as he went, he hovered over her face, grinning. "I'm not done with you yet, sweetheart."

He hurriedly lowered his pants and boxers. Reaching for the condom on the bed, he tore the package open and quickly slid it on. Raising her legs in the air, he rested them against his chest and wrapped her ankles about his neck. Bringing her hips to the edge of the bed, he entered her with one powerful thrust. She sucked in a loud breath as he filled every inch of her. Pulling out, he rammed into her again. First, that familiar burn made its way up from his groin, and as he hungrily moved in and out of her, the burn morphed into a white fire. When his eyes connected with hers, he was suddenly lost. He slowed down his rapid thrusting, and began to fight for control. When her face contorted in a mask of pleasure as the tension in her body began to crest, Cary clasped the bedspread in her hands. He waited, and when she let go, Hunter smiled as her guttural scream filled the bedroom. As the fervor of her orgasm diminished, he mercilessly dove into her. Driven by his demand for release, he grunted as the white fire in his gut spread outward, and when he could feel his climax rising, he pounded into her until he cried out her name.

Reclining next to her on the bed, he was breathing hard into her neck when her fingernails lightly raked all the way down his back to his hard, round butt.

"Now that was something. I think I like your way better."

He rose up on his right elbow. "See? You should let me take control more often."

She combed her fingers through his curly brown hair. "You were different tonight."

Hunter rolled on his back. "I wasn't tied up." He tossed the condom to the floor.

She cuddled against his chest. "I'm not talking about the sex; I'm talking about this entire evening. For the first time since we met, you haven't been pushing me away."

He put his arms about her. "I haven't been pushing you away."

"Yes, you have. You've been trying like hell to keep me at a distance. So what changed?"

Hunter kissed her shoulder. "I guess you're growing on me."

"Growing on you?" She sat up and shimmed to the edge of the bed. "Somehow I get the impression you don't let women grow on you."

He tossed his arms about her and pulled her back to him. "You talk about me keeping you at a distance. What about you, Cary?" He nipped at her earlobe. "You're always pretending to be this cool and elusive woman, when I know deep down you're not."

When she faced him, Hunter swore he saw a hint of fear shimmering in her eyes, but then it was gone. She smiled and brushed her fingertips along the dark stubble on his chin. Her eyes were glowing with contentment, making Hunter want to hold her in his embrace and keep her safe forever. She kissed his lips, gently at first, and then she kissed him again, more insistent than before. Her arms went around his neck and she crushed her body against his.

When Hunter kissed her back, he could feel his desire building. They fell back on the bed as her kisses burned against him; her eager hands stroked his chest and butt, driving him mad. Unable to hold back, he moved her hips beneath him as his mouth tasted her right nipple. Her hands were running through his hair as he spread her knees apart. Frantic, he dove into her, letting out a long satisfied breath as her hot, wet flesh closed around his shaft. His body trembled with the overwhelming sensation and Cary lifted her hips, begging him to go deeper. Ramming into her again, Hunter lost all sense of control. He held on to her, driving into her with all the force he could muster. Clinging to each other, their bodies moved together as one, and as their desire mounted, Hunter felt something change. He could have sworn that she was finally opening up to him and revealing her true self; the gentle woman behind the rough exterior.

As his climax catapulted forward, her body arched against him. When she screamed into his chest, Hunter gave one last thrust and exploded into her. She held him against her as he shook with the last remnants of his orgasm, and when he collapsed on top of her, she rubbed her cheek against his.

"That was even better," she whispered.

He squeezed her tight. "Best yet." As he held her, a jolt of panic hit him. He immediately sat up. "Shit. We didn't use anything. I got so caught up I forgot to—"

She put her fingers to his lips. "It's all right. I'm not in any danger of getting pregnant."

He flopped back on the bed. "But what about the other stuff?"

"Before Winter and I slept together, he insisted we get tested. He refused to wear condoms, so I started on the pill. I've been on it ever since."

He rolled over on his side, facing her. "What about the others?"

She turned to him. "Others?"

"The other men you met in those clubs?"

She eased back on the bed. "There haven't been any others, Hunter. You're the first man I have had in my bed since Winter."

He sat up, bowled over by her confession. "That's been what? Four years?"

"Four and a half, actually," she calmly commented.

"But how...you knew about handcuffs, and ties, and you—"

"Everything we did I read about in books, talked to people in the clubs. I've never actually tied a man up before you."

His arms slipped about her. "Why didn't you say anything before?"

"I wanted to appear experienced, like Smut Slut. You liked her, and I was hoping if I acted like her, you would like me, too."

"What makes you think I liked Smut Slut?"

She hesitated for a moment. "The way you…spoke about her. I thought you wanted a woman like her."

He laughed into her short brown hair. "Jesus, Cary. I wish you would have told me this before. Maybe then I could have saved myself the trip to the ER and avoided spending a small fortune on Advil."

"Are you angry?"

"No, I'm not angry, but it makes a lot of sense. I've always gotten the impression that all is not what it seems with you." He held her away from him, staring into her eyes. "No more secrets, okay? Just tell me whatever it is ahead of time and we will work it out." He paused as a thought occurred to him. "But you do know about erotica, right?"

She punched his chest. "Yes!"

"Oww!" He put his hand to his chest. "All right. I believe you." His arms embraced her, bringing her back to him. "Are there any other bombshells we need to discuss?"

She relaxed against him. "No, Hunter. Now you know my secrets."

"Not all of your secrets. I'm sure there is more for me to learn about you. Understanding a woman is like catching shadows. Once you think you have them figured out, the light changes, and all your efforts vanish in the blink of an eye."

"Eloquently put. And yes, I still have a few more secrets up my sleeve."

He sighed into her cheek. "As long as you weren't a man or anything like that before, I can live with them."

"No, I wasn't a man, just a tomboy," she confessed with a giggle.

"Did that come from growing up with three older brothers?"

"Yeah. I used to get picked on a lot, but that wasn't all bad. Some days were better than others and when we used to play games they would always let me win. There was this one Christmas, when we were...."

As Hunter listened to her soft voice, he felt a rush of victory as she opened up to him about her life. This was better than the nights he had spent being her bound lover. It was as if the intimacy of what they had shared was finally spilling over into their conversation. But as he considered the days and weeks to come, a strange sense of irony rolled across his mind. They had left behind the handcuffs only to embrace a different kind of bondage; one that bound the heart and not the hands. Hunter wanted to snicker as he mulled over the concept. It seemed that no matter how hard he had tried to avoid relationships here he was...beginning one with a woman he would have never pictured for himself, and considering a future he once thought he never deserved.

Alexandrea Weis

Chapter 15

Hunter awoke with the taste of fur in his mouth. When he opened his eyes, orange and white fluff blocked his vision. Thinking he was hung over, or worse, dying, he popped up from the bed to discover Sex Kitten curled up on the pillow next to him. Rubbing his eyes, he gazed about the blue bedroom and noted the yellow rays of light streaming in through the windows by the canopy bed. Looking over to the spot in the bed next to him, he sighed when he found Cary's petite body was no longer there.

He rubbed the cat's head. "Where did she go?"

Sex Kitten stretched and purred, but gave no hints as to Cary's whereabouts.

Sitting up on the edge of the bed, Hunter ran his hands over his face, felt his five o'clock shadow, and then yawned. Standing from the bed, he searched the floor for his clothes. Finding his boxers and khaki pants, he quickly slipped them on and headed to the closed bedroom door.

Out in the small hallway that led to the kitchen, he briefly listened for any movement in the apartment, but all he could hear was the mild din of the traffic outside. Heading along the cool hardwood floor, he was making his way to the kitchen when he spotted the open door to the second bedroom Cary used as an office. Peeking inside, he spied her laptop sitting open on her desk. The faint light from the screen filled the dark room with an eerie glow.

Intrigued, Hunter made his way to the computer and glanced down at the screen. To his surprise, he found words written there, a chapter of a book. As he read the first few lines, he realized it was the story he and Cary had discussed a few nights before. It appeared as if she had found her opening. Eagerly he read the page, impressed with her ability to convey emotion. But after four pages the screen turned white again. He sighed with disappointment. It was a good beginning, a very good beginning.

Curious to see if she might have penned anything else on the computer, he pulled up her files and began perusing the titles. Knowing he was going beyond the bounds of decency, he hoped she would not mind, then again he reminded himself that she had sought out his advice for her books and maybe he could offer her more on another work. A few of the titles he recognized as Smut Slut's published works, and figured Cary had kept some of the manuscripts in her computer after she had finished editing them.

One title caught his eye, *Of Love and Bondage*. Interested to see what this story entailed, he opened the manuscript and read the title page and discovered that the book was written by Smut Slut. Excited that this could be another possible title for Donovan Books, he began to read the story. He was about ten pages into it when the screen suddenly went white and the work came to an end in the middle of a paragraph.

Stunned, Hunter sat back in the chair. *Why would Smut Slut send Cary something unfinished?* A sickening sense of unease came over him as he sat at her desk. Quickly, he opened her e-mail page and began combing through the long list of addresses, but nowhere did he see Smut Slut's e-mail.

Panic-stricken, he began rifling through her desk, desperate for something that would confirm his suspicions. In a bottom drawer, he found her checkbook. Lifting the black binder from the drawer, he flipped it open. The first sheet of checks had Cary's name and Cary Anderson Editing Services written beneath it. But in the middle of the binder was a black divider and the checks listed there were for a very different business.

Cary Anderson DBA Smut Slut Enterprises

Hunter's heart caught in his throat. All the instances of meeting Smut Slut whipped across his mind. He began to put together hints in the size and stature of the two women; their lips, voice, and delicate features were almost identical. Why had he not seen it before?

Infuriated he stood from the desk, knocking the checkbook to the floor. Right at that moment, he heard the front door of the apartment close and footfalls coming from the living room toward the hall.

Hunter thought about hiding the checkbook and not letting her know that he had discovered her secret, but then he remembered all that they had shared the night before. He had thought she was being honest with him, only to discover she had been playing him all along. He began to doubt everything Cary had told him ever since the day she had walked through his office door.

The footsteps were passing right outside of the room when they stopped. He waited as she slowly pushed the door open and peered inside. At first, when she saw him at her desk, she smiled and held up two tall paper cups from Starbucks. Then, she noticed the checkbook on the floor and her smile dropped.

"You're Smut Slut. All this time you were pretending to be something you're not." His anger saturated his words. "The bondage clubs, the handcuffs…why didn't I see it?"

She walked into the room. "I can explain."

"Explain!" He rushed up to her and grabbed her arms. The coffee spilled to the floor, grazing his khaki pants and splashing against the blue jeans she had on. "What kind of twisted bitch are you? Do you get off leading men on? I was beginning to—" He let her go and rushed to the door.

"I never meant to lie to you," she called behind him.

Hunter stopped at the door.

"But when I saw you at the Book Expo, I knew I couldn't tell you the truth, so I told you to call me, the real me, and I hoped you would want Cary and not Smut Slut." She wiped her hands over her jeans. "All the men want Smut Slut. And for once I wanted to meet a man I could be me around, and not some fantasy."

He turned to her and for the first time noticed the coffee strewn about the hardwood floor. "Why lie to me? That first day at my office you should have told me the truth."

She shook her head and walked out of the room. Turning down the hall, she headed toward the kitchen. He quickly pursued her and at the kitchen counter, she grabbed a roll of paper towels from the rack by the sink and faced him.

"You hit on me at the Book Expo when you thought I was some experienced woman who would be a real tiger in bed. But I could never let you know how I really am. That Smut Slut is nothing more than a name to sell books and not a real person." She tossed her hand in the air and stormed past him. Hunter followed her back to the office and waited in the doorway as she scattered the paper towels about the floor. "If I had shown you the real me that day we met, you would have run away. I know. Every man I wanted to be with and told the truth about me in the past ran. So, I decided not to say anything to you, to live a double life, which wasn't easy. I had to find out if you could like me for me, or if you were just like all the others; only interested in a woman who could show you a good time."

He shook his head as she kneeled on the floor and began to soak up the spilled coffee with the paper towels. "Cary, I wanted more than that with you."

"Oh, come on, Hunter! You didn't want me at all." She stood from the floor, her jeans drenched with coffee. "I was never your type and I knew it. All you ever wanted with any woman was a quick roll in the sack and a kiss good-bye. I would have been no different. If I had approached you as Smut Slut, you would have had your night of fun and been gone in the morning, just like you've probably done with every other woman. But I couldn't do that. I wanted to get to know you, and I figured if we worked together you might give me a chance."

"But it was all a lie. Last night was a lie. Everything you said to me was a lie."

"Last night was not a lie; that was the real me, and it was the real you." She stomped her foot on the floor. "You know that."

Feeling trapped, he backed out the door. "I don't know a goddamned thing anymore."

Heading down the hall, he went to the bedroom and quickly collected his shirt and shoes. Bolting across the living room for the apartment entrance, he paused for a split second, letting his emotions get the better of him. Hunter considered going back to her, forgiving her and starting over, but she had lied to him. Opening the front door, he hardened his determination to banish her from his heart. Once in the hallway, he slammed the door and bounded toward the elevator. Cary Anderson had been a mistake; a mistake he had every intention of putting behind him for good.

* * *

Later that morning in his office, he was not surprised when Cary didn't appear. After their altercation, he figured she would never set foot in Donovan Books again, at least not as Cary Anderson. Smut Slut, however, still had an ironclad contract to submit two more erotica books and three romances to the publishing house.

Sitting at his desk, Hunter ran his hand over the dark stubble on his chin as he tried to come to terms with the deception Cary had been playing. Now faced with years of working with her as Smut Slut, he wondered how on earth they would ever be able to get along. The idea of seeing her again only fueled his anger, but at the same time tugged at his heart. How was he going to survive this?

"Hey Hunter, you got a minute?" Jesse asked from his open office door.

Hunter sat back in his desk chair and waved the hulking man into his office. "Sure, Jesse, what's up?"

As Jesse's bulky figure strode across the room, he glimpsed Cary's desk. "Where is she?"

Hunter cleared his throat, buying time while he thought of an excuse. "Ah, she had some kind of family illness. She might be out for a few days, I'm not sure."

Jesse raised his black eyebrows with concern. "Hope it's nothing serious. I know she is real close with her family back in New Orleans."

Hunter was surprised by the comment. "She told you about them?"

Jesse nodded as he rested his hip against Hunter's desk. "Yeah, we talked for hours about our families. I told her all about my crazy Aunt Marion, you know the one who knits me socks every Christmas?"

"Yeah, I remember."

Jesse eyed Hunter's downturned lips. "You okay? You seem put off by something."

Hunter debated how much he could confide in his IT expert. "Jesse, have you ever had a woman lie to you?"

Jesse's boisterous chortle resounded about the office. "Hell yeah. Plenty of times. Every woman lies in some way or another. Mostly about their weight. I don't know what it is, but you can spend all night making love to a woman in a hundred different ways, but the next morning put her near a scale and she acts like you're a serial killer."

"No, I'm not talking about that, Jesse. I meant has a woman ever been someone they're not with you."

Jesse took a moment, folding his thick arms over his wide chest. "Not sure I've run across that, unless a few of the one-night stands I had told me a fake name or something. Why?"

Hunter dragged his finger over the smooth edge of his desk, thinking of Cary's soft skin. "What would you do if a woman was hiding their identity from you? If she was pretending to be two different women?"

Jesse smiled, flashing his bright white teeth. "Be thankful. I don't know about you, but I have always fantasized about one woman being both sweet and innocent on some nights, and then a real sex kitten on others."

Hunter smiled and whispered, "Sex Kitten."

"Is something going on with you and Cary?"

Hunter's smile washed away and he sat up in his chair. "Me and Cary, no way."

Jesse just laughed. "Man, if I had it as bad as you, I would have done something about it by now. Having a good employee is one thing, but finding a good woman like Cary is something else."

"What makes you think she's a good woman?"

The mountain of a man grinned. "Come on, Hunter. You can always tell. Bad girls can't be good, but good girls...well, they're the best of both worlds, aren't they?"

Wanting to avoid any further discussion about Cary, Hunter demanded, "What is it you came in to tell me, Jesse?"

"Oh, yeah." He stood from the desk. "I got the website ready to go. You just let me know when you want to launch it. I know you have the book launch slated for early September, but I didn't know if you wanted the website to go live then or before."

"Let's get it up as soon as possible."

"You sure about that?" Jesse's dark eyes narrowed. "Your old man will get wind of the new line before it launches."

"To hell with what Jim Donovan thinks. It's my company now, right?"

Jesse pounded his fist on the corner of the desk. "Damn right. Glad to hear that. Your old man's shadow has been hanging over this place for too long." He waved toward the bookcase of statues. "Now maybe you'll get those creepy things out of here." He was about to turn away when he paused. "Oh, let Cary know I've finished the touch ups on the cover she wanted. It's good to go."

"Go ahead and send it to me, Jesse. I'll probably be filling in for her until she gets back."

"Okay, Hunter." Jesse gave him one last nod and walked out of the office.

As Hunter sat at his desk, he became deluged with images of Cary. The night they had spent together and the way she had made him feel. Perhaps he had been too hasty not to accept her reasoning for her trickery. Turning to his cell phone on his desk, he deliberated on whether or not to call her. As the minutes ticked by, his longing to hear her voice overwhelmed him. Disgusted, he picked up the phone.

After three rings, she answered the call. "What is it, Hunter?" Her voice was cold and harsh.

He sighed into the phone, rubbing his forehead. "I'm sorry about what happened."

Silence filled the line and his gut twisted in suspense.

"I think it would be best if I didn't return to Donovan Books. Consider this my resignation."

"Cary, don't do this," he softly pleaded. "We have the Hot Nights line to launch and—"

"I will honor my commitment of books outlined in our contract. But I think any communication we have from now on should be strictly about business. Good-bye, Hunter." She abruptly hung up.

Staring at his phone, Hunter's heart slowly sank to his knees. Now what in the hell was he supposed to do?

* * *

Later that night, Hunter was sitting on his sofa, staring at the copy of his book opened before him on the glass coffee table. Cradling the empty old-fashioned glass in his hand, he refilled his drink. Banging the bottle of vodka on the table glass, he gulped back a mouthful of the alcohol.

It had been a long time since a woman had made him feel this low. Not since Kathleen had walked out on him had he been so torn up. That was how he really felt about Cary, torn; ripped in two by her absence and the lack of her support. In a short amount of time, he had become dependent on her. With her encouragement, he had considered going back to writing. He had pulled out his manuscript and begun editing it because she had believed in his talent. The night they had spent discussing story lines had been the most fulfilling time he had shared with any woman in…he couldn't remember how long.

"Finally found a woman I can relate to and she is…." He let the words slip from his lips. Despite all Cary had done, he could not see her as anyone other than that adorable little girl in a woman's body. Her kisses haunted him, her girlish giggle breezed in and out of his mind, and the profound contentment he felt in her presence confused him.

The chime from his doorbell roused him from his melancholy. Rising to his feet, he went to the door, secretly hoping Cary had changed her mind. But when he opened the door, Kathleen was waiting. Decked out in a sleek, silky black dress that hugged her alluring curves, with her long brown hair draped around her shoulders and her face painted to perfection, she was as beautiful as the first day he had met her at a friend's party.

"I thought I would find you here."

As she walked in his doorway, she kissed his cheek.

"What is it?" He closed the door behind her. "You and Frank have another fight?"

"Not exactly." Her attention drifted to the bottle of vodka on the glass coffee table.

"Then what exactly happened, Kat?"

She strolled into the living room and wrapped her hand around the neck of the bottle. "Why are you reading that?" She pointed to the open spiral-bound book on the coffee table.

He went to the coffee table and closed the book. "Why are you here?"

"Frank couldn't get me a deal in New York." She took a long swig from the bottle.

"I'm sorry. I know what it meant to you to get to New York."

She wobbled on her feet. "All he could get me was some shitty show in New Orleans."

He examined her glassy eyes. "Are you drunk?"

Kathleen held up the bottle. "Not completely, no, but I plan on getting there real soon." She shot back another big gulp of vodka.

Hunter sighed, knowing that soothing Kathleen's bruised ego could take a while. "So what's wrong with a show in New Orleans?"

She lowered the bottle from her lips and let go a contemptuous laugh. "It's not like that's the cultural Mecca of the country, Hunter. It's smaller than Atlanta."

"It's a pretty cultural town, Kat. A lot of big artists got their start in New Orleans."

She slapped the bottle on the glass table, sending a loud clang echoing about the first floor. "I'm not a jazz musician or a writer, Hunter. I'm a photographer. To be anyone I have got to get into New York galleries, and Frank promised he would get me there." She pouted her lips together, sparking Hunter's ire.

"Stop acting like a spoiled child. I'm sure Frank did the best he could." He grabbed the bottle from the table and went back to the kitchen.

"His best? And how would you know if he did that?" she debated, coming behind him. "Did you ever do your best for me?"

He stopped at the breakfast bar and turned to her. "What is that supposed to mean? I took the job with the publishing house for us."

She sashayed up to him, swinging her hips enticingly from side to side. "We both know that's not true. You said you were going to be this big writer and buy me the moon."

Ignoring her attempted seduction, he replaced the cap on the bottle of vodka. "I could have bought you the moon as a publisher, but you didn't want me then."

She snorted and swiped at the bottle. "That's because you gave up being an artist. I'm an artist; I need another artistic type to understand me."

He held the bottle out of her reach. "Frank's a lawyer, Kat, and far from artistic, but you're going to marry him."

"I'm only marrying him because he's rich, baby."

He gawked at her, upset by her admission, but not that surprised by it. "Maybe that's all I was to you; some rich man's son." He slammed the bottle down on the bar. "All those years together you kept telling me I was creative and talented, but you never read my book, never read anything I ever wrote, no matter how many times I asked. How could you possibly know if I was artistic…or even good enough to make it as a writer?"

"You had an artistic vibe, Hunter. I knew one day you would make it as a writer. But you gave up writing and everything changed between us."

"Jesus, Kat. Everything changed between us when I went to work at the business. But we needed to eat, and I had an obligation to my family."

"Hey, you had an obligation to me, asshole. I was there for you when you wanted to be a writer, but as soon as you sold out I couldn't be with you anymore. You were just like me when we started out, but when you began working at Donovan Books you changed."

"I grew up!"

"You gave up," she fired back. "You don't get it, Hunter. I could have lived with you as a publisher if you hadn't walked away from your dreams. You gave up being a writer the moment you took over that company. It was like the guy who used to be filled with ideas and stories just disappeared. That's how I knew you were a writer, Hunter, because you embraced your imagination and didn't...run from it."

Tightly gripping the bottle of vodka, he went around the breakfast bar and into the kitchen. "You're drunker than I thought."

She slinked to the stairs. "I want to sleep here tonight."

"No, Kat. Go back to the fancy apartment Frank got you."

"I'll be alone there." She held on to the metal railing along the stairs, steadying herself. "I don't want to be alone."

"Where's Frank?"

She sagged against the railing. "Visiting his kids at his wife's house. He won't be back until morning."

He marched to his front door and opened it. "Go home, Kat."

Gliding up to him, she ran her hand up the front of his button-down shirt, grinning suggestively. "Don't you want me, Hunter?"

For a split second he thought of Cary standing before him, saying the same words. "We've played this game too many times, Kat. I need...I want something more."

She stared at him, slightly taken aback. "You've never turned me down before. I thought you liked it this way. No ties, no commitments. You said you never wanted a relationship."

"Well, maybe now I do." He removed her hand from his shirt. "Go back to Frank. He's going to be your husband, Kat, and you need to start acting like his wife."

"His wife? What is that supposed to mean?"

"It's time you invested your heart in the future, and stopped holding on to the past." He kissed her forehead. "You have a great life. I wish you only the best." Shoving her into the hallway, he quickly shut the door.

Resting his hand on the door, he felt the thrill of accomplishment. For years they had been stealing moments together, adding to his self-loathing. He had never wanted to admit it before, but Kathleen's lack of support for his writing had been discouraging. Now he had finally found a woman who could feed his muse and not stifle it. But how could he win her back?

Glancing toward the living room, the book on his coffee table called to him. Making his way across the hardwood floor, he remembered what Cary had told him about releasing his inner demons, and suddenly he understood that she had been right. He needed to vent his raging emotions. With a tentative hand, he lifted the book from the table.

Climbing the metal steps, he reviewed the notes he had made in the margins. Perhaps he should consider taking one more crack at his book to see if he could make it work. It would give him a chance to rediscover the Hunter Donovan he had once been; the young man who had been filled with so much…hope. But could he be that man without Cary by his side to inspire him?

Peering up the stairs, Hunter willed the image of Cary out of his heart. "Let's find out."

Chapter 16

Over the next few weeks, Hunter threw his energy into preparing for the launch of the Hot Nights erotica line. Determined not to think about Cary, he stacked his pile of manuscripts on top of her desk—attempting to blot out the ever-present reminder of her—and told the staff that she had to take a leave of absence due to a family crisis. When that did not help to rid his mind of her, he redecorated his office. Removing his father's bookcase of dusty Alexander the Great statues, he bought some cheerful potted plants, and even put a few of the green leafy shrubs around her desk. However, all of his feeble efforts to erase her memory proved to be in vain, and when he wasn't staring at her empty desk, Hunter was wondering what she was doing or if she was thinking of him.

Luckily, work was the only thing that kept him going. When not bogged down with his usual pile of day-to-day management duties, Hunter's time was occupied with phone calls to bookstores and other connections in the business, touting the new line and the premier of *The Bondage Club*. Hours were spent on the computer, notifying book bloggers, reviewers, and making last minute changes to the new website before it went live. But the e-mails to Cary were the hardest for Hunter. Preparations for the new book had to be finalized, and with every communication, there was not a hint of the woman he had come to know. Her words were always businesslike, and every message he read from her only added to the heaviness in his heart.

Despite the demands of his business, at the end of the day, he still had to return to his condo. Every evening when he shuffled through his front door, he would be unhinged by the emptiness of his home. The restlessness that had consumed him since parting ways with Cary only burned stronger at night. To ease his burdens he would occupy his mind with his manuscript and a bottle of vodka. But as time went on, he discovered that the margins of his book, *The Other Side of Me*, were becoming filled with more corrections and his need for vodka was dwindling.

On one particular night, when he was lying in his bed and looking up at the full moon through the skylights above, he kept mulling over endings for his novel. Frustrated with tossing and turning, he threw the covers aside. Tugging at his green pajama bottoms, he walked from the bedroom and across the hall to the second bedroom he used as an office. After switching on the lights, he went to the laptop on his white metal desk and flipped up the cover. As he waited for the machine to come to life, he cracked his fingers and let out a loud breath between his gritted teeth. It had been a long time since he had written anything, but tonight, more than any other, he felt compelled to give it a try.

As the blinking curser called his attention to the white page before him, he placed his hands on the keyboard. Instantly, the images in his mind came to life and the words began to appear on the page. Caught up in the frenzy of his imagination, Hunter lost himself in his writing. He could not remember when he had felt so overcome by words. For the first time in years, Hunter Donovan felt...alive.

* * *

Two days after the website had launched, Hunter was making last minute arrangements for Smut Slut's cover shoot later that evening at The Hole. The early summer sun was pouring in through his arched office window as he sat at his desk reading through a pile of e-mails, when a shadow darkened his office door.

"You and me are gonna have a serious talk, boy," Jim Donovan bellowed, and then slammed the door with a loud bang.

Hunter flinched in his chair at the sound. He had been expecting a visit from his old man. Despite being retired, Hunter knew his father still kept tabs on the company, and figured he had seen the new website and the announcement for the Hot Nights erotica line.

Sitting back in his chair, Hunter braced himself for what was to come. "I guess you saw the website then."

Jim Donovan waved the end of his cane at his son. "Are you out of your goddamned mind? An erotica line?" He pounded the cane on the floor. "That's not what we publish at Donovan Books."

Hunter took in a calming breath and rose from his chair. "You don't know the market, Dad. You've been out of it for ten years now and we need—"

"We need to stick to the kind of wholesome books we've always published," Jim Donovan interrupted. "If you take us in that direction we will lose a lot of loyal customers. Bookstores won't touch us and all the steadfast connections I spent years cultivating will be wiped out by one book." He held up his right index finger. "Just one filthy book, Hunter, one. That's all it will take."

Hunter remained defiant and kept his eyes locked on his father. "I've already spoken to all the bookstore chains we deal with, as well as a few of the independents, and they're all very interested in carrying this new line. Our reviewers at all the big newspapers are interested. I've even picked up new reviewers and have gotten hooked into a slew of new bloggers because of this book." He went around his desk. "The market is changing. It's not about wholesome books anymore. It's about sex—hell, it's always been about sex. But today everyone isn't afraid to talk about it."

Jim Donovan sighed, filling the room with all the apprehension and doubt Hunter had always sensed from his father whenever they discussed business. There were times when Hunter felt as if he were ten years old again, trying his damnedest to please a man who saw him as nothing more than a silly child.

"Son, I know the market has changed, but that doesn't mean we have to change with it. This is my company and—"

"No, Dad, it's my company. You gave it to me to run, so let me run it."

The office door flew open and Chris strutted inside, grinning from ear to ear. "Little son of a bitch still insisting on that new line, eh?"

Decked out in a fitted black suit and fancy Italian leather shoes, Chris reeked of success and snobbery. His blue eyes weighed his father's face and then he shifted his gaze to Hunter. "I called Dad when I saw the new website hit." He shook his head and rested his hands on his slender hips. "You should have talked to both of us before doing this, Hunts. You've made a big mess and it will take all three of us to clean it up."

Hunter balled his hands into fists. "You called Dad?"

"Of course," Chris snickered. "I drove him down here to talk some sense into you."

Incensed, Hunter lunged at his brother, and he was just about to wrap his hands around Chris's skinny neck when his father's cane whipped in front of his face.

"Stop it, both of you!" Jim Donovan shouted. "How did I get saddled with two sons that can't spend five minutes in a room without trying to kill the other?" He waited until Hunter backed away before he lowered his thick, wooden cane. "Yes, Chris called me and told me about the new line, and yes he drove me down here, but it was not to argue with you about your business decisions, Hunter. It was to remind you that we have a duty to the readers that we have spent years cultivating. I cannot with good conscience allow you to ruin—"

"Aw, for Christ's sake, Dad," Hunter clamored. "We're not a church or religious group. We're publishers. We publish books, and if some of those books are a little risqué, then so be it. You always treated this place like it was some kind of sanctuary, but it's a business. And if we're going to stay in business, we have to keep up with the market." He took a moment to calm down and collect his thoughts. "Remember the time you were afraid to start publishing romance novels because you thought everyone would say they were cheap, and Mom told you to do it and ignore what everyone told you. She was right and your company tripled in size after that. Well, this is the same thing. I have to start publishing erotica novels if we are going to continue to have a business."

"Don't listen to him, Dad," Chris bellowed. "He just wants to publish erotica so he can sleep with the lurid women who write that crap."

Hunter leapt toward his brother.

"Enough!" Jim Donovan turned to Chris. "You're the one who sleeps with all the authors, not your brother."

Hunter silently rejoiced when his brother lowered his eyes to the floor, appearing set in his place.

"Go wait in the car for me, Chris," Jim Donovan ordered. "I want to speak with Hunter alone."

"What am I, five?" Chris barked.

"Just do it!"

Chris's angry blue eyes glowered at his brother and then he turned for the door.

After Chris had left, Jim Donovan progressed across the office to Hunter's desk. "I know you, Hunter, and you don't act without thinking, unlike your idiot brother. Chris was always so damned headstrong, always having to be first in everything." He had a seat in the chair in front of Hunter's desk. "But you…your mother said you were the thinker, and she was right. Before she died, she said you would be the one who made something of your life." Placing his cane before him, he lowered his bold blue eyes to the carved wooden handle. "I gave you the company to run because your mother always believed in you, and I figured it was time I did, too. I'm not saying I agree with you about this erotica thing, I'm dead set against it, but you are right…this is your company now, and I need to leave you to make your own mistakes."

"It won't be a mistake," Hunter insisted, coming up to him. "The advanced buzz we have on this book has been fantastic, and I already have pre-orders for ten thousand units."

Jim Donovan furrowed his brow. "Ten thousand?"

"Bookstores are hot for this, Dad," Hunter exuberantly told him. "I know once we launch the advanced sales on Amazon will be just as good. This author has a really big following."

He tapped his cane on the floor. "Yes…this Smut Slut. After I saw the announcement on the company website, I researched her on the Internet. You can imagine how surprised I was to recognize the woman you introduced to me as Ms. Simms." He frowned. "Is Simms her real name?"

Hunter went around the side of his desk. "No, her real name is Cary Anderson. She is the woman who was working as an editor in my office."

Jim Donovan regarded Cary's desk piled high with manuscripts and dying potted plants. "Now I see why you're excited about publishing her book."

"The only thing is I didn't know that she was Smut Slut at the time. She...." He scratched his head. "She kept her identity hidden from me."

"You mean you couldn't tell the two women were one in the same?" Jim Donovan chuckled. "Hunter, it was pretty obvious to me that day when I came to see you."

"Come on, Dad. It wasn't that obvious."

Jim Donovan's rollicking chortle rattled Hunter's nerves. "Son, you really don't pay attention to women, do you? Those two women had the same build, same round face, and the same great legs. I guess it takes an old man to appreciate the finer points of a woman." He took a moment, contemplating his son. "So which one are you in love with?"

"Neither." Hunter lowered his eyes, unaccustomed to sharing his feelings with his father. "I...I, ah, had something with Cary...but it's over now."

"By the look on your face I would hazard a guess that it's not quite over."

Hunter shook his head. "Nah, we're done."

Jim Donovan stood from his chair leaning on his cane. "You're only done with a woman when your heart tells you so, not your head. Like you and that Kathleen Marx girl you shacked up with. I thought you would never get rid of her."

"Why didn't you like Kathleen, Dad?"

"Your mother and I never liked what she did to you. She made you dependent and weak. But if how you are today is any indication of what Cary has done for you, then I like her. She's given you a backbone."

"What about the new line?" Hunter asked, timidly sliding his hands in the pockets of his black trousers. "Are you going to fight me on it?"

Jim Donovan stood for a moment, observing his son. "You said this was your company, so let's see what you do with it."

A swell of pride washed over Hunter. It was the first time in his life he could remember ever winning an argument with his father. It made him feel ten feet tall. "Thank you, Dad, for trusting me."

"Trust you?" Jim Donovan clucked, raising his eyebrows. "We'll see about that. You just keep me updated on how this Hot Nights line does." He turned for the door. "Maybe I'll have to read one of Smut Slut's books."

"Might make you blush, Dad."

Jim Donovan stopped at the office door. "Son, I could tell you a few things that would make you blush." He turned his gaze to the two tall plants that filled the spot where his bookcase of statues used to be. "Glad to see you've finally made some changes around here."

"Don't you want to know where I put your statues of Alexander?"

"Not particularly." His father grinned. "It's your office now."

After his father had stepped through the door, Hunter returned to his desk infused with even more determination to make his new line a success.

But how will it be a success without Cary by your side? The unwanted thought echoed about the hollows of his heart.

Slumping down in his chair, Hunter's enthusiasm fizzled. He hated to admit it but his father had been right; his heart wasn't done with Cary despite what his head kept insisting.

Flipping up his laptop, he spied the assortment of e-mails waiting in his inbox. When he spotted the one from Cary, he quickly opened it.

Editing done. Final draft to you at end of the week.

It was like all the other messages he had read from her; curt and cold. Could he spend the next two or three years being bothered by her every e-mail?

"I have to do something about this," he vowed, tapping his computer screen.

But how did he convince her to give him another chance? He was better at walking away from relationships, not struggling to hold on to them. His mind raced ahead to their meeting at the cover shoot later that evening. It was a golden opportunity to change her mind about him.

Easing back in his chair, he felt his eagerness return. "And if not tonight...."

She was his writer after all, and as long as he published her books, Cary would have to interact with him. Sooner or later, Hunter was convinced she would have to give in.

* * *

Hunter entered through the black curtains of the Dungeon Club at The Hole, and was surprised to find the room lit up and the atmosphere only half as sinister as it had been that first night he had gone there with Cary. The blue neon lights had been turned off and the silver chains and handcuffs along the walls scintillated in the revealing glare of the photography lamps. The black couches and booths appeared a little dingy and the corner bar seemed a lot smaller. Scattered along the top of the black-painted bar were camera bags and a selection of different lenses, along with a light meter. Standing at the end of the bar beneath the blaze of the bright lights, and basking in the attention of a makeup woman and the photographer, was Smut Slut.

With a silver chain around her neck, a black leather jumper, her blonde wig, and dark glasses, Hunter found it hard to believe that Cary was hiding underneath such a costume. But as his father's words came back to him from earlier in the day, his eyes traveled the curves of face, along her fitted black leather dress, and down to her black, knee-high boots. He wondered why he had not seen the similarities before; it was obviously the same woman.

"I'm such an idiot."

When she saw Hunter standing at the other end of the bar, she waved off the makeup woman touching up the shiny spots on her nose. Saying something he could not hear to the dark-haired man in jeans holding a camera next to her, Hunter waited as she came toward him, her heart-shaped red lips pressed tightly together.

"You don't need to be here. I can handle everything," she said in a flat voice that sounded nothing like the sweet, high intonations he had grown addicted to in the past.

He took her elbow, and firmly gripping her arm, pulled her to the side. "We need to talk."

She tried to fight against him, but after glancing back to see the photographer, his assistant, and her makeup woman taking in their every word, she allowed him to escort her to a discreet corner of the room.

"We really have nothing to discuss," she briskly informed him.

He let go of her arm. "Bullshit."

Cary glimpsed the group by the bar. "Keep your voice down."

"You owe me an explanation, Cary," he began, lowering his voice.

"I don't owe you a goddamned thing, Hunter."

"Why didn't you tell me the truth from day one?"

"You preferred what I am now to Cary Anderson."

"What?" he shouted. "You can't believe that? I didn't take Smut Slut to bed. I took you."

"But you wanted her. From that first day you saw me at the Book Expo you were attracted to Smut Slut, admit it. She was what you perceived a woman to be. But I—"

"Will you take off that stupid wig and glasses?" he cut in. "I can't talk to you like this."

"But this is the woman you want." She placed her hands on her hips and stuck out her chest. "She's the woman every man wants. Do you know how many times men have hit on me as this character, and then when they meet me as Cary, they won't give me the time of day. You're no different than the rest."

"I am different, and I did get to know Cary Anderson, not this...drag queen you pretend to be. I like Cary. I like being with her and talking to her. You hide behind this persona because you're too damned afraid to show the world who you really are; just like you're too afraid to publish a book under your real name."

"I may be scared of putting my name out there as a writer, but you're just as scared of putting your heart on the line with a woman." She adjusted the sunglasses on her face. "Now if you will excuse me, I have a cover to shoot."

"This isn't over, Cary."

"It's over, Hunter. Go back to selling books. It's what you're good at."

As she walked away, an invisible weight pressed down in the center of Hunter's chest. There was more he needed to say to her. He wanted her to know how much she had changed him. Cary had chased away the foggy cloud that had been enshrouding him. She had re-awakened all the dreams he had harbored before taking over Donovan Books. He wanted to write again, to create, and to have a chance to be the man he always knew he could be. But how could he tell her all of that?

The photographer positioned Smut Slut at the end of the bar and adjusted her shoulders. As the flash of the camera lit up the room, Hunter's anger returned. But instead of rushing to the bar and forcing her to listen, he returned to the black curtains at the entrance. He was about to step through them when a short man, carrying a heavy tray of glasses, appeared in the doorway.

"Hey, sorry," the muscular man said as he moved out of Hunter's way.

"No problem," Hunter mumbled.

"Are you here with Cary's group?" He smiled and nodded to Cary dressed as Smut Slut. "Or should I call her Smuttie during this photo shoot?"

Hunter noted the man's black leather chaps and silver chain necklace. "You know about Cary?"

He put the tray of glasses on a nearby table. "Yeah I know." He held out his hand to Hunter. "I'm Wes, the manager here."

"Hunter Donovan, owner of Donovan Books." He shook Wes's hand. "We're publishing her new book."

"Yeah, she told me. Cary's a regular, and the one who asked me to set up the shoot for her." He motioned to the tray of glasses on the table. "I usually run the bar back here a few nights a week; that's how we met." He folded his thick, hairy arms over his chest. "The first time she came in wearing that outfit I laughed out loud. After a while we got to talking and she told me why she dressed that way. I even read one of her books." He held up his wide hands. "Not my thing, but hey, my wife loved it."

"I'm surprised she said anything to you. She's very...guarded about being Smut Slut," Hunter admitted

"Well, when she first came in, I was worried about her hanging with this crowd. They can get a little rough, so I kept an eye on her. When she came in one night as Cary and not Smuttie, I pretty much figured it out right away. But I can understand why she dresses that way."

Hunter smirked. "You can?"

"Sure. It's tough being a woman doing what she does. No one takes her seriously; at least that's what she told me. She said that it was easier to be Smuttie. She could lay it on the line as Smuttie and not be criticized."

Hunter remembered how outspoken Cary had been as Smut Slut. "But she can't hide behind her alter ego forever."

Smut Slut pouted her red lips and struck a sexy pose for the camera.

"She's not hiding; she's giving people what they want...the fantasy," Wes clarified. "I've seen how men interacted with her at my bar, expecting her to be the woman she appeared to be, and she gave them that. I think she was trying to figure out a way to be Cary and Smut Slut, so she could please a man. Lucky man that gets those two women; he gets the best of both worlds." Wes hefted the tray of glasses. "I've got to set up for tonight. Good meeting you, Mr. Donovan."

Wes walked over to the end of the bar and put the tray down as the photographer snapped some more pictures of Cary. Turning from the room, Hunter walked through the black curtains. As he rushed out of the building, the bartender's words kept repeating in Hunter's head. Then, an idea struck him.

He thought of his book and how he had intended to write about a man searching for purpose in his life, but the main character of Stone became so caught up in his quest that he lost sight of what he was hunting for in the first place. Starting the engine of his roadster, Hunter wondered if the character of Stone might have been better suited to a woman; a woman pretending to be someone she wasn't in order to find love.

Hunter's deep, boisterous laughter rolled about the small car. "Damn, I think I just found my inspiration."

Anxious for home, Hunter gunned the car out of the parking lot. He needed to get back to his book.

Chapter 17

The cooling breezes of September teased the city of Atlanta with hopes of the fall weather ahead. As Hunter beheld the sleek copper and neon entrance to Thrive Restaurant, he grinned. Having purposefully planned the launch party for Smut Slut's new book at the restaurant, he knew Cary would be reminded of the time they had dined there. As he strolled through the main entrance, he felt that usual sense of frustration pull at his heart whenever he thought of her. The two and a half months since the photo shoot had been productive for him, and the launch of the Hot Nights line had taken up most of his time, but he still missed her. Many times he had reached for his cell phone to call her, but would always change his mind. He had to make her want to come back to him.

The lounge-like dining room had been cleared of furniture and the chrome tables had been set against the side to be used as a buffet line. White plush couches and chairs were strategically placed about the room, and set out on the chrome sushi bar were display posters of *The Bondage Club* book cover. At the back of the room, a long table was piled high with paperback copies of the book for signing.

"We have everything just as you requested, Mr. Donovan," a slender blonde in a short black dress that accentuated her long legs said to Hunter as he surveyed the room.

"It looks great, Angelique." Hunter gave the blonde a sexy smile, accentuating his dimples. "It's exactly what I wanted."

Her pink lips curved into a bewitching grin. "Mixed drinks and wine will be served at the bar while appetizers are passed around by the waitstaff. After you have finished with the introduction and signing, the buffet will be opened to serve your guests, and coffee will be brought out an hour after dinner." Her blue eyes searched his. "I hope that will be satisfactory."

"Perfect, Angelique." He rubbed his hands together. "My staff and a few other guests, as well as our author, will be arriving early."

Angelique waved a slender arm toward the main bar to the right of the entrance. "They should be ready to serve drinks at the bar in about ten more minutes for your early guests." Her eyes swerved back to him. "I'll be here all evening, Mr. Donovan, to handle any problems."

"Thank you, Angelique."

"And I will be available after the party," she assured him with a hopeful tone in her smooth voice. "In case there is anything else you need."

Hunter's gut twitched at the thrill of Angelique's proposition, but then Cary's deep chocolate eyes came to mind. The idea of taking the slender blonde up on her offer suddenly lacked the satisfaction of being with Cary. Giving the woman a fleeting smile, he added, "I'll keep that in mind."

Two men wearing black T-shirts emerged from deep in the restaurant and eased behind the glass and chrome bar at the entrance to the main dining room. Angelique gave Hunter a brief nod and then headed to the bar. As she walked away, he wondered what was wrong with him. Why was he turning down such an attractive woman? But he knew where a night with Angelique would lead and he didn't want that kind of relationship anymore. He needed to share his thoughts and dreams with someone, and not just his bed.

As Angelique oversaw the bar preparations, Jesse walked in the entrance on the arm of a dark-eyed beauty with luscious olive skin, silky black hair, and a tight, muscular figure. Sporting a fitted suit that showed off his eye-popping physique, Jesse waved when he spotted Hunter in the main dining room.

"Quite a spread," Jesse stated while firmly shaking Hunter's hand. He turned to the stunning woman next to him. "This is a friend from my club, Max."

Hunter took her hand. "Max, it's a pleasure."

"Thanks for having me, Mr. Donovan."

"Hunter, please, Max."

"Is Cary coming?" Jesse asked.

Hunter shook his head. "I seriously doubt it."

"I can't wait to meet this Smut Slut woman. Heard a lot about her from Cary." Jesse pointed to the woman next to him. "Max has read all of her books."

"When he told me who this party was for, I made the big lug bring me." Max elbowed Jesse's side.

Out of the corner of his eye, Hunter saw his father and Chris enter the restaurant. He politely smiled at Jesse and Max. "Excuse me, my father just walked in."

"Can't believe he came," Jesse commented.

"Neither can I," Hunter mumbled.

As Hunter hurried to the entrance, he saw the way his father was taking in the restaurant. The discerning glint in his eyes made Hunter cringe. *Here we go*, Hunter thought. *He's going to rip everything to shreds.*

"Dad." Hunter nodded to his father. "Glad you made it." He eyed his brother's double-breasted charcoal suit and Windsor knotted black silk tie. "Chris, why are you here?"

"I asked him to bring me along," Jim Donovan confessed. "It seems your brother is representing your new author."

"What?" Hunter moved toward his brother. "Since when?"

Chris raised both his hands, attempting to soothe his brother's fury. "Hey, calm down. She called me. She wanted representation for future events. Seems she expects to go far with our publishing house and said she wanted me to get her some more publicity." Chris cracked a lecherous smile. "Very interesting woman. We met for lunch last week and inked a two-year contract." He patted Hunter on the shoulder. "Don't worry, little brother. I'll make her look good, so she sells a lot of books."

The clink of glasses from the bar to the right distracted the men. Two thick-necked bartenders waited at the ready behind the bar for the party to begin.

"I'll just get something to drink," Chris declared and then turned to his father. "What do you want, Dad?"

"Just soda water," Jim Donovan commented.

Chris patted his father's shoulder and then veered toward the bar. After he was out of earshot, Hunter shifted his focus to his father.

"Does he know about Cary and Smut Slut?"

Jim Donovan snorted as he placed both of his hands on his cane. "Are you kidding? Your brother has his moments, but where women are concerned he only sees form and function; he's blind to anything else." He shook his head. "I'm sure one day he'll catch on though. She can't hide behind that wig and glasses forever."

"I think she likes keeping everyone from knowing who she really is."

"But she showed you who she really is, didn't she?" He raised one hand from his cane and waved about the restaurant. "That's why you're doing all of this. The new book line, the new website, it's all been for her, hasn't it?"

Hunter avoided his father's piercing eyes and hunched his shoulders while shoving his hands in the pockets of his dark blue suit trousers. "No, I wanted the new line long before I met Cary. She just…helped bring it to life."

"Bring it to life?" Jim Donovan tapped his cane on the stone floor. "That's what your mother did for me. She brought my dreams to life."

"What are you talking about?"

"I was working this dead end job selling textbooks for a local publishing house when I met your mother. I always dreamed of owning a publishing company and your mother believed I could do it. She's the reason Donovan Books exists today."

Hunter was floored by the acknowledgement. "You never told me that before. I always thought you were the force behind the company."

"No, she was." He paused and his stern eyes softened. "Your mother and I had to get married because she got pregnant with your brother. After Chris was born, I thought I would never be able to afford opening a publishing house. But your mother kept encouraging me, saving our money, and making plans for the business. Hell, she even signed my first author. My Gracie helped me bring my dream to life, just like Cary helped bring yours to life."

"Starting the line wasn't exactly a dream, Dad."

"But it was a start, Hunter." Jim Donovan observed Chris at the bar chatting with Max and Jesse. "Your brother's dream was always to be…famous. He only aspires to get his name in the paper or rub elbows with celebrities." He pensively eyed Hunter. "You're the one who wanted to be a writer."

Hunter could feel the tension building in the back of his neck. "Yeah well, writing was just hobby, nothing serious."

"And why not make it serious?"

Hunter was flabbergasted by the suggestion. "I thought you said I made a better publisher than a writer."

Jim Donovan tugged at his casual black jacket. "At the time, I needed you to be a publisher and not a writer. Your mother had just died and I wanted out of the business. I knew Chris couldn't handle it, but you could."

Hunter studied his father's square face, not sure what to make of him. "Why are you telling me this?"

"Ever since you told me about this erotica line, I have been doing some research. I think this could go big for the company and I have some ideas I want to try. I was hoping I could come back to the office and help out, part-time of course."

"You want to come back to work?" Hunter's jaw dropped. "I'm…shocked. I thought you liked retirement."

"Son, no one likes retirement. Retirement is boring. I may be old, but I still want to accomplish things with my life. And if I come back, you might be able to concentrate more on your writing. Be the kind of writer you always wanted to be. Someone once said, 'There is nothing impossible to him who will try.'"

Hunter snickered, shaking his head. "Let me guess, Alexander again?"

Jim Donovan slowly nodded. "The man knew a thing or two about life."

Hunter thought on his father's proposition. "It's your company, Dad. Come back whenever you want," he proposed, keeping the enthusiasm from his voice.

"No, Hunter. Donovan Books stopped being mine the day you told me to butt out. She's your baby now; I just want to help her become everything you want her to be."

Hunter held out his hand to his father. "Glad to have you on board."

As Hunter and his father were shaking hands, Smut Slut walked in the restaurant door. Decked out in a form-fitting black leather bodysuit, spiked black heels, platinum wig, and round dark sunglasses, she looked more like a porn star than a writer of erotica. But when Hunter caught sight of the muscular blond man on her arm, wearing only a painfully tight pair of black leather shorts, a thunderbolt of jealousy seared through him.

Smut Slut saw Hunter standing with his father and beamed a brilliant smile. "Well, Mr. Donovan, what a nice surprise." She came up to Hunter's father and kissed his cheek, leaving a bright red lipstick stain.

"Who's that?" Hunter snapped, pointing to her date.

"Ah, there she is," Chris exclaimed, coming from the bar. He leaned over to Smut Slut, kissing her cheek. "I see my escort arrived."

Hunter turned to his brother. "Your escort?"

"Promo, little brother. It's all about the promotion." Chris nodded to the black dog collar about the man's neck. "Where's the leash?"

Smut Slut frowned. "I left it in my car. It's really too much, Chris."

He waved a slender hand at the hulking man in the obscenely tight shorts. "Serge is getting paid fifty bucks an hour to dress like this. He's a book cover model. He doesn't care what it looks like."

The blond Adonis next to Smut Slut shrugged his thick shoulders. "I'll wear whatever as long as I'm paid."

Chris pointed to the door. "Serge, go get the leash from the car before the guests start coming in."

Smut Slut opened her black leather purse and handed him her keys. "It's on the back seat."

Serge took the keys. "I'll be right back."

He was heading back out the door when Jim Donovan patted Chris on the shoulder. "Let's wait at the bar for the other guests."

"But I need to talk with my client," Chris objected.

Jim Donovan pushed him forward. "I think your brother needs a word with her first, Chris. Let's leave them to talk."

As Chris allowed his father to direct him toward the bar, he gave a concerned glance back to Smut Slut.

"I can't believe you signed with him, Cary," Hunter whispered.

"If this book takes off, I'll need a manager. Don't you want *The Bondage Club* to be a big success? That's why you planned this event right?" She shook her head. "Why did you have to book this restaurant? Were you trying to piss me off?"

"Why are you acting like this?" He stared at her tight bodysuit. "And that outfit...why did you wear that?"

"Did you expect me to come as Cary Anderson?" A cold snicker escaped from her lips. "Now that would have really set tongues wagging."

"Why can't you just come as yourself, be yourself? Why do you need to be her?" He itched to pull the round, dark glasses from her face.

"I tried being Cary Anderson with you, and we both know how that ended."

He took a step closer to her. "I was wrong. I shouldn't have gone off on you like that. What else do you want me to say?"

"Forget it, Hunter. What's done is done."

She was about to move toward the bar when he held her arm. "I want you to know you were right about my book. It is good, and I've been going back through it making notes, making changes."

She hesitated as the cruel grin on her lips abated. "You're writing again?"

"Thanks to you."

"I had nothing to do with it. You're a writer, Hunter. You're just starting to accept it, that's all." She gestured to his father by the bar. "I guess your father knows about the new line, then."

"Knows and likes the idea. He even wants to come and work with me." He paused and took in her perfect profile. "He knows about you, too."

The light changed, and for a second Hunter swore he could see her brown eyes beneath the glasses, but then the vision was gone. Serge reappeared at the door, carrying a black leash in his hands.

"You want to put it on?" He held out the leash to her.

Hunter noted the faint blush on Cary's pale cheeks. "You just hold on to it, okay?" She took his arm. "Come on. Let's get a drink."

As Hunter stood by the entrance, Cary proceeded to the bar on the arm of her scantily clad model. He felt about as low as the day he had gone to work for his father's company. Hunter had walked away from one dream then, and for the second time in his life he questioned if he was giving up another with Cary. With his stomach churning and at his wits end, he went to the opposite end of the bar from Cary and her date, dead set on getting good and drunk.

* * *

Packed with staff, business associates, and other authors represented by Donovan Books, the small restaurant became thick with the din of conversation. For most of the evening Hunter kept close to the bar, greeting the occasional guest and casting a wary eye out for Smut Slut as she worked the room. She flitted about, dragging her book cover model with her, flirted with a book reviewer from the *Atlanta Journal-Constitution*, did shots with a reporter from the *Creative Loafing* newspaper, seductively posed as a photographer took some pictures, then chatted with every one of the dozen booksellers there from the Atlanta area. As she made her way around the room, laughing and flaunting her leather outfit, Hunter kept sipping on his vodka and soda.

"You keep staring at her like you're getting ready to poke pins in her voodoo doll," Jim Donovan said as he came up to the bar.

"I'm hoping the woman I know will appear at some point in the evening." Hunter took a long pull from his drink as Smut Slut teasingly patted Chris's arm and laughed at something he had said.

"Does she know how you feel about her?" Jim Donovan took the stool next to his son.

Hunter frowned into his vodka. "How I feel?"

"The last time I saw you so infatuated with a woman was when you were living with that photographer. But your mother said it wouldn't last, and she was right."

He peered over at his father. "When did Mom say that?"

"Right after you moved in with her. Your mother said she was 'a vain woman looking to fuel her ego and not your heart.'" His father pointed across the room to Smut Slut. "But she's different. She cares about you."

"How would you know that?"

His father waved down a bartender. "I'm not an idiot, Hunter. She's been watching you, just as much as you've been watching her." A thick-necked man in a black T-shirt came to the end of the bar. "Can I have a black coffee?" Jim Donovan told the bartender.

After the bartender had turned away, Jim Donovan pushed Hunter's drink out of reach. "You've had enough of that. You need some coffee."

Hunter glared at his father. "I'm fine."

"You're not fine, Hunter. Drinking is what you do after she leaves you, not before."

Hunter shook his head. "She's already left me."

"She hasn't left you; she's just waiting for you to make the next move."

"What next move?"

Jim Donovan rested his cane on the bar. "If you want that woman back, you have to let her know how much you need her. I had to do it all the time with your mother. Prove to her that she was the one I needed in my life." He held up his hand when Hunter opened his mouth to speak. "Don't remind me. I know we didn't have the best marriage, but she knew I loved her. The other women...well, they were just flings. But I was wrong to hurt her. I was stupid and selfish, sort of like your brother. I fear he's repeating my mistakes with women, but you...you're not like me, you're like your mother." He sighed and shook his head. "Getting older can be a blessing and a curse. You get to see life go on, but you also get time to live with your mistakes. I'll never forgive myself for not fixing things with your mother, but you've still got a chance with Cary. Tell her how you really feel."

"I don't know how I really feel, Dad."

"Yes, you do." Jim Donovan gripped his cane. "Perhaps you should put your feelings on paper. After all, you're a writer. Isn't that what writers do?" He stood from his stool. "I'm going to get your brother to take me home." He eyed Chris who was deep in conversation with a pretty, petite blonde. "I better get him out of here before does something we will both regret."

After his father had moved away, the bartender placed the cup of black coffee before Hunter. The warm aromatic steam from the cup rose to his nose, tempting Hunter to take a sip. Lifting the cup to his lips, he took in a deep gulp of the hot liquid, easing the queasiness in his belly.

"Glad to see you're drinking coffee," Smut Slut said beside his barstool. "After three drinks you need it."

Holding his cup in his hand, he faced her. "I didn't realize you were keeping track."

"I couldn't help it. I've been wondering when you were going to get off your high horse and entertain your guests. Donovan Books is hosting this party after all."

"No one cares about Donovan Books. They came to see you. Tell me, is there any man in the room you haven't hit on?"

She smirked. "I haven't hit on you."

He put his cup down on the bar. "I'm not interested in Smut Slut hitting on me."

She took the barstool next to him. "I think it's time you and I came to some kind of understanding. I can't have you sulking at all my book launches in the future. It's bad for business."

"Is that all you're worried about? The business?"

"It's what you need to be worried about, too, Hunter. We're going to have to put the past behind us."

"What if I'm not willing to do that?"

"Cary Anderson is not who you want."

"Don't tell me who I want, Cary," he griped.

"Fine." She placed her hands on the bar. "I just came over here to say that despite how things ended, I want to make peace. I have a long-term contract with Donovan Books and we will have a lot of functions like this to attend together. Smut Slut is going to be in your life for a while and you'd better get used it."

"And what about Cary Anderson? Am I ever going to see her again?"

Her red lips smashed together in an angry frown. "No, I think you've seen enough of her."

"And what about your dream of writing under your real name? Are you going to give up on that, too?"

She obstinately held up her head. "I'm only writing under the name Smut Slut from now on. No one wants to read anything from Cary Anderson."

"I do."

"Drink your coffee and go home, Hunter." She put on a fake smile as she stood from her barstool. "You're just making a fool of yourself, and putting a damper on my party."

As she walked away, Hunter banged his fist on the bar. He didn't know what hurt more, having her shut him out, or having her shut out the passionate and wonderful woman he had come to care for. Fed up, he rose from his barstool and was heading toward the entrance when Jesse came up to him.

"You heading out already?"

Hunter pulled his keys from his jacket pocket. "Yeah. Our Smut Slut has everything in hand. She doesn't need me."

"Are you sure about that?"

Hunter closed his hand over his keys. "I'm not sure about anything, Jesse."

"Yeah, it takes a woman to turn day into night."

Hunter shook his head, confused. "What is that supposed mean?"

"Only a woman can turn a man's world upside down. No other creature on the planet can be so beguiling and at the same time so infuriating. But once you strip away the makeup, wig, and black leather," Jesse smiled, "she's just like you; terrified."

Hunter softly chuckled. "You figured it out too, eh?"

"From the moment I saw the way you looked at her." Jesse's thick paw patted his shoulder. "I'll drive you home."

Hunter waved off his offer. "I'm fine."

Jesse clamped his hand about his shoulder and shoved him toward the entrance. "You're not fine, my friend. You're in love."

Chapter 18

Two weeks after the launch party, Hunter was sitting in his roadster outside of the Charis Bookstore. As he spied the group of women milling about the entrance of the purple-painted cottage, he wondered why Smut Slut had arranged a signing at such a place. He knew Chris had set up signings for her at several bookstores in and around Atlanta, but Hunter had only learned of this event when his brother had called him earlier that morning to complain about Smut Slut's insistence on hosting a signing at the small, and very controversial, feminist bookstore.

"You need to speak with her, Hunter," Chris had barked into his cell phone. "I've got her booked into some top-notch stores and then she goes behind my back and does this."

"What do you want me to do?" Hunter had asked, smirking.

"Talk to her. Tell her you need her to think about her future with Donovan Books. This isn't a wise business move. A feminist bookstore? Is she crazy?"

Hunter had refrained from laughing as he viewed the small green park across the street from his arched window. "Maybe she knows the owners or something, Chris."

"Just go and talk to her, Hunter."

"Why can't you do it?"

"She won't listen to me!" Chris had yelled into the phone speaker. "You're the owner of the company. Go and make her listen to you."

Eyeing the eclectic bookstore once more, Hunter gathered up the courage to face Cary. He dropped his eyes to the printed manuscript on the seat next to him. *The Other Side of Me* was still in need of editing, but he had revised the original story, basing the main character on Cary. When he had started, he never thought he would complete the book so quickly. Now staring at the finished manuscript, he longed to show it to Cary. He wanted her to see what he had accomplished, and more to the point, he needed her to read what he had written. He had poured his soul into the work; he had emptied his emotions onto the page and written his feelings for the woman Cary was. All the confusion, angst, happiness, and fear she had caused him were embedded in those pages. His soul was laid bare for her, and he just hoped she read the damn thing instead of pushing it away.

Climbing from the car, he gripped the manuscript in his hand. Making his way past the cluster of women, he jogged up the few steps to the entrance and then pulled the narrow glass door open.

It was a small bookstore with shelves set into the pale lime green walls and a purple-painted ceiling. There was a children's section in one corner, and a reading area for authors in another. He sighted Smut Slut's platinum blonde hair poking out from behind a bevy of women standing around a table in the fiction section of the store. The crowd appeared very interested in what Smut Slut was saying. As he moved closer, he caught a glimpse every now and then of her dark, round glasses, deep red lips, and the top of her almost demure yellow shirt. He was surprised as he came closer that she did not have on her usual array of tight leather, and instead was decked out in blue jeans and black high heels. She was laughing with the group of women, but when she saw Hunter emerge from behind one tall redhead, her laughter ceased.

"Well, well, I never thought I'd see you in here, Hunter." Her tone was peppered with sarcasm.

"Chris sent me." He moved toward her table. "He wanted you to know that your being here is a dangerous career move."

"He would," she laughed. "But what does my esteemed publisher think?"

"Ex-publisher," he corrected. "I'm taking a leave of absence."

Her red lips parted in surprise. "You're leaving Donovan Books?"

"Just for a year. My father and Chris will be overseeing things for a while. I have some place I have to go."

"Where?" she loudly demanded.

He noted the gaggle of women taking in their every word. "Can we talk in private?"

She waved to a pile of books on the table next to her. "I'm in the middle of a signing, Hunter."

"Fine. If this is how you want it?" He plopped the manuscript down on the table before her. "This is for you. You wanted me to rewrite it, so I did. It's about you, or at least the woman I knew. Read it, burn it, do whatever you like with it. I thought you should...." He surveyed the eager faces around them, drinking in their conversation. "Good-bye...Smuttie."

Turning on his heels, he made a beeline for the entrance, suddenly eager for a clean getaway. Dashing down the steps, he was almost across the parking lot when he heard her voice behind him.

"Why did you come here?"

He stopped and let his shoulders sag forward. *So much for the clean getaway.*

"You could have just mailed this to me, Hunter."

He slowly faced her. She was standing at the bottom of the steps, clutching the manuscript in her hands. "Mailed it to you? Come on, Cary. Did what we have mean nothing to you?"

She warily inspected the faces of the women still standing around the entrance, and then walked up to him. "I thought that was behind us."

"Is that what you really want?"

She came to a halt in front of him. "I thought that is what we both needed."

He removed the dark glasses from her face. When he saw her deep brown eyes, his insides warmed with happiness. "You told me once that what I needed as a writer was inspiration, my muse to finish my book. Well, I found that…in you." He pointed to the manuscript in her hands. "It's all in there. Everything I should have said and wanted to say to you, but didn't have the nerve." He tucked the glasses into the collar of her yellow blouse. "You can pretend to be Smut Slut as long as you want, but I know the woman behind the glasses, Cary. That's the woman I wrote about in my book."

Stepping aside, he went to his car, fighting the urge to look back. As he hastily turned over the engine of his BMW, he caught a glimpse of her still standing where he had left her. She was holding the manuscript against her heart, waiting for him to drive away.

Pulling the car onto the street, he felt the unbearable emptiness that had been pressing down on him for the past few months begin to recede. He had said good-bye, and though he may not have been cured of her, he was ready to move on. Cary Anderson had taught him not to give up on his desires, and if he could not have her, at least he could set free that part of his soul that he had been stifling. It was time to get back to being the Hunter Donovan he had always envisioned. It was time to open up his heart…and dream.

Alexandrea Weis

Epilogue

Sitting on the third-floor balcony of his New Orleans French Quarter apartment, Hunter scanned the courtyard below. Surrounded by lush greenery, the inner courtyard was made up of a single wide, circular fountain with a stream of water rising from the mouth of a large brass fish perched on a rock in the center. To the right, a black wrought iron table with a multi-colored umbrella was used by the neighbors below to take in the crisp fall evening air. Beyond the courtyard, the bustling sounds of the French Quarter intruded as the din of traffic, people, and a hint of jazz music wafted over the high rooftop.

Hunching over a wooden table, Hunter returned to the words he had written on his laptop. He wasn't happy with how this chapter was going. Stretching out, he decided perhaps the time had come to take a stroll around the streets of the Quarter to give his creative muse a little air. Rising from his flimsy chair, he collected his mug of coffee and walked back through the open white french doors to his apartment.

The living room beyond the balcony was small, with only a few pieces of old, worn furniture that his landlord had given him. The peach-colored walls were covered with a selection of posters of the city which he had bought at a local gift shop. To the left of the living room was an efficiency kitchen with a half-refrigerator, sink, a few shelves above the sink for dishes, and a small stove next to the refrigerator. The pantry was a bookcase with a curtain in front of it, and a microwave took up most of the counter space, along with the coffeemaker. Leaving his mug in the sink, Hunter went to his bedroom to find a clean T-shirt.

Reaching over the single-sized bed he had bought after arriving in the Big Easy, he grabbed a T-shirt from a second-hand, white-painted dresser. Checking his five o'clock shadow in the small bathroom mirror, he raked his fingers through his hair and decided that he was good enough for public display.

Making his way back into his living room, he snagged his sunglasses, keys, and wallet from the pine table by the front door. He was stuffing his wallet into the back pocket of his jeans when he heard a light rapping on his apartment door. Curious as to who would be stopping by so early in the morning, he turned the brass knob.

She was standing on the landing outside of his doorway with her hands behind her back, wearing one of her light cotton dresses that clung to her petite figure. Her short brown hair appeared windblown, her cheeks pink from climbing the two flights of stairs to his apartment, and her lips were painted deep red. But when Hunter connected with Cary's eyes, his heart skipped a beat.

"Where's your wig?"

She slowly smiled for him. "I left it in Atlanta with Sex Kitten. He's using it as his new play toy."

"I thought you were on your book tour for *The Bondage Club*."

"I am, but I told Chris I needed a few days off after I read *The Other Side of Me*." Pulling her hands from behind her back, she held up the tightly rolled manuscript. "What you wrote in here…the things Max said, the words he used to tell the heroine, Stone, how he felt…was that meant to be you? Did you—"

"Took you long enough to read it," he said, cutting her off. "I was beginning to think you had forgotten about me."

"Yeah, well, it sat on my desk for a month before I read it. Then when I went to Donovan Books looking for you, your father told me you were here, in New Orleans, taking some time off to write." She hesitated, as if searching for something else to say. "Your father seemed really excited about the Hot Nights line."

"Yeah, Dad is so impressed with how your book is rising up the New York Times Bestseller's List that he's getting more authors for the line." He paused, still unsure of how to take her visit. "Why are you here, Cary? You didn't come all this way to ask me about my book," he added, playing it cool.

She fingered the manuscript in her hand. "No, that's not the only reason. I'm also here to see my family." She peeked beyond his front door. "So is this your new place?"

"It's just a small apartment." He stepped in front of her. "You once told me you pictured me living in something simpler, so I decided to follow your advice."

She leaned against the doorframe. "What did you do with your fancy condo?"

"Dad's staying in it for now."

A nervous silence settled between them. As Hunter stood in his doorway, trying to appear unfazed, Cary's eyes swept over his angular features.

"So am I to stand out here all day, or are you going to invite me in?" she insisted, breaking the tension in the air.

"Why should I invite you in, Cary?"

"I want to see how a talented writer lives."

He skeptically cocked one eyebrow. "Talented writer?"

She held up the manuscript. "It's good, Hunter. Better than before. I especially liked the heroine, Stone. The way you had her pretending to be someone she wasn't to impress Max. And how they found love in the end…nice touch. I didn't like her first name though." She wrinkled her brow. "You should come up with something better than Cory."

He scratched his head. "I'm not good at coming up with names. I tried to think of something other than Cary."

She tipped her head to the side. "I'm great at coming up with names for characters. Maybe I could help you with that."

"In that case…." He stood back from the door and waved her inside.

"I also think she's a little too pushy in the book." She breezed in through his door. "You know how she ties the guy to the bed and practically rapes him?" She shook her head. "It's not very realistic."

"It felt pretty realistic at the time." Hunter reveled in the aroma of her floral perfume as he shut the door. "What would you recommend?"

"A rewrite. Maybe change the location of the book, too. Perhaps a city with a little rougher edge to it."

Hunter followed her as she walked into his cramped living room. Placing his keys and sunglasses on the table by the door, he considered her comment. "What's wrong with Atlanta?"

"Nothing." She dropped the manuscript on his shabby gold and white overstuffed sofa. "But I think if you put the characters in New Orleans, made them meet up in the French Quarter, it might make for a more intriguing love story. You could have them taking in the sites of the city, perhaps dining at a restaurant or two. Maybe make Max a jazz musician instead of a writer."

He waited as her eyes drank in the compact room. "Anything else?"

She went to the french door that led to the balcony. "I have a few ideas."

Hunter waited as she moved to his bedroom and pushed the tall cypress door open, peering inside.

"Is this where you sleep? The bed is so small."

He came up to her. "It's fine for me."

Her eyes took a turn of the apartment. "Not a lot of room in here, and it's going to get a bit cramped with two of us. We will probably have to get a bigger bed."

"We? I don't remember asking you to move in with me."

"How else are we going to work on your book?" She gingerly placed her hand on his chest. "We will have to spend our days writing and our nights experimenting."

"Experimenting?" He scowled at her. "I'm not sure I like the sound of that."

"You want to make sure your love scenes are accurate, right?"

Hunter wrapped one arm about her waist. "No more handcuffs. I'm still having nightmares."

"All right, but you do know that New Orleans has some great bondage clubs, and I was thinking we could—"

Hunter kissed her lips, silencing her. When she clasped her hands behind his neck, pressing her body into his, he lifted his head. Touching his forehead to hers, he asserted, "No more bondage clubs. Let's try writing this story without all of that."

"Then what would we write about?"

He wrapped his other arm about her and began pushing her back into the bedroom. "Why don't you move in here with me, and we can spend our days writing and at night...well, we will figure it out. Once we finish my rewrites, we can talk about collaborating on more books."

"More books? That's sounds kind of...permanent."

His hands went to the buttons on the front of her dress. "Maybe we could talk about making this a permanent partnership. What do you think?"

"Are you sure you're ready to get tied down with me, Hunter?"

He gazed into her lovely brown eyes and was instantly whole. "Cary, I can't imagine being tied down by anyone else."

The End

Alexandrea Weis is an advanced practice registered nurse who was born and raised in New Orleans. Having been brought up in the motion picture industry, she learned how to tell stories from a different perspective and began writing at the age of eight. Infusing the rich tapestry of her hometown into her award-winning novels, she believes that creating vivid characters makes a story memorable. A permitted/certified wildlife rehabber with the Louisiana Wildlife and Fisheries, Weis rescues orphaned and injured wildlife. She lives with her husband and pets in New Orleans.

Facebook: https://www.facebook.com/pages/Alexandrea-Weis/289566081083949
Twitter: https://twitter.com/alexandreaweis
Goodreads: http://www.goodreads.com/author/show/1211671.Alexandrea_Weis
Website: http://www.alexandreaweis.com/
Watch for Alexandrea's coming releases:
That Night with You Coming February 5, 2015 (read the teaser on the next page)

Alexandrea Weis

Enjoy a Teaser from *That Night with You*
By Alexandrea Weis

"He said his friends called him Harry, so I called him Harry." Madison lifted her beer and took a sip. "We spent about an hour at the bar talking." She smiled and let go a small giggle. "Well, he asked questions and I talked. I seem to remember he asked me a lot of questions."

"What kind of questions?" Charlie intruded.

"Where I was from, what I was studying in school. I told him my name was Mary. I remember thinking he knew a lot about architecture. He was pretty smart. I think he talked about how hard architecture school was, but I'm not sure if he mentioned going to architecture school. He asked about my family, what I liked to do outside of school…stuff like that."

"Get to the good part," Lizzie insisted as she moved her chair closer to Madison. "Did he take you to his place?"

Madison played with her beer glass in her hands. "He drove me in his Porsche to his apartment. More like a penthouse, really. It had this wall of windows with great view of the UT campus. I remember he had a bar." She tilted her head, lost in her memories. "Really nice paintings on the wall. He told me the name of the painter, but I've forgotten."

"Sounds nice." Charlie grinned. "He must have been rich to have a place like that."

"He led me into his apartment, turned on this song 'Feeling Good.' I remember asking him about it. He told me it was by his favorite singer, Nina Simone." She paused and smiled.

"Is that the song you always play? You know…I'm feeeliiinnn' gooood," Charlie sang out. "I hear it coming from your bedroom sometimes."

Madison nodded. "But I listen to the Michael Bublé version."

"Oh, I love him," Lizzie squealed.

"So you play that song for him, don't you?" Charlie probed.

Madison nodded. "I always wonder what it would be like if he was there with me; dancing with me again. Sometimes I daydream about it. You know, being with him again." She rubbed her arms, feeling she had said too much. "Silly, huh?"

"I think it's romantic." Lizzie giggled. "You and Harry have a song."

"Enough about the song," Charlie clamored. "What happened next?"

Madison sighed. "He wanted me to sober up a bit before…anyway, he made me some coffee in his kitchen. I was sipping on the coffee and we were standing in the kitchen talking when I slipped or got dizzy…I'm not sure. He went to grab me and I spilled some coffee on his nice shirt. I was mortified and kept apologizing, but he just laughed at me." She smiled lost in her thoughts. "He had this great laugh. Deep, soulful; the kind that vibrates inside of your bones. The one thing I clearly remember about that night was his laugh."

"And then what happened," Lizzie inserted.

Madison was awakened from her memories. "I grabbed for some paper towels and started wiping his shirt." She rolled her green eyes. "I must have looked like a total idiot. He took the paper towels from my hands and then he kissed me."

"Good kisser?" Charlie pressed.

Madison nodded, blushing. "Really good. The kind you don't want to stop kissing."

Lizzie's grip on her glass of beer tightened. "Then…."

Madison lowered her eyes to the table. "He took my hand and led me from the kitchen to the master bedroom. When we got to the bedroom door, I think I had a mini panic attack. I was so nervous...never having done it before. But he put his arm around me, kissed my cheek and gently eased me into the room." She raised her head. "After that, I wasn't quite as nervous."

Charlie's blue eyes grew round. "And the sex? How was it?"

"He was very gentle." Madison shrugged her shoulders. "I thought it was going to hurt more, but he...he went really slow...I'm not sure he if he knew I was...." She chuckled. "He made me feel comfortable, or as comfortable as I could feel in that situation. But the second and third times were even better."

"Second and third times?" Lizzie shrieked, then she glanced around the bar. "Jesus." She reached for the shot glasses still piled in the middle of the table and took one. "He must have been really good. After my first time, I did want anyone to touch me for days." She shot back the small glass of tequila.

Charlie nudged Madison's hand on the table. "But what exactly happened? How did he do it?"

Madison's jaw dropped. "What do you mean 'how did he do it'? You're kidding, right?"

"No, Mads, I'm talking about before he took off your clothes. How did he seduce you? You know, what kind of moves did he put on you? Or did you two just get right to it?"

"Oh that." Madison became silent for a few seconds. "Yeah, well, he, ah, danced with me. After we walked into the bedroom, he took my hand and held me close. I don't know how long we swayed like that to the music, but he made me feel really...special."

"Special?" Charlie laughed. "What about the morning after? How did you feel then?"

Enjoy a Teaser of *Something Great*
by M. Clarke/Mary Ting

From the corner of my eye I saw a figure moving, but dismissed it as I shifted my eyes to the right and spotted the elusive restroom sign. I was just about to head in that direction when someone spoke to me from behind in a deep, manly voice, sending shivers down my back.

"I'm your prescription. Let me be your new addiction." His words glided like butter, smooth and cool.

Startled, I twitched, and turned my body toward his voice. There he was; all six feet of him, peering down at me with a smile that could make me do just about anything. Though there was nothing to laugh about, especially seeing this hottie in front of me, I couldn't help but giggle from his words.

He wore beige casual pants and a black sweater that fit perfectly to his toned body. His hair was brushed to the side, showing his nice forehead. Whatever kind of cologne he had on made me want to dive right into his arms...ok, maybe it wasn't the cologne, but just him.

"Pretty cheesy, huh?" he chuckled.

I shyly giggled, as I stared down at my shoes. What's wrong with me? Answer him. "Umm...kind of," I smiled as I peered up, only to have him take my breath away again.

"Sorry. I just had to say that. You looked so lost and vulnerable. Did you need some help?"

Great! To him I was just a lost puppy...lost and vulnerable. "I actually found what I was looking for." I was staring into his eyes, melting, feeling myself sink into him. Snap out of it!

"You certainly did," he said with a playful tone.

Arching my brows in confusion, I thought about what I'd said. From his perspective, I guess he thought my words had been about him.

"We meet again, for the third time."

He was counting?

"You left so abruptly from Café Express, I didn't get to ask your name."

"Umm...my name? Oh...my name is Jeanella Mefferd, but you can call me Jenna."

Extending his hand, he waited for me. "I'm Maxwell. But you can call me Max."

Nervously, I placed my hand in his. It was strong, yet gentle...just right, and heat blazed through me from his touch.

"Are you here with someone?"

"Yes." I looked away shyly.

"Are you lost? Do you need some help?"

"Actually, I was looking for the restroom. I didn't know where it was, so I thought I'd ask the bartender, but I guess there isn't one back here, but I spotted it anyway, and I'm on my way to the restroom," I rambled nervously. I slowly pulled my hand back to point in the direction I needed to go. I had just realized we were holding hands during our short conversation. "So...I'd better go."

"I'll walk you there."

What? "Oh...no need. I'm sure I won't get lost." Feeling the heat on my face again, I turned before he could say another word, but it didn't matter what I had said. His hand was gently placed on my back, guiding me to the Ladies room. I turned my back to the bathroom door to thank him, but he spoke first.

"I think this is my stop," he murmured, looking straight at me. "I'm not wanted in there. What do you think?" He arched his brows, and his tone held a note of challenge.

Huh? He wants to go in with me? I gasped silently, as I was still lost in his eyes. "I think the women in there (will is right) throw themselves at you." I couldn't believe I'd said those words. I couldn't take it back. What was I doing, flirting with him?

He seemed to like what he heard. His arms reached out, his muscles flexing as he placed one on each side of me on the wall. With nowhere to go, I was trapped inside the circle of his arms. He leaned down toward the left side of my face and brushed my hair with his cheek. "You smell…delicious," he whispered. His hot breath shot tingles to places I hadn't expected.

Out of nervousness and habit, my left index finger flew to my mouth. Max gave a crooked, naughty grin and slowly took my hand out of my mouth. "Did you know that biting one's finger is an indication one is sexually deprived?" His words came out slowly, playfully, but hot. "I can fix that for you, if you'd like."

He did not just say that to me! I parted my lips for a good comeback, but I couldn't find one. Feeling my chest rise and fall quickly, I tried to control the desire that burned through me. Sure, he'd helped me once, but that didn't mean we were friends, or flirting buddies, or that I would allow him to fix my sexual deprivation. Oh God…can guys tell if you haven't done it in a very long time? This had to stop or else…oh dear…I wanted to take him with me into the restroom.

Needing to put a stop to the heat, I placed my hand on his chest…big mistake. Touching him made the heat worse, and tingles that were already intensifying, burst through every inch of me. I had to push him away.

As if he knew what I meant to do, he pulled back, but his eyes did the talking instead. There was no need for words; I felt his hard stare on my body, as if he was undressing me with his gorgeous eyes. His gaze was powerful, as if his eyes were hands; I felt them all over me, completely unraveling me.

Just when I thought I was going to faint, his eyes shifted to mine again. "It was really nice to meet you, Jenna. I'm sure we'll see each other again, real soon. I better let you go. Your someone must be waiting for you. By the way…." There was a pause as he charmed me with his eyes again. "You…took my breath away. If I were your someone, I wouldn't let you out of my sight for even a second, because someone like me will surely try to whisk you away." He winked and left.